REACH OUT AND GRAB SOMEONE

As the great Randal T. Rumpp's secretary, Dorma Wormser was used to brushing off tough callers. But this one was different. "Oh, God," she moaned at what came out of the receiver.

It was white from the hairless top of its bloated head to the tips of its very white feet. But there were golden veins under its smooth white skin, pulsing with fleet golden lights. Even weirder was the way the manlike thing floated just under the high ceiling, like a white corpse filled with helium.

Worst of all, it had no face.

The greatest menace America ever faced had arrived—and no way could it be put on hold. . . .

GHOST IN THE MACHINE

The Destroyer

#90

GHOST IN THE MACHINE

Created by
WARREN MURPHY & RICHARD SAPIR

A SIGNET BOOK

SIGNET
Published by the Penguin Group
Penguin Books USA Inc., 375 Hudson Street,
New York, New York 10014, U.S.A.
Penguin Books Ltd, 27 Wrights Lane,
London W8 5TZ, England
Penguin Books Australia Ltd, Ringwood,
Victoria, Australia
Penguin Books Canada Ltd, 10 Alcorn Avenue,
Toronto, Ontario, Canada M4V 3B2
Penguin Books (N.Z.) Ltd, 182—190 Wairau Road,
Auckland 10, New Zealand

Penguin Books Ltd, Registered Offices:
Harmondsworth, Middlesex, England

First published by Signet, an imprint of New American Library, a
division of Penguin Books USA Inc.

First Printing, October, 1992
10 9 8 7 6 5 4 3 2 1

Ⓢ REGISTERED TRADEMARK—MARCA REGISTRADA

Printed in the United States of America

PUBLISHER'S NOTE
This is a work of fiction. Names, characters, places, and incidents
either are the product of the author's imagination or are used ficti-
tiously, and any resemblance to actual persons, living or dead,
events, or locales is entirely coincidental.

BOOKS ARE AVAILABLE AT QUANTITY DISCOUNTS WHEN USED TO PROMOTE
PRODUCTS OR SERVICES. FOR INFORMATION PLEASE WRITE TO PREMIUM
MARKETING DIVISION, PENGUIN BOOKS USA INC., 375 HUDSON STREET,
NEW YORK, NEW YORK 10014.

For the Cryptic Robert M. Price.

And the Glorious House of Sinanju,
P.O. Box 2505, Quincy, MA 02269.

1

Randal T. Rumpp lived by the telephone.

The lowly telephone was the symbol of his empire, his great fame, his vast wealth. In his hands, it was transformed from a mere instrument for idle conversation into a lightning rod for raw money.

Randal Rumpp was never far from the telephone. A bank of them sat on his office desk. Cellular units filled every car and yacht he owned. When the maid set his table, there was a cellular handset where the salad fork should be. In restaurants, the maître d' would see to it that Mr. Rumpp's special table—and he had special tables in restaurants throughout Manhattan, Paris, and other world-class cities—was set with a telephone to the immediate left of the dinner fork.

For alleged billionaire Randal Tiberius Rumpp was a maker of deals. And deals were best made by telephone.

On the day the telephones stopped ringing all over the Rumpp Tower, Randal T. Rumpp, for the first time in his life, lived in fear of their clarion call.

He arrived at six in the morning and put to his executive assistant the crisp question always asked of her.

"Any calls, Dorma?"

"No, Mr. Rumpp."

And for the first time in his meteoric career, Randy

Rumpp—as the tabloids and gossip columnists styled him—was pleased to hear that there had been no messages lying in wait for him. Usually, the messages were stacked to the ceiling. From Tokyo. From Hong Kong. From Zurich. There were always deals swirling around Randy Rumpp's pompadoured head.

Those kind of calls had long ago ceased to pour in.

Now, the only people who called were his creditors. If there were no messages, then the banks hadn't yet foreclosed on Randal Rumpp's last major trophies of an ill-spent business career: the Rumpp Tower, overlooking New York's Fifth Avenue, and the Rumpp Regis Hotel, up on Third.

Still, it was a blow to his ego.

"Are you sure?" he asked.

"I think the phone company is having problems again."

"Well," he said, "if anyone does call, take names and numbers. And try to give the impression that I'm too busy to get back time anytime soon. Okay?"

"Yes, Mr. Rumpp."

"Remember, we're selling success here."

"Yes. Mr. Rumpp."

Self-consciously, Randal Rumpp patted his famous sandy crown of hair and entered his sumptuous, cathedral-like office overlooking Central Park. He set down the Spanish leather briefcase that contained the cellular telephone that was his lifeline when he was between stationary phones, and removed the handset. The way the phone company was plagued by service interruptions these days, one couldn't be too careful.

Once, Randal Rumpp, on his way to a major deal, had had the misfortune to be stranded in an elevator.

First he called his broker, obtaining the latest market quotes. Second, he called for help.

It took twenty minutes for the maintenance people to pry the elevator doors apart and haul him from the cage that had been stuck between the fourteenth and fifteenth floors. In that short span of time, Randal Rumpp made a cool two million in a series of brilliant stock transactions. Flushed with success, he strode into his business meeting and, simply by announcing his good fortune, demoralized his business adversaries, who had in fact arranged for the elevator to malfunction in a blatant attempt to put him at a psychological disadvantage. Rumpp greenmailed them into bankruptcy court in less time than he had spent in that elevator.

Now, surrounded by the very instruments that had, during the heady days of the 1980s, made him into a multibillionaire who oversaw a real-estate empire that spread faster than lymph node cancer, Randal Rumpp fervently prayed they would start ringing again on this final day in October.

He strode over to his magnificent view of upper Manhattan. Directly across the street was a skyscraper of silvery polished glass, not nearly as tall and fine as the tower that bore Rumpp's proud name.

When the rival building had first been proposed, Randal Rumpp sued to have it quashed, claiming that it would ruin his unique view. When the higher courts threw out the suit, he resorted to other types of legal harassment.

Finally, the thing was finished. It had been intended to tower over the Rumpp Tower, but Randal Rumpp's law firm had so drained the financial resources of the development company that they were forced to strike the top ten floors from the original design. In its final form, it stood one story shy of matching the lofty eminence of his own Rumpp Tower. That single story was all that Randal Rumpp required. He had never cared much for the view, anyway. But he simply despised being bested in business.

While the dedication ceremony was taking place many floors below his twenty-fourth-floor aerie, Randal Rumpp dictated a memo to his head of PR stating that the offending building was the ugliest dwarf since Quasimodo.

The press, then in love with his every loutish witticism, printed it on page one. It became a *Newsweek* "Quote of the Week."

After the furor had died down, Rumpp dictated another memo.

"I've changed my mind," Rumpp said of the silvery skyscraper. "I like it. Every day when I come to work, I look out my office window and there it is: the Rumpp Tower, and me, reflected in the most expensive mirror ever built. And it cost the Rumpster nothing."

That was Randal Rumpp in his salad days. A gracious victor.

On this last day in October, Randal Rumpp stared out at the mirror-like surface across busy Fifth Avenue, and the reflection of his greatest holding.

The Rumpp Tower was as brassy as its namesake. It looked like a phantasm of polarized bronze-colored glass, and steel. Fragile enough to be shattered by the throw of a common stone.

The illusion was closer to the truth than Randal Rumpp would have cared to admit. The Rumpp empire had been erected of steel and glass and concrete and debt. Debt had never bothered Randal Rumpp in the 1980s. Debt wasn't real. It couldn't be cut like glass, drop-forged like steel, or poured like concrete. Yet it was the true foundation of Randal Rumpp's mighty real-estate holdings. The more he borrowed, the more Randal Rumpp was able to build and buy. And the more he built and bought, the more the banks would lend him. He went on the biggest buying spree in human history. There were only two criteria to catch his interest: The prize had to the best of its kind, and it had to have a blank area large enough to accommodate his last name in six-foot-high letters.

That pretty much limited his major purchases to

buildings, luxury yachts, and private aircraft. Once Randal Rumpp had considered making an offer on the world's largest diamond, and hired the premier diamond-cutter in the world as a consultant. He changed his mind when the respected jeweler informed him that cutting his name into the Hope Diamond would seriously reduce its value.

"How seriously?" asked Randal Rumpp cautiously.

"Seriously enough to make it unsalable at any price."

"Listen, I've put my name on classier buys than that gaudy rock and resold them at a tidy profit."

"Worthless, Mr. Rumpp."

Disappointed, Rumpp went on to purchase a shuttle service, and soon had RUMPP SHUTTLE emblazoned on a fleet of 727s traversing the Northeast air corridor.

It all started to unravel with the junk bond fiasco. Still, even as his debts mounted, they were just numbers on a computer. The buildings still stood, the planes still flew, and the flow of cash, although not flowing overwhelmingly in Randal Rumpp's direction or favor, continued to flow. Payrolls were met. Rents came in. The bottom line, although fluctuating wildly, continued to be written. The top line was staggering. Best of all, the press continued to print his brash pronouncements.

As long as Randal Rumpp got publicity, he knew he would eventually come out on top.

Yet the debt continued to mount and mount, until one day his accountant—the best number-cruncher money could buy—took him aside and whispered, "You're broke."

"Broke!" roared Randal Rumpp, in disbelief. "How can I be broke? I have assets of over two billion dollars."

"It's very simple. You have a combined debt of three and one half billion."

"So? I'll sell off a few trifles. That white elephant

of a yacht. The Florida dump. It's no fun since the divorce, anyway."

"In today's market, Mal-de-Mer is worth half what you originally paid for it."

"We'll subdivide. That ought to piss off those Palm Beach jerk-offs who wouldn't let me join their private club, even after I gave them some of my beach front-age as inducement."

"You don't understand. In today's market, your current holdings won't fetch back the outlay."

"It's a temporary phenomenon. The market will bounce back. I'll call a press conference and announce I'm buying something big. Word will get out that Randal T. Rumpp is bullish on the economy. That should kick-start the commercial real-estate market just long enough for me to sell off a few soot-catchers and make a fast buck or two. Then I'll retire and leave the suckers holding the bag."

"There are no profits out there, Mr. Rumpp," the accountant said morosely.

"No one with assets of more than two billion dollars can be broke. Get real."

"Mr. Rumpp, let me explain this in simple terms," the accountant said carefully. "If you had seventy cents to your name, but you owed a dollar twenty, how would you describe yourself?"

"A pauper."

"A kinder term would be 'over-leveraged.' Which is what you are. Your acquisition debts exceed your assets by almost two-to-one. And the debt service on outstanding loans is costing you a healthy six figures a day."

Randal Rumpp paused in his pacing. "You're not listening to me, Chuck. I have assets of two billion. You said so yourself. I can't fall. No one is going to let me fall. What are the banks going to do—foreclose?"

"They could."

"Ridiculous. Nobody forecloses on multimillion-dollar skyscrapers. My Atlantic City casinos alone are going to put me back in the black. Shangri-Rumpp is gonna bounce back."

The accountant shook his head sorrowfully. "The numbers just aren't there. I'm sorry."

"You're *not* sorry!" Randal Rumpp snarled back. "You're terminated! You just don't understand how business works! I *am* the economy!"

Slowly, the accountant got to his feet. He closed his briefcase gently. "I will submit a final bill for services rendered."

"Submit all you want!" Randal Rumpp snapped. "I'm not paying."

"And why not?"

"Take your pick," sneered Rumpp. "Either you're right, in which case you're way at the bottom of the creditor list. Or you're incompetent, and don't deserve to be paid. In fact, I should probably sue you for trying to pass off this garbage as accounting. You're a cheap fraud. Get out of my sight."

Stiffly, the accountant retreated to the door.

After he had gone, Randal Rumpp buzzed his executive assistant.

"Yes, Mr. Rumpp?"

"Have maintenance shut down the elevators. I want that fraud to walk all twenty-four stories to the ground."

"Yes, Mr. Rumpp."

Satisfied, Randal Rumpp hit the telephones. The world was full of businessmen who thought they were smarter than anyone else. Randal Rumpp had two PR firms working round the clock promoting the notion that Randal Rumpp was the man to beat in business. That always brought out the climbers. They were the easiest to fleece. They walked in the door with a chip on their shoulders—and usually left without their shirts.

It took only an hour to discover that none of the usual fish were biting.

"What the hell's going on here?" Randal Rumpp shouted into the telephone.

The voice at the other end of the line said in a cool, detached matter, "I read your book, Rumpp."

"*The Scam of the Deal* is earning me thirty grand a month in royalties!" Randal Rumpp snapped back.

"It has also shown the world how you run your shoddy business, you simpering egotist."

"Listen, Chuck. Randal Rumpp has the biggest ego money can buy, and don't you forget it!" shouted Rumpp, slamming down the receiver. But in the vast emptiness of his palatial office, the self-styled Rumpp-ster made a rare admission.

"Okay, so maybe the book wasn't a good idea. I'll transcend this."

But mounting debt, he soon found, was not so easily transcended.

The holdings of the Rumpp Empire may have been as solid as the materials they were built of, but they were static. Debt, on the other hand, although as insubstantial as electrons in a bank mainframe, grew inexorably.

One by one, markers were called in. One by one, his trophy assets had to be sold off at fire-sale prices. After each sale, Rumpp put the word out that he had gotten the best of the buyer. But this time, not even Randal Rumpp believed his own PR.

Randal Rumpp was forced to hire the second best number-cruncher that money could buy, hoping to consolidate his affairs. After a month's time, the accountant broke the bad news.

"You're hopelessly in debt."

"I own the biggest yacht in the world," Rumpp retorted. "The owner of the biggest yacht afloat cannot possibly be broke."

"According to my records, you sold the *Rumpp Queen* three months ago."

Randal Rumpp's bee-stung mouth pursed. "I did? Oh, right. I forgot. I hardly go near the thing anyway. I'm allergic to water, or something."

"Your interest payments alone obviate any hope of recovery, Mr. Rumpp. I recommend Chapter Eleven."

Intrigued, Randal Rumpp picked a copy of *The Scam of the Deal* off his desk and began leafing through it, saying, "*Now* you're talking my language."

When he came to the right chapter he looked up, scowling.

"My football league scam—I mean, deal? How will that help?"

"That's not what I meant," the accountant said dryly.

"Oh, right," said Rumpp, dropping the book and grabbing the sequel, *People Hate a Winner*. He had written it before his fortunes had changed, and now it was an embarrassment. Still, if Chapter Eleven got him out of this mess, it would have been worth it.

"What's this? Chapter Eleven is about that has-been boxer, Tyson."

"I meant," the accountant put in, "declaring bankruptcy."

Randal Rumpp clapped the book shut, his eyes glittering. "No chance. I just won't pay my creditors."

"The banks will have to foreclose."

"Then they'll be foreclosing on their own future," Rumpp snarled. "I'll drag them down with me."

"That doesn't change your bottom line."

"The hell it doesn't! All my life I've been playing financial chicken with the old-money crowd, the banks, the insurance companies, speculators. Well, now I play for keeps. From this day forward Randal Tiberius Rumpp pays out no money. Not one red cent. Let's take this to the edge. Let's see who swerves first."

*   *   *

Within a month, the bankers had started foreclosure proceedings. First it was the Florida estate. Then the surviving casinos. Then they came after his Manhattan holdings. Each time another trophy was seized, the phones lit up. For a day. But when the Rumpp organization put out the word that its CEO was no longer giving press interviews, even those flurries of interest ceased.

On the day the phones fell totally silent, Randal Rumpp was down to the Rumpp Tower and his Rumpp Regis Hotel.

"There's gotta be a way out of this black hole," he muttered. "Maybe I'll buy Russia on credit and rename it 'Rumpponia'."

The intercom buzzed.

"What is it?" demanded Randal Rumpp.

"There's a representative from Chemical Percolator's Hoboken Bank down in the lobby asking to see you."

"Is he alone?"

"I'm told there's a man from the sheriff's office with him."

"Sheriff's office? What do they think I am, some nickel-and-dime Savings and Loan?"

"What shall I tell the guard captain?"

"Don't let him in. In fact, have security throw them out on their asses."

Randal Rumpp severed the intercom connection.

A phone rang. At first, Rumpp didn't know which phone had rung. There were so many in the office it looked like an AT&T showroom. A beeping red light on his desk cellular console began flashing.

It was his private direct number, available only to his main squeeze of the month and close friends. The number was changed often.

Smiling, he picked it up. "This is the Rumppster," he announced, primping the four and a quarter pounds of hair that squatted on his head like a startled sea anemone.

"And this is your ex!" a throaty voice purred.

"Igoria?"

"Of course, dahling. A little birdie tells me you're about to undergo foreclosure. I just wanted to be the first to say how very, very sorry I am."

"You're not sorry at all," Rumpp snarled.

"You know, dahling, you're right. And how is that little blond thing? The one with the inverted nipples?"

"How did you know about those?"

"You should never have canceled your subscription to *Spy*, dahling."

Randal Rumpp's simpering expression went prim. "Igoria, you know how you're going to end up? Like Zsa Zsa Gabor—your face stretched to the tearing point, slapping traffic cops to get ink."

"If you ever need a place to crash, dahling, I just bought this insouciant little Louis XIV couch. Bring your own bedding."

Randal Rumpp hung up. "Hag."

His face screwed up into his trademark scowl. He thought a moment. "I gotta get back. I gotta get back." Rumpp snapped his fingers. "I know. I'll leak the name of her plastic surgeon to *Vogue*."

He picked up the main phone. It was dead. He tried another. It, too, was dead.

"What's going on with the phones?" Randal Rumpp demanded of his executive secretary through the intercom.

"Sir?"

"I can't get a dial tone."

"Let me see."

Soon, it became clear that none of the phones in Randal Rumpp's suite of offices was working.

"Maybe . . . maybe the phone company cut service," Dorma Wormser ventured.

"They wouldn't dare!"

17

"They *have* been threatening to terminate if the bills weren't paid."

"Call them. Tell them the check's in the mail."

"How? The lines are all dead."

"Go down to the corner and use a pay phone. Get it done."

"Right away, Mr. Rumpp," said Dorma, hurrying into her coat and out the reception area.

Randal Rumpp threw himself behind his massive desk, which looked like a cherry wood pool table without pockets, thinking that if he docked the broad for her time out of the office he not only wouldn't have to reimburse her the quarter, he'd come out half a buck ahead. These days, a businessman needed every cent.

Dorma hadn't been gone long when suddenly every phone in the office began ringing. It was as if a starter gun had been fired. Every phone erupted into song at once. Some beeped, others warbled, and still others buzzed shrilly.

Seated at his desk, Randal Rumpp goggled, wide-eyed, at the banks of insistent instruments. They sounded angry. Like electronic rattlesnakes.

He decided not to answer any of them.

Then the faxes started emitting warning beeps and whistles.

"Incoming!" Randal Rumpp shouted, lunging to the table on which four fax-phones sat like circled wagons. Paper began rolling out in long white tongues. He hit the OFF switches. Just in time.

The exposed sheets were all blank. He didn't know if it was legal to fax foreclosure notices, but there was no sense taking unnecessary chances.

Back at his desk, the phones kept up their discordant accompaniment.

Randal Rumpp worked his way down the bank, picking up receivers and instantly hanging up again.

This helped not at all. The phones continued to compete for his attention.

In desperation, he grabbed one up and shouted into the receiver, "Leave me alone!"

To his surprise a weak voice responded. It said, "Help me. I am stuck in telephone."

"Dammit! What's going on with these things?" Rumpp complained, slamming the receiver down. It resumed its annoying ringing. Only the cellular unit was silent.

A moment later, his executive assistant stumbled into the office, glassy-eyed and white-faced.

"Mr. Rumpp . . ." she began breathlessly.

"I asked you to restore service, not test the electronics! What is this crap?"

Then Randal Rumpp saw the ghostly pallor that had drained his executive assistant's face.

"What's with you?"

The woman took a deep, steadying breath. "Mr. Rumpp! I . . . never . . . left . . . the . . . building."

"There goes my profit," he muttered. Aloud, he said, "Why the hell not?"

"Because I didn't want to . . . fall in. Like the . . . others."

"Fall into *what*?"

She gulped more air. "The sidewalk, Mr. Rumpp. People were sinking into the sidewalk. It was awful. Like quicksand. They couldn't get out."

Randal T. Rumpp had ascended to the pinnacle of his chosen field because he knew how to read people. He read his secretary now. She wasn't drunk. She wasn't high. She wasn't trying to scam him. She was frightened. She was serious. So no matter how inane it sounded, Randal Rumpp knew he would have to look into her story.

"Are the people from the bank still down there?" he asked firmly.

"Yes."

"Did they see what you saw?"

"I don't think so."

"Did the guard?"

"No, Mr. Rumpp."

"Go back downstairs and tell the guard to throw them out."

"But Mr. Rumpp!"

"Out the main entrance. So I can see what happens."

The secretary was in tears. "But Mr. Rumpp!"

"Or I can go down there myself and have him throw *you* out."

"Right away, Mr. Rumpp." She hurried off, sobbing.

Randal Rumpp's executive assistant stumbled away. Rumpp went to the north wall, which was decorated with framed magazine covers depicting his own face. He opened the *Vanity Fair* portrait. It revealed a closed-circuit TV monitor.

There were cameras concealed throughout the building. Rumpp hit the button labeled CAMERA FOUR. A clear picture appeared. It showed the atrium entrance and the Fifth Avenue sidewalk beyond.

Randal Rumpp noticed that a crowd had gathered. Like at a fire. They were pressed close to the building facade, touching it curiously. He wondered why they were doing that.

Then, through the main entrance, came one of his black-coated guards, escorting a man in gray flannel and another uniformed person. These would be the bank officer and the sheriff.

They had taken no more than four steps beyond the brass-and-pink-marble confines of the atrium lobby when all three men threw up their hands, as if losing their balance. They twisted on their feet like surfers trying not to go under, faces incredulous.

Randal Rumpp watched curiously.

Then, they began sinking into what was apparently solid pavement.

It was a slow process. The crowd recoiled from

the sight. Some scattered, as if afraid that the ground under their feet was going to swallow them, too.

But only the three men were affected. The video monitor captured no sound. Randal Rumpp fiddled with the volume control without success. All he got was the desultory gurgle of his eight-million-dollar atrium waterfall.

The way the three sinking men's faces and mouths worked was enough to convince Randal Rumpp that he would rather not hear their screams of terror anyway.

They were up to their waists within a minute and a half. They started to beat at the sidewalk with their fists. Their fists simply dipped into the ground. They yanked them back, undamaged, eyes astonished.

When their chins were only an inch or so above the pavement, the bank officer began to cry. The tower guard just shut his eyes. The sheriff was flailing his arms like a panicky blue bird. His arms appeared and disappeared, as if he were sinking into calm gray ice water.

At one point, he found something solid. The apron of marble lobby floor that projected beyond the entrance doors. His fingers slipped and slid along the edge. Hope leaped into his eyes. Then, inexorably, the weight of his sinking body was more than his strength could overcome, and he lost his grip.

The unforgiving line of the pavement crept up to their noses, past their wide eyes, and closed over their heads. Their hands were the last to go, clutching like those of drowning men.

Then they were gone. The sidewalk was empty. Everyone was gone.

Randal Rumpp stared at the bare sidewalk where three human beings had disappeared, in defiance of all natural law. He blinked. He looked to his desk calendar. It read: "October 31." Halloween. Then he blurted out the personal mantra that had exalted him to the heights of business success and dashed him back onto the rocks of near-bankruptcy.

"There's gotta be a way I can hype this disaster as a positive!"

2

His name was Remo, and he was attending the twenti-
eth reunion of the Francis Wayland Thurston High
School, Class of '72.

The reunion was being held in the Pickman Neighborhood Club, outside Buffalo, New York, a white
mansion of a place built by a turn-of-the-century industrialist that had been reduced to a function rental.

At the door, Remo gave the name he had been told
to give.

"Edgar Perry."

The woman looked up from the list, blinked, and
said, "Eddie! It's been ages!"

"Forever," Remo agreed. He looked at her name
tag. "Pamela."

"Pam, remember? Here, let me get your photo
badge."

As Remo waited patiently, Pamela dug into a folder
in which splotchy photocopies of the 1972 class year-
book portraits had been clipped and then inserted into
separate laminated badges. She handed Remo one
that showed a bland face with staring eyes and the
name "Edgar Perry" printed underneath.

"Yep, that's me," Remo said, clipping on the
badge.

The face that stared out from the laminated holder
in no way resembled the face of Remo Williams. Not

in shape, head contour, or bone structure. Had it been in color, the eyes wouldn't have matched either.

"It sure is," Pamela agreed, giving Remo a smile that probably had been dazzling back in 1972 but was just teeth in a too-pink mouth today.

"Lewis here yet?" Remo asked casually.

"Lewis Theobald?"

"Yeah."

"Oh, now he's *really* changed. You'd never in a million years pick him out of the crowd."

Remo looked over the main function room. It was done in smoky brick and boasted an ancient fireplace that was as cold as the air outside. There was no need for a crackling fire, the room being warmed by the combined body heat of nearly two hundred "thirty-something" people. Had his eyes been closed, Remo could have accurately counted the exact number of attendees just from the BTUs. Remo had no idea how much heat made a British Thermal Unit, but long ago he had learned how to sense the exact number of lurking enemies in a dark room from the heat radiation. He remembered the steps he had been taught. The rewards, which were few, and the punishments, which were many, before he could do it every time without thinking. Gradually he lost the specifics of that learning experience. All that remained was instinct. Now he just walked in, felt the heat, and a number popped into his head.

Remo's deep-set brown eyes roamed the sea of heads. None of the faces was familiar. He knew that Lewis Theobald's would mean nothing to him, either. But he wasn't looking for a face. He was looking for ears.

"That's him," Remo said, pointing at an animated, blond-haired man whose small ears had almost no lobes.

Pamela asked, "Which one? Come on, be specific."

"The blondish guy with the reddish mustache," Remo said confidently.

"You're right! You're absolutely right! You must have a fantastic memory. How did you *do* that?"

"I have a fantastic memory," said Remo, who just hours before had been shown pre-plastic surgery photographs of his target. There were no post-plastic photos available. But that wasn't a problem. There was no such procedure as an 'earlobe augmentation.' Remo had recognized the shape of Lewis Theobald's ears as if they had played basketball together every day since graduation.

Remo pushed through the crowd, ignoring a waitress in a vampire outfit who offered orange-tinted champagne in tiny glasses, slipped up to the man who wore Lewis Theobald's ID badge, and slapped him on the back hard enough to pop his contact lenses.

"Lew!"

The man with the Lewis Theobald name tag turned from his conversation and looked at Remo's face with a mixture of shock and surprise. His startled eyes went from Remo's familiar grin to his name tag. He absorbed the name and quickly grabbed Remo's hand. "Edgar! How'd you recognize me?"

"Your ears," Remo said, smiling thinly.

"Huh?"

"A joke," Remo said. "Long time no see. What's it been—almost twenty years?"

"You tell me," said the man wearing Lewis Theobald's name tag, pointedly ignoring the person whom he'd been talking to. The other man soon drifted off.

"Twenty years. You haven't changed a bit," said Remo.

"Neither have you, Eddie. My God, it's great to see you. Just great."

"I knew you'd say that," said Remo. "Hey, remember that time in biology class when we had to dissect the frog?"

"How could I forget?"

"And you took the scissors, cut off its head, and dropped it into Mrs. Shields' coffee?"

"That was great!" said Lewis Theobald, forcing a hearty laugh. He slipped one heavy arm over Remo's shoulder.

"Listen, Eddie. I can't tell you how relieved I am to see you. I've been in Ohio since '77, and I've lost touch with everyone."

A redhead with too much sun in her lined face slipped up and said, "Eddie! How nice to see you again!" She gave him a peck on the cheek.

Remo said, "Remember Lew?"

The blonde looked over the supposed Lewis Theobald, went momentarily blank, and finally forced a smile of recognition. "Lewis! Of course. So nice to see you!"

"Same here."

She slipped away, saying to Remo, "Let's catch up, shall we?"

"Count on it," Remo said straight-facedly. It was working. Just as Upstairs had said it would. Twenty years is a long time. People change. Hairlines recede, or change color. Beards come and go. Poundage settles in for the long haul. No one suspected that Edgar Perry wasn't Edgar Perry, who happened to be serving twenty to life on a manslaughter beef down on Riker's Island, and whose reunion invitation had been intercepted before it reached his prison post office box.

It had been a lucky break that the only living member of the Class of '72 who couldn't make the reunion happened to have the same hair color as Remo Williams, who had never heard of the Francis Wayland Thurston High School until a few weeks ago. Lucky for Remo. Not so lucky for the man trying to pass himself off as Lewis Theobald.

"Listen, Eddie," said the man who wore Lewis Theobald's name tag, "I've been out of touch a long

26

time. Catch me up on some of these people. A lot of them don't remember me as well as you. it's awkward."

"No problem," said Remo, smiling to a pert brunette who blew him a kiss and mouthed the words "Hello, Eddie." No doubt the incarcerated Perry's once-and-future prom date. Remo picked a man at random, who had hair like a Chia pet, and said, "Remember Sty Sterling?"

"Vaguely."

"Sty's been dry three, four years now. On his second wife and third career change. He used to be a computer programmer for IDC. Now he not only owns Hair Weavers Anonymous, he's their best client."

"The economy brings them down, doesn't it?"

"And that's Debby Holland. Her LSD flashbacks finally settled down after she had the two-headed baby."

Lewis Theobald made a face. "Our generation has seen its trials, hasn't it? What about you?"

"Me?" said Remo Williams, looking the man directly in the eye. "I did a tour in Nam, in between pounding a beat."

Lewis looked his disbelief. "You're a cop?"

"Not anymore. I moved up. Work for the government now."

"Doing what?"

"Hunting weasels."

The man calling himself Lewis Theobald locked gazes with the man pretending to be Edgar Perry. Neither man flinched.

Finally Theobald said in a cool, toneless voice, "Weasels?"

"Yeah. The human kind. Guys who can't be caught any other way."

"I don't follow. . . ." Theobald said, his voice edgy.

Remo shrugged nonchalantly. "Serial killers. White-collar types. The big bad guys even the Feds can't touch. Super-secret stuff."

"FBI?"

"Not even close," Remo said.

An overweight woman wearing too much Chanel No. 5 dragged a balding, bespectacled husband over and said, "Eddie! Eddie Perry! Pam said you'd shown up! How *are* you?"

"Young as ever," Remo quipped.

"Go *on*. You look ten years *younger* than the rest of us."

"More like twenty," Remo quipped.

The overweight woman smiled through her confusion, and Remo said, "You remember Lew."

"Lew?"

"Lewis Theobald."

The supposed Lewis Theobald smiled hopefully.

"Did you go to school with us?" she asked doubtfully.

"I've been in Ohio since '77," Theobald said, flushing. "I'm the one who chopped the head off the frog in Biology."

"Do tell."

The woman dragged her compliant husband off.

"Where were we?" Remo said.

"Discussing your work. With weasels."

"Right. I'm the top weasel-catcher for Uncle Sam."

"Why have I never hear of you?"

"Only weasels ever hear about me. And when they do, it's already too late for them."

The supposed Lewis Theobald took a sip of pumpkin-colored champagne and smiled knowingly. "Who would have thought that Edgar Perry would go to work for the Central Intelligence Agency?"

Remo smiled back. The smile, under his deep-set dark eyes, made his high-cheekboned face resemble a death's-head. He was rotating his hands absently. It was a habit he had when he was about to zero in on a hit. The unaccustomed shirt cuffs chafed his thick wrists. He hated wearing jacket and tie, but this was a class reunion. Besides, Upstairs was especially nervous about excessive exposure. Especially after Remo's most recent plastic surgery.

Let Manuel "The Weasel" Silva think he worked for the CIA. It wasn't true. And Manuel the Weasel was not known to be afraid of the CIA. He was not known to be afraid of anything.

Here, at the Class of '72 reunion, no fear showed in the eyes of the man pretending to be Lewis Theobald. He had no reason to suspect that the person he thought was Edgar Perry was anyone other than who he claimed to be. To think otherwise would have been too unbelievable a coincidence.

Ever since the Gulf War, and the collapse of his main patron, Soviet Russia, Manuel "The Weasel" Silva had become a human hot potato. The most feared and successful terrorist of the last twenty years, responsible for masterminding a horrific string of hijackings, political murders, and bombings, Manuel had been kicked out of Syria several times. Usually to Libya. The Libyans, who had more to fear from U.S. intervention than the Syrians, invariably kicked The Weasel back to Damascus. Even Baghdad didn't want Manuel the Weasel.

Finally, Manuel disappeared on his own. He had been traced to Montreal, traveling on a falsified Australian passport. There, the trail had disappeared. Washington put its security forces on a higher state of alert, fearing a direct attack by Silva. None had come.

Upstairs, through his vast computer network, had picked up a few clues. Nothing definitive. But through careful work, a pattern had emerged. A bizarre one.

Manuel had not entered the U.S. to commit random acts of terror. He had come to assume a new identity.

The identity of Lewis Theobald, who was found dead in his Akron, Ohio, apartment, his spinal cord severed by a thin, flat blade that had entered through the back of his neck.

It had been a trademark of The Weasel to assassinate his victims in that way. It was the first solid clue Upstairs had gotten. And when Lewis Theobald's parents were both found murdered in the same way in their Miami condominium, Upstairs recognized what no law enforcement agent in the nation could have: The Weasel was erasing anyone who could prove that Lewis Theobald was no longer Lewis Theobald.

When the new Lewis Theobald relocated to Buffalo and opened up a print shop, Upstairs decided to act. The occasion of the class reunion had provided the perfect neutral ground, where Manuel would never dream of coming armed.

Just as he would never imagine that he would meet his assassin.

"Who said I worked for the CIA?" Remo whispered.

The Weasel shrugged. The dead face of Lewis Theobald looked at Remo through the laminated holder with blank, uncomprehending eyes. The eyes of Manuel held a hint of suspicion. He was trying to figure out if he was being stalked or not.

"If you're not FBI or CIA, then who could you work for?"

"It's called CURE," Remo volunteered brightly.

"CURE? That's one I never heard of."

"No surprise there," Remo said easily, smiling to put the man off his guard. "Officially we don't exist."

"Oh?"

"They set it up back in the sixties," Remo went on casually. "Strictly as a counterintelligence organization. One guy runs it. Directly answerable to the president. No official staff, no official payroll. Not even an office in Washington. That way, if things go wrong, it can be shut down inside an hour."

"Are you saying you're the person who runs this organization?"

"Nope. I'm its one agent. The enforcement arm."

Manuel the Weasel allowed himself an easy smile. His confidence was returning. Remo knew what he was thinking. He was thinking that Edgar Perry was trying to impress him with a cock-and-bull story. That Edgar Perry probably only worked for the Defense Investigative Service, or some similar low-level federal organization, and was trying to make himself sound more important than he was.

"Not much of an organization," The Weasel remarked. "One spymaster. One agent."

"Remember what they said about the Texas Rangers."

Manuel looked blank. Naturally, he would. He was a Basque Separatist, and wouldn't know the Alamo from a car rental agency.

Remo said, "One Riot. One Ranger. I'm sort of like that."

"Ah, I see. This is very interesting."

"Look," said Remo, looking furtively around. "I shouldn't really be talking to you about this. After all, we *are* a secret."

Manuel made no attempt to conceal his amused smile. "Supersecret, you said."

"Yeah. Yeah. Right."

"Why don't we retire to the other room?" Manuel suggested. "I would like to hear more about this . . . CURE."

"Why not? After all, we dissected frogs together."

Manuel threw back his head with a nervous laugh and guided Remo into the dining area. He shook his free arm and Remo heard the thin, flat knife slide from a hidden sleeve pocket and into The Weasel's hand.

Good, Remo thought. He's going to make it easy.

The dining room was decorated in a Halloween motif. Halloween was only hours away. The walls were a riot of witches, ghosts, and goblins. Every table bore a carved jack-o'-lantern, in which a lit candle had been set. The jack-o'-lanterns' triangular eyes quaked angry light at them as they took seats.

"This CURE," said Manuel. "How exactly do you function in its table of organization?"

"Between the tight-ass and the pain in the ass," Remo said. "The tight-ass is Smith, my boss. Affectionately known as 'Upstairs.' The pain in the ass is my trainer. A Korean."

"I am not following thees," said The Weasel, his suppressed native accent slipping out.

Remo leaned closer, hoping his target would go for his throat. "Like I said, I'm the weasel catcher. You see, long ago a president saw the country falling apart. Crime was riding high. Terrorists were operating with impunity. The Soviets were threatening to bury us. And our system of government was being twisted by low people in high places who perverted the Constitution so they could get fat, rich, and powerful pulling stuff."

"Stuff?"

"Heavy stuff."

"I follow," said The Weasel, who didn't follow at all. "But I still do not understand your function."

Remo looked around the empty dining room conspiratorially. Only hot-eyed jack-o'-lantern faces stared back.

"Swear not to tell?" Remo whispered.

"I swear."

"Not good enough. You gotta swear The Oath of the Headless Frog. Like in the old days."

"I swear by the Headless Frog," said Manuel "The Weasel" Silva, humoring this fool of an American.

Remo leaned closer, wondering what was taking this idiot so long. "My job description says 'assassin.' "

"Ah. You must be very good at what you do."

"I had a lot of training. CURE doesn't just hire anybody, you know."

"Naturally not."

"First they framed me for killing a nothing pusher. I was still a cop then. Then they gave me a new face, a new name."

"New name?"

"Yeah," Remo said, deciding to cut to the chase. "I used to be Remo Williams."

"But your badge says—"

"A crock," admitted Remo.

Manuel shifted so that his free hand—the one clutching the knife—could snake out without warning. He lifted his glass to cover the action.

"Then they made me learn Sinanju," Remo added.

Manuel the Weasel was in the act of swallowing the last of his champagne. It must have gone down the wrong pipe, because he started coughing.

"Here, let me help you with that," Remo said, taking the empty champagne glass from his fingers and grabbing Manuel the Weasel by the back of his neck. He literally lifted Manuel out of his chair and jammed his entire head into the table's guttering jack-o'-lantern. The thin, flat knife slipped from his fingers and struck the floor, quivering on its point.

Manuel the Weasel's face met the flame of the candle, bent the hot wax candle out of shape, and was pressed into the puddle of clear liquid wax that had melted at the bottom of the hollow gourd.

Manuel would have screamed, but Remo had paralyzed his spinal column. The man could no longer move, or yell, or do anything of his own volition.

Except listen. He could listen. Remo had not bothered to squeeze off his sensory receptors. Although he could have.

Since he had the time, Remo finished his story. He waved away a tendril of smoke that was seeping from the pumpkin. It smelled sickly sweet. Like burning flesh.

"I figured you might have heard of Sinanju. I mean,

you're an assassin. And I'm an assassin. General Motors knows about Toyota, right?"

Manuel didn't answer. He didn't do anything except smoke quietly and twitch.

"Speaking as one assassin to another," Remo went on, "not to mention victor to victim—or is that 'victee'?—I gotta tell you my boss was really worried about my nailing you. I mean, you've got a reputation. That's the problem. Having a rep. It's good for the image, but bad for security. Nobody knows I exist, so I can come to one of these dippy reunions pretending to be someone I'm not and no one knows different. Even if they figured out I wasn't Eddie What's-his-face, they still wouldn't tip to anything important. After all, Remo Williams is buried six feet under. The backtrail's cold. They pulled my prints and burned every existing photo."

Remo squeezed the man's neck harder. The quivering settled down to a spasmodic tremble.

"You, on the other hand, Weasel my friend, have left a methods trail a mile wide. You've got limited technique, so when the pieces started coming together it was easy enough to figure your game. Take off Lewis Theobald and everyone connected with him. Move back into the old neighborhood and strike up acquaintances with the old crowd. After twenty years, and a little plastic surgery, who could say you weren't Lewis Theobald? Pamela? I'll bet if you kissed her, she'd say you kiss just like the old days." Remo eyed the inert form bent over the table. "Or did. Hot wax tends to distort the lip contours."

Remo paused to listen. Manuel the Weasel's breathing was becoming ragged. Probably his nose was full of hot wax. His lungs were laboring. His heart, however, still beat strongly. It was usually the last major organ to give out.

Remo reached over and pulled Manuel the Weasel

back into his seat. The jack-o'-lantern came with it. It sat on his lolling head like a topsy-turvy helmet.

Remo rose to get up. "Well, Weasel old pal, guess I'd better call it a night. Before I go, let me show you what CURE does to weasels."

Remo took the pumpkin in his hands and turned it to the right. He did it so fast that Manuel's head moved right with it, his neck snapping from the deliberate force.

Remo restored the head, so that Manuel "The Weasel" Silva would look natural when the Class of '72 poured in for dinner an hour or so from then.

Or as natural as a dead terrorist with an upside-down jack-o'-lantern for a head could look.

"That's the biz, sweetheart," Remo said, slipping out through the kitchen.

A hour later, Jennifer "Cookie" Friend, secretary-treasurer of the class of '72, threw open the doors and beheld the novel sight of a supposed classmate seated in perfect Halloween form.

"Oh, now who is *that*?"

The general consensus was that it was Freddy Fish, the class clown. Until somebody remembered that Freddy had died attempting to hotwire his front door bell into a car battery three April Fools' ago.

Somebody got the courage to pull off the pumpkin. It refused to come off. But a lightning bolt of blood did trickle down from under the man's neck.

Someone laughed and said it was colored Karo syrup. He rubbed a fingertip in the goo and brought it to his mouth. When it tasted salty instead of sweet, he started heaving.

Cookie screamed.

When the paramedics arrived, naturally they removed the jack-o'-lantern so as to give the victim CPR. The moment the pumpkin came off, a woman shouted "My God! It's Lewis!"

"Who?"

"Lewis Theobald."

"Jesus, you're right. He's hardly aged at all!"

"Well, he ain't gonna age anymore."

"Poor Lew. What will his parents say?"

It was unanimously decided to turn over the proceeds of the Class of '72 raffle to Lewis Theobald's survivors. Cookie went along with a sick smile. She had had the raffle rigged so she would win.

By that time, Remo was miles away. He felt sad. He knew that if he could ever have attended one of his own high school reunions, he would have had no more in common with his old classmates than he'd had with the roomful of strangers he'd just fooled.

For everything he had told Manuel the Weasel—destined to be dumped into a potter's field when the coroner learned that Lewis Theobald was already buried in Ohio—was true. Remo Williams *had* been officially erased so that he could become CURE's enforcement arm. He *had* lost his name, his identity, his friends—he had no family—and his face. Only recently, he had gotten that back through plastic surgery. But as comforting as that was, it wasn't enough. Remo wanted more. He wanted a life. A normal life.

Remo had long ago ceased to be normal when Chiun, the elderly Master of Sinanju, had taken it upon himself to train Remo in the assassin's art known as "Sinanju." From this training, Remo had emerged a Master of Sinanju himself, the first and greatest martial art. There was almost no feat the human body was capable of that Remo could not match. Or exceed. He had become, in a literal sense, a superman, albeit an inconspicuous one.

It wasn't enough. He wanted more. Or perhaps it was less. He wanted a home of his own and a family.

He decided he would take it up with Upstairs. Chiun was in the middle of contract negotiations.

Pulling over to a roadside pay phone, Remo picked up the receiver and thumbed the 1 button. He held it down. That triggered an automatic dialer sequence that rang a blind phone in an artist's studio in Wapiti, Wyoming, and was rerouted to Piscataway, New Jersey, before finally ringing on a shabby desk in a shabby office overlooking Long Island Sound.

"Smitty. Remo. The Weasel is a dead duck."

"Remo," said the lemony voice of Harold W. Smith, director of Folcroft Sanitarium, in Rye, New York—the cover for CURE. "You have called just in time. There has been an event on Manhattan's Fifth Avenue."

"Nuclear?"

"No."

"Then what do you mean by 'event'?"

Smith cleared his throat. He sounded uncomfortable. That could mean anything.

"Smitty?" Remo prompted.

"Sorry. Chiun has already left for the site."

"Chiun? Then it must be serious, if you're rash enough to let him run loose unsupervised."

"It is unprecedented, I agree."

"Is it something you can explain in twenty-five words or less?" Remo wanted to know.

The line was very quiet. "No," Smith said at last.

Remo switched ears. "I'm not up for charades, Smitty. I've been strangling weasels, remember?"

Smith cleared his throat again. Whatever was bothering him, obviously it was big. Remo decided to press his advantage.

"You know, Smitty," Remo began casually, "I've been thinking. Ever since you threw Chiun and me out of our own house, we've been footloose vagabonds. I'm sick of it. I want a permanent campsite."

"See Randal Rumpp," Smith blurted.

"The real-estate developer? You got an in with him?"

"No. The—er—event is at the Rumpp Tower."

"There's that word again. 'Event.' Can I have a tiny clue?"

"People are—um—trapped inside the building."

"Okay."

"And people who go in—ah—never come out again."

"Terrorists?"

"I wish it were only that," Smith sighed. Then the words came rushing out. "Remo, this is so far beyond anything we've ever faced before, that I am at a complete loss to account for it. Please go to the Rumpp Tower and evaluate the situation."

Harold Smith sounded so ragged-voiced that Remo forgot all about pressing his advantage.

"Is Chiun in any danger down there?" he asked.

"We may all be in danger if this event spreads."

"I'm on my way."

Before Remo could hang up, the normally unflappable Smith said a strange thing.

"Remo, don't let it get you, too."

3

The Rumpp Tower occupied half a city block at the corner of Fifth Avenue and Fifty-sixth Street, abutting the quiet elegance of Spiffany's.

By day, it gleamed like a futuristic cigarette lighter cut from golden crystal. By night, its sixty-eight stories became a mosaic of checkered light.

Day or night, its brass and Maldetto Vomito marble lobby atrium, containing six floors of the finest shops and boutiques, attracted thousands of shoppers. Offices occupied its middle floors, and above the eighteenth the sumptuous duplex and triplex luxury apartments began.

On this late Halloween afternoon, no one was shopping in the atruim shops. The tourists who had been caught in the building when the phones went dead were huddled at the ground-floor windows looking out with fear-haunted eyes, waiting for rescue.

No one dared leave. They had seen the terrible thing that had happened to any who made that mistake.

It was the same at the Fifty-sixth Street residential entrance. The doorman had opened the door to let a blue-haired matron out. He stepped onto the street, one hand on the brass door handle. It was very lucky for him that he kept his hand on the handle. The second he felt no solidity under his polished shoes, he pulled himself back in.

"What is it? What's wrong?" demanded the perplexed matron.

"My God! It felt like the sidewalk wasn't there."

"Are you drunk? One side, please."

The matron had a poodle on a leash. She let the poodle go ahead of her.

The poodle gave a frisky leap, yelped as if its tail had been run over, and the leash was pulled out of the surprised matron's hand.

"Joline!"

The matron started to step from the lobby, but the doorman pulled her back.

She whirled and slapped him.

"What are you doing?"

"Saving your life," said the doorman, pointing at the poodle's curly butt as it slipped into the pavement, like sausage through a meat-grinder.

"Joline! Come back!" The tail disappeared from sight, and she grabbed the doorman by his charcoal-gray jacket. "Save my Joline! Save my Joline!"

Any thought of rescue evaporated when one of the basement garage elevators rose to sidewalk level and a white stretch Lincoln rolled out.

Momentum carried it into the street. It was still moving forward as the wheels slipped into the asphalt. The grille tipped downward.

When the hood ornament dipped to ground level, the driver jumped free. His leap carried him clear of the car—and straight down into the unsupporting street.

People do strange things when confronted with danger. The chauffeur was up to his chest in gray street, and only a few feet away the stretch Lincoln was slipping from sight. Like a man grasping at a sinking straw he tried to flounder toward it, as if he were swimming in an unreal sea.

The chauffeur's head was lost to sight bare seconds after the Lincoln had vanished.

Not even an air bubble was left to show that they had sunk from sight on that mundane spot in midtown Manhattan.

"I think we'd better stay put," the doorman gulped.

The blue-haired matron said nothing. She had fainted.

Even now, three hours into the crisis, people were still stepping off the elevators, unaware that the Rumpp Tower had undergone an invisible but very dramatic transformation.

Whenever an unwary resident stepped off an elevator, a knot of the trapped would rush to intercept him.

"Please, don't leave the building!" they would implore.

The exchange was almost always the same. Beginning with the inevitable question.

"Why not?"

"Because it's not safe."

After the first dozen people had stepped out onto the sidewalk, and then *into* the sidewalk, the would-be samaritans gave up telling the truth. The truth was too unbelievable. So they pleaded and cajoled, and sometimes held the person back by force.

Sometimes a simple demonstration was enough. Like the time two people demonstrated the unstable nature of the world beyond the Rumpp Tower when they rolled an R-shaped brass lobby ashtray to the Fifth Avenue entrance and shoved it out a revolving door.

The ashtray wobbled, tilted, and slowly began to sink. It tipped sand, and the sand seemed to melt into the cheerless gray pavement.

It was a convincing demonstration—and saved several lives—but soon they ran out of ashtrays.

Once, a brave fireman approached the Fifth Avenue entrance. By this time the block had been cordoned off with Public Works sawhorses and emergency vehicles. The fireman wore the black-and-yellow slicker and regulation fire hat of the Fire Department, which made him look like a sloppy yellowjacket with an attitude. He carried a pole normally used to pick apart burning debris. He carried this like a blind man's cane, tapping the ground before him as if attempting to find a solid path through the apparently unstable concrete.

A cheer went up when, apparently by chance, he found a solid patch of pavement.

The door was thrown open for him. Hands reached out to shake his, to thank him, to touch the brave public servant who had defied an unbearable fate to rescue his fellow human beings.

No sooner had the fireman set foot on the splotchy pink marble apron extending from the lobby than he slipped from grateful hands and began sinking into its gleaming surface.

The fireman managed a stunned comment. "What the fuck!"

People rushed to his side. "Grab him! Don't let him sink!"

Gripping hands tried. They only slipped through the man's seemingly solid form. No one could touch him.

When he saw the marble floor creeping up to his waist, he screamed. It was a long scream. It went on for as long as he continued to sink and a little while after.

The last thing to go was his black fireman's hat.

Wide-eyed shoppers shrank back from the spot where the poor fireman had last been seen. They could see him scream, but no audible sounds reached their ears.

After that, those trapped in the lobby lost all hope and stared out the great windows like dull creatures in a zoo.

*   *   *

The Master of Sinanju regarded the lines of frightened faces from a position behind police lines.

He stood barely five feet tall, yet he stood out of the crowd like a lapis lazuli fireplug. This, despite the fact that several New Yorkers had crawled into their trick-or-treat costumes early.

His blue-and-gold kimono shimmered like the finest of silks. He carried his hands before him, tucked into the garment's wide, touching sleeves. His face was a webwork of wrinkles, like a papyrus death mask upon which spiders had toiled delicately over centuries.

In contrast to the stiffness in his visage, his young, hazel eyes looked out with a sharpness belying his full century of life.

"Nice costume," said a red-faced ghoul at his elbow.

"Thank you," Chiun replied in a chilly voice, not wishing to acknowledge the interruption.

"Love the mask."

Chiun's eyes narrowed. He looked up. The crown of his head, bald as an amber egg, wrinkled above the eyebrow line. There were two puffs of cloudy white over each ear. A tendril of similar color clung from his tiny chin.

"Mask?"

"Yeah. What are you supposed to be? Bozo the Chinaman, or what?"

The steely eyes lost their hard glitter. They flew wide.

"I am Korean, white!"

"No offense. The mask looks Chinese."

The Master of Sinanju's tiny mouth thinned even more. What manner of imbecile was this, who could look upon the sweet face of Chiun, Reigning Master of Sinanju, and mistake it for that of mask?

"I wear no mask," he said frostily.

"Ha-ha," laughed the ghoul. "That's so old, it's almost funny again."

This was too much for Chiun, who slipped the toe of one of his sandals onto the man's instep. The man never felt any pressure when his toe bones impacted all at once, sending waves of searing pain up into his nervous system.

This had a predictable result. The man screamed and began hopping in place.

Inasmuch as this had taken place but minutes after the fireman had vanished in plain view of everyone, it was enough to ignite the low spark of hysteria.

"The sidewalk! It's going here too!"

In a mad rush, the area surrounding the Master of Sinanju and the hopping wretch who had had the misfortune to insult him was cleared. The fire trucks pulled back. Word that the instability in the sidewalk was growing raced about like wildfire.

Normally, New York crowds have to be beaten back with mounted police and water cannon. But in this case, panic was enough to motivate even the stubbornest gawker.

In less than twenty minutes, a four-block area surrounding the Rumpp Tower was clear to the last person. A new perimeter was hastily established.

From a place of concealment in the deserted B. Dalton's bookstore, the Master of Sinanju smiled thinly. With one blow, he had reprimanded an insolent idiot and created space in which to work without attracting undue attention or angering his employer, whom he believed was the secret emperor of America, known privately as Harold the Mad.

Now all that remained was to learn the nature of this sorcery before Remo arrived.

For not even in the five-thousand-year annals of the House of Sinanju, greatest house of assassins in human history, was there recorded any such magic as this taking hold of a building.

And that, more than the quiet horror that had befallen the most opulent landmark on Manhattan's gold coast, was what troubled the Master of Sinanju's parchment face more than anything else.

4

Word of the bizarre fate that had overtaken the Rumpp Tower reached the ears of Broadcast Corporation of North America superanchorwoman Cheeta Ching, while she was giving an interview in her office.

"Don't bother me now!" she blazed, when her assistant poked her head in.

"But Miss Ching . . ."

All cameras and microphones turned from Cheeta's angry glare to that of her white-faced assistant.

Realizing that she was courting a PR disaster, Cheeta slapped the angry lines from her face and put a little sugar in her tone.

"All right. You may speak."

"It's a story. A *big* one."

Cheeta Ching had been in the midst of recounting her latest triumph. It was bigger than her Jell-O breast implant exposé, or her four-part series on testosterone dementia, or the classic "Why Men are Bad."

It was the culmination of her three-year campaign to become with child. From the moment word had gotten out, Cheeta, who had walked off *Eyeball-to-Eyeball with Cheeta Ching* to undertake "the heroic struggle," had become a celebrity in her own right. The ultimate career woman who was having it all.

Even flush with biological triumph, she still wanted it all. All, in this case, meant the anchor chair at her network.

"One moment," Cheeta said crisply, excusing herself. She moved quickly to the door.

"What's this about a story?" one of her interviewers inquired nervously.

"I'll find out for you," Cheeta said helpfully.

She shut the door. The last sight they had of Cheeta Ching was of her treacly professional smile, set in a flat face so heavily made up it looked like a petri dish overwhelmed by mold spores.

Then they heard the lock click.

Shocked glances were exchanged.

"She wouldn't . . . !"

Then came Cheeta's loud, screeching voice.

"Don't let them out until I'm on the air with this thing, whatever it is!"

"That Korean shark!" a reporter screamed.

Cheeta's next words were, "Does Cooder know about this?"

"No," said her nervous assistant.

"Perfect. Let me break it to him."

She hurried down the corridor to Dan Cooder's office and poked her glossy head in. "Hi Don," she said sweetly.

"Get lost!" snarled BCN anchor Don Cooder, not bothering to look up from his latest Nielsen standings.

"Hear about the Lincoln Tunnel collapse?"

"What!"

"I'd take it myself, but I'm giving an interview on the state of my world-famous womb."

"I owe you one," said Don Cooder, blasting past her like a hurricane with hair.

Ten minutes later, Cheeta Ching was piling out of a microwave van and tearing through the crowd like a bulldozer in high heels.

"Who's in charge here?" she asked a cop.

The officer pointed to a fire marshal. "The marshal is. At least, until the National Guard gets here."

Cheeta thrust her flat face into the fire marshal's grizzled, weatherbeaten features. "Sheriff . . ."

"Marshal."

"Let's have your story."

"No time. We're still stabilizing the situation. Now get back."

"I will *not* get back," Cheeta hissed. "I demand my rights as a dual minority—female and Korean."

"I am woman, hear me roar," the fire marshal muttered.

Cheeta lifted her mike to his face. "What was that? I didn't catch that."

"I said, 'Get back, please.' "

Cheeta Ching turned on her cameraman, snapping, "Follow me."

The cameraman meekly followed. Cheeta skirted the crowd until she found an opening.

She reached back, found the cameraman's tie, and using it as a leash, yanked him through the opening.

"Miss Ching! What are you doing?"

"Just keep your eye to the viewfinder and the tape rolling. I'll get you through the rest. Trust me."

The cameraman swallowed hard. He had no choice. Cheeta Ching could have a man hired and fired on the spot. It was rumored she had eaten her last cameraman alive when he'd screwed up. Not chewed him out, but actually cannibalized him. At least, that was the way he'd heard it. If the story had been about anyone but the Korean Shark, he would have laughed it off.

Cheeta worked her way to Fifth Avenue and boldly strode up to the sidewalk before the brass-framed Rumpp Tower entrance. Under the huge letters RUMPP TOWER, anxious faces stared out.

"Pan along the building," she directed. "I want every gut-churning, scared-white face on the six o'clock news."

"Yes, Miss Ching."

The cameraman began to pan. Evidently some of the trapped recognized the unmistakable features of Cheeta Ching.

They waved and seemingly called her name. But their voices didn't penetrate the thick glass.

"What're they saying?" Cheeta asked, frowning.

"I dunno. Can't hear them."

"Peculiar."

"What is?"

"They're supposed to be trapped, but it looks to me like a person could just walk right out the front door."

"Then why don't they?"

The moment the words were out of his mouth, the cameraman knew he had made a mistake. There were two kinds of mistakes a cameraman working for Cheeta Ching could make: recoverable ones and irrecoverable ones.

The cameraman understood, as if by divine revelation, that he had made a mistake of the irrecoverable variety.

His fears were confirmed by Cheeta's next orders.

"Go up to the door and ask them."

He gulped. "Is it safe?"

"I'll let you know," Cheeta said flatly.

"Miss Ching, we're already in violation of the fire marshal's orders."

Cheeta whirled, teeth flashing. "What's your problem? Are you leaking testosterone out a pinhole in your scrotum? This could be your chance to become a hero."

The cameraman wasn't concerned about his heroism. He was just hoping to live through the assignment. All he had been told was that there was a big story at the Rumpp Tower. From the looks of it, it was a terrorist thing. Someone had wired the tower and was holding its occupants hostage, or something.

"Miss Ching," he croaked. "I'd rather not. Please."

Cheeta Ching got around in front of him. She was

in stiletto heels, which made her almost as tall as the cameraman, who stood five-foot seven. Cheeta Ching slowly rose up on her heels, like a creeping yellow vine. As she came up to his exact eye level, her poisonous red mouth broadened to expose her too-perfect teeth.

"Has anyone ever told you how . . . *tasty* you look?" she asked in a glittering tone.

Suddenly the cameraman had no fear of terrorists or high explosives or any ordinary threat to his bodily integrity. He was staring right into a flat, predatory face with dark, glittering eyes and excessively sharp incisors. If human evolution could be traced back to sharks and not apes, he thought, the face of Cheeta Ching would represent the highest state of mankind's long evolutionary climb.

"For God's sake," the cameraman pleaded, "I have a family!"

Cheeta grinned wickedly. "I'll bet the baby would taste just great microwaved."

The cameraman's eyes rounded perfectly. "But— but you're going to have a baby yourself!" he stammered.

"More oxygen for my baby, if yours stops breathing."

The cameraman reacted as if a brick had knocked him between the eyes. He took a faltering step backward. Then he turned woodenly, like a man ascending the scaffold to the hangman's noose. Except that he was heading straight for the Rumpp Tower.

A police officer stationed within shouting range spotted him and yelled for the cameraman to stop.

He walked on, oblivious, his footsteps as leaden as a sponge diver's.

Cheeta Ching had taken possession of his camera and now had it up on her padded shoulder, tape running.

"Pick it up, will you?" she said spitefully. "I don't want to run out of tape."

Someone had a bullhorn, and he began exhorting the cameraman to turn back. Inside the tower, the trapped grew panic-stricken. They tried waving him away. A man picked up a clothes rack in a famous clothing store and rammed it toward the glass, in an attempt to frighten the cameraman into changing his mind.

He didn't know his own strength. The heavy rack went through the glass, shattering it.

The expensive bronze solar panel didn't shatter in a normal fashion. It cracked apart. But there was no crystalline sound of breaking glass. There was no sound at all.

And because there was no noise, the cameraman, his dull eyes fixed on the looming entrance, completely failed to notice what happened to the glass.

Cheeta Ching noticed. With instinctive speed, she swung the videocam lens over toward the action. The camera recorded the glass falling and striking the ground.

The big triangles and trapezoids of solar panel might have been raindrops, or glass spun of candy cane touching a moist surface. The glass immediately melted into the broad sidewalk.

Cheeta blinked and brought the camera off her shoulder, a stupefied look on her heavily pancaked features.

"Am I seeing this?"

Under the circumstances, it was an intelligent question. Cheeta thought briefly of commanding her hapless cameraman to walk over to the mysterious spot and investigate, but decided that getting one of the hostages to speak on camera was more important. The chump could do that later.

The cameraman was almost to the door now. Inside

the lobby, a security guard and several others were trying to hold the doors shut.

The cameraman's body blocked Cheeta's view, so she didn't really catch what happened next.

It appeared that the cameraman had reached for the door handle of polished brass. His hand jumped back, as if it had received a shock.

His voice was shocked, too.

"I can't touch the door!" he screamed.

"Try kicking it," Cheeta shouted.

"You don't understand! I can't *touch* it!"

"Yum-yum, baby!" Cheeta called.

If the cameraman hadn't already been frightened out of his wits, he never would have attempted what he next attempted to do.

He stepped back and, lifting his right foot, drove it toward the unyielding door.

He went through the glass door like light through a screen. Literally. The glass remain intact. He kept going.

Inside, trapped shoppers recoiled.

And the cameraman fell into the floor and kept falling. He twisted, as if in quicksand. His mouth was making horrible shapes. Oddly, no screams reached Cheeta Ching's pointed ears. Or worse, her directional mike.

Keeping the camera balanced, Cheeta tried to get his attention with a waving hand.

It worked. The horrified cameraman looked imploringly toward her. His eyes were wounded. It was as stomach-churning a sight as any ever captured on half-inch tape.

Cheeta shouted encouragement.

"Scream louder! I'm not getting a sound level!"

5

Because of the nationwide cutback of military bases, Remo Williams was forced to catch a commercial flight out of Buffalo for New York City.

That was bad enough. Since nearly two-thirds of the nation's airlines had slipped into bankruptcy, there were no direct flights to Manhattan, and Remo was forced to change planes in Boston.

At the Boston gate, unmistakable signs that it was Halloween were apparent. The lounging stewardesses wore paint masks. A passing pilot lent a ghoulish air with his plastic skull face.

Remo noticed the passenger in flowing black especially.

It was hard not to notice her. She was tall and willowy, with jet-black hair parted down the middle of her pale scalp, lashes that resembled hair on a tarantula's legs, and a lipsticked mouth that might have been caked with blood.

Her gown made her look like she had been dragged through a mixture of coal dust and old cobwebs. All she needed was a conical black hat and broomstick to complete her ensemble.

The moment Remo entered the passenger waiting area, her eyes went to his lean body. Remo had shucked off his coat, shirt, and tie, leaving only a white T-shirt above the waist and exposing his wiry, understated musculature and unusually thick wrists.

The woman in black was looking at his wrists in particular. Women sometimes did that. It was not the wrists themselves that attracted them, but an indefinable something that made Remo what he was. A combination of perfect balance and coordination that was as alluring to the opposite sex as animal musk.

Remo found the attention as boring as playing gin rummy with blank pasteboards.

He found sex even more boring. The techniques of Sinanju extended to sexual ones. Just as Remo had learned the myriad arts of the silent assassin, he had mastered perfect sexual technique. Unfortunately, for Remo, perfect sexual technique was as mechanical as changing a flat.

Remo pretended not to notice the weirdly pale woman. It wasn't easy. Everyone else was staring at her, which only made Remo's feigned indifference all the more obvious.

A little boy in a Transformed Tae Kwon Do Teen Terrapin trick-or-treat outfit walked up to the woman and asked, "Where's your broom?"

Instead of answering directly, the woman made a pass with one hand and said, "I cast a spell on you, impertinent boy!"

The boy started sneezing uncontrollably and ran away crying, "Mommy! A witch hurt me!"

Everyone in the terminal laughed at the over-imaginative boy except Remo, whose sharp eyes caught the sprinkling of black powder and the scent of fresh pepper in the air.

All eyes were on the mysteriously smiling woman. She moved in Remo's direction. Remo moved off. She followed. Remo ducked into the men's room and washed his hands slowly.

He was relieved when his flight was called. When first-class boarding was announced, Remo started for the gate.

The cobwebby apparition slinked in front of him, throwing a sickly smile over her black shoulder.

"Hi!"

"You look it," said Remo sourly, hoping to quash further conversation.

The hope died when he found that she had the seat next to him. First Class rapidly filled up, killing any hope of his sliding into another seat.

The seatbelt sign came on, and the plane moved quickly to the taxiing position and thundered into the sky.

It droned out over Boston Harbor and turned south.

At that point, the tall, languid woman in black asked, "Are you aware of witches?"

"I'm aware of the one sitting next to me," Remo said thinly. "But only because she smells like rotting toadstools."

"It is not enough to look the part. One must smell the part."

"I'd rather smell car exhaust."

"My name is Delpha. Delpha Rohmer. I come from Salem."

"Figures."

One brush-stroke eyebrow rose. "You have not heard of me?"

"No."

"You must not read very much. I've been on all the talk shows, and profiled in everything from *People* to *Boston Magazine*."

From her low-cut cleavage, Delpha Rohmer produced a warm white business card that smelled like a stinkweed potpourri. She offered it.

Without touching, Remo glanced it over. The card read:

DELPHA ROHMER
OFFICIAL WITCH OF
SALEM, MASSACHUSETTS

In small Gothic letters in one corner was the legend: "President, Sisterhood for Witch Awareness."

This motivated Remo to ask, " 'Witch Awareness'?"

"You think I am in costume for the holiday, mortal?"

"Halloween isn't what I'd call a holiday."

"Correct. It is a sacred day to those who practice Wicca."

"Wicca?"

"Wiseness. The religion of pre-Christian womanhood. It is the oldest religion known to woman."

"Never heard of it," Remo said flatly.

"You're a man."

"What's wrong with men—don't they count?"

Delpha Rohmer looked Remo up and down, in a way that made him think of a vulture eyeing something that was not quite dead.

"They have their place," she said breathily, restoring the card to its nesting place.

Remo decided not to ask where that place was. He hadn't a clue, but he knew he didn't ever want to end up there.

The stewardess came by to inquire of their needs. Delpha pulled down her tray and demurred. Remo asked for mineral water. "Straight up. No ice."

Remo noticed Delpha dealing out a pack of oversized cards on her tray. At first he thought she was playing solitaire, until he noticed the faces of the cards. They were crudely drawn and crude, period. They depicted medieval figures, mostly female, all nude. The few men included one called "The Fool," who was dressed as a priest, and another called "The Hanged Man." One card, titled "The Lovers," showed two naked women embracing.

"Tarot," Delpha said, noticing his gaze.

"I didn't ask."

"You asked with your eyes. It was enough."

"Forget my eyes asked, then."

"Shall I do your Tarot?"

"Only if you'll do it out on the wing," Remo said.

"Men fear what they do not understand. It has always been thus with my kind. In the Middle Ages, we were persecuted. Those were the Burning Times. Today, those who practice the Craft are ridiculed. But after tonight, I will change that."

"Good for you."

"Tonight," Delpha went on in her sonorous voice, "the entire world will see that Wicca is no mere fantasy. For tonight is Samhain, November Eve, the night the Great Goddess sleeps."

"Your night to howl, right?"

"No. My night to break the spell that has fallen over one of the most pretentious idols of pagan malehood."

Delpha continued to turn over cards and look at their faces. To Remo, it looked exactly like solitaire.

"Yes," she went on, examining a card. "It is definitely an omen of evil."

Remo looked at the card. It said, "The Hanged Man."

"No argument there."

"There can be no doubt, the Rumpp Tower has been owl-blasted."

Remo started to blurt out, "Rumpp Tower?" but "owl-blasted?" slipped onto his tongue first.

"The ignorant would call it 'bewitched,' " Delpha murmured.

"The smart would call it bullshit."

"You would not say this, if only you knew what has happened to the great modern Tower of Babel."

"Okay," Remo said. "I'll bite. What's happened to the Rumpp Tower?"

"I am still attempting to divine the exact forces at work. But retrograde spirits have seized it for their plaything."

"Uh-huh."

Delpha turned over another card. "Their intent is

unclear. This may be only a sign of their coming in force. Or perhaps Baphomet merely intends to claim one of his own."

"Baphomet?"

"The Great Horned One. The Lord of Death."

"That anything like the devil?"

"Baphomet is the All-Satan. He is also known as Lucifer, Shaitan, and Beliel. There is no doubt that Randal Rumpp has sold his soul for gold, and Baphomet has come to claim it."

"You can tell all that by playing Go Fish?" Remo asked.

"The Tarot does not lie."

"It doesn't even whisper. And I'm still waiting to hear what happened to the Rumpp Tower."

Delpha Rohmer looked up from her cards. She regarded Remo's strong, skeptical face with its prominent cheekbones.

"People who go in, do not emerge," she whispered. "And those who attempt to flee its enscorcelled confines fall through the earth."

"I heard that. Yeah," Remo said vaguely.

"But if Ishtar is with me, I may be able to undo his black sorcery."

"Sort of fighting fire with fire?"

"I am a *white* witch!" Delpha Rohmer said indignantly.

"Then why are you tricked out like Morticia Addams' third cousin, Moronica?"

"White lace yellows like crazy," said Delpha Rohmer flatly.

At that, Remo grabbed a passing stewardess in clown face.

"Any empty seats back in coach?"

"Yes. Is something wrong, sir?"

"I have this urge to sit with people who come from the same planet as me," Remo explained, without a hint of humor.

The stewardess looked momentarily blank. Remo jerked a surreptitious thumb in the direction of his spidery seatmate. The stewardess nodded. "I'm sure I can fix you up, sir."

"It's been ooky," Remo told Delpha, as he vacated his seat.

"We are destined to meet again," said Delpha Rohmer in a sepulchral voice.

"Not if I see you first."

"You cannot escape your destiny, mortal man."

"Maybe not. But I *can* hightail it back into coach. Regards to Margaret Hamilton."

"A pox on you."

Remo settled into a seat over the wing. After the luxury of First Class, it felt like a baby's high chair. But at least the woman seated next to him wasn't wearing cobra-green eyeshadow.

The descent of the 727—it was one of the former Rumpp Shuttle fleet, now taken over by another carrier—brought it over Manhattan.

Curious, Remo tried to see past his seatmate, hoping to catch a glimpse of the Rumpp Tower—and maybe a hint of what all the trouble was about.

The pilot's voice came over the ceiling speakers.

"Ladies and gentlemen, the sawtoothed skyscraper over to our right is the fantastic architectural triumph known as the Rumpp Tower. Most of you have heard the reports of what's going on down there. And if any of you understand it, let us know," he added with a dry chuckle.

A hush fell over the aisle. Then the buzz of conversation rose anew, more animated than before.

Remo attuned his hearing and began separating out snatches that interested him.

"There it is!"

"They say over six hundred people are trapped inside."

"Do you think they'll condemn it?"

"How? They can't even touch it!"

The 727 banked, and the tower suddenly appeared framed in Remo's window. Under the rays of the setting sun, it was a thing of golden panels and monumental ego. Remo thought it resembled a set of high-tech disposable razor heads welded together. It was smaller than he had expected.

"Incredible," the woman seated next to him murmured.

"Excuse me," Remo said politely. "I've been out of touch. What happened to the tower?"

The woman turned, blinked, and said, "Why, it's disappeared."

It was Remo's turn to blink. He pointed out the window at the unmistakable shape of the Rumpp Tower.

"But it's right there. In plain sight."

"Yes," the woman said dreamily. "Incredible, isn't it?"

"Excuse me," Remo said, slipping from his seat. He found another vacancy, thinking that all the loons come out on Halloween night.

There was a serious-faced businessman in the seat next to Remo. He looked normal, so Remo asked, "Hear what happened to the Rumpp Tower?"

"Of course. Chilling."

"Then clue me in. All I hear is rumors."

"It's not there anymore."

Remo's returned "Thanks" was very small. Okay, he told himself, everybody's a joker tonight. Must be a new thing. Halloween Fools.

The seatbelt light came on and Remo buckled up, figuring he'd just keep his mouth shut and tough out the last few minutes until touchdown.

At La Guardia, Remo caught a cab.

"Rumpp Tower," he told the driver. "And step on it."

"Where you been? Nobody can go to the Rumpp Tower."

"Why not?"

"They got it cordoned off."

"I'll settle for the cordon."

The cabby shrugged. "It's your twenty, pal."

On the way into the city, Remo decided to take another stab at the riddle.

"So what happened to the Rumpp Tower? *Exactly.*"

The cabby looked into his rearview mirror in surprise. "You don't know?"

"No."

"Then why're you so hot to check it out?"

"Just answer the question."

"The tower ain't there anymore."

"Pull over," Remo said suddenly.

"Huh?"

"I said, 'Pull over.' "

"Suit yourself."

The cabby pulled over, and Remo reached forward for the safety shield that separated the driver's seat from the passenger. He grabbed it by the money slot.

The stuff was Plexiglas. Not brittle enough to shatter under an ordinary blow.

"If this is a heist, you're wasting your time," the cabby warned.

Remo used both hands to rub circles in the glass. His right hand rubbed clockwise, and the left counterclockwise.

The Plexiglas soon began to warp and actually run, like melting wax. It became very warm in the taxi.

The driver, seeing the impossible thing that was happening to his safety shield, tried to get out from behind the wheel.

He was too late. Remo put one hand through the widening hole and got him by the back of his neck. With the other hand, he swatted the Plexiglas away.

It fell into the front passenger seat like a tangle of lucite taffy.

"How'd you do that?" the cabby croaked.

"Tell me what really happened to the Rumpp Tower, and I'll be happy to oblige," Remo said in a reasonable tone.

"It's not there anymore," the cabby repeated.

Remo squeezed. The cab driver's red face turned purple.

"It's the truth!" the driver yelped. "You can see it, but you can't touch it. It's like—what do call it?—'intangible.' "

"Intangible?"

"Yeah. It's there, but then again it's not. You can see it clear as day, but you can't touch it. People who go in, fall right smack through the floor. People coming out fall through the sidewalk. It's spooky."

"Anybody know what caused it?"

"If they do, they ain't sayin'. The betting is Randal Rumpp did it, on account the banks are about to foreclose."

"I don't think he's that smart."

"How 'bout lettin' go now?" the cabby suggested.

Reluctantly, Remo released him.

"Still want to go to the Tower?"

"Yeah."

The cab returned to traffic. After the cabby had the sputum cleared out of his throat, he resumed speaking in his normal Brooklyn growl.

"You were going to tell me how you did that trick with the Plexiglas."

"Sinanju," Remo said flatly.

"What kind of an answer is that?"

"A truthful one."

The cabby, mindful of the steel-like hand that had realigned his upper vertebrae in a way his chiropractor would have envied, decided to accept the answer as definitive. He drove north along Fifth Avenue.

He got only as far as Fiftieth Street and Saint Patrick's Cathedral. Traffic was backed up. The howl of sirens seemed to chase one another through the growing dusk. National Guard trucks were cutting back and forth along the cross streets, trying to find their way to the cordon.

Blocks ahead, the Rumpp Tower gleamed like a monument to the mirrored sunglass industry.

"Blocked," said the cabby. "I gotta let you out here. Sorry."

"It'll do," said Remo, throwing a twenty into the front seat and stepping out.

This stretch of Fifth Avenue was pure gridlock. Not only was the avenue locked up tight, but the sidewalks too. Cars, mostly cabs, had attempted to work around the stalled traffic and ended up on the wide sidewalks. The few open spaces were packed with people pushing forward against others.

Seeing the hopelessness of getting through the crowd, Remo simply climbed up onto the cab and began jumping from roof to roof. He willed his body mass to the approximate weight of a pillow, so that when he alighted on each roof the drivers remained unaware, and he left no telltale dents.

To the few bystanders who bothered to pay any attention, it looked like Remo was trampolining from roof to roof. It should have been impossible, but it wasn't. Correct breathing was the key. Remo had been taught to breathe with his entire body, turning every cell into a miniature, super-efficient furnace.

Control over breathing was the essence of the art of Sinanju. Once that had been mastered, the body would respond to any achievable demand required of it. Great strength. Uncanny stealth. Inhuman speed.

In a matter of minutes, Remo had reached the cordon. Kegs of barbed wire were being unrolled to keep back the crowds. National Guard APCs and sentries were stationed at every corner and lamp post. They didn't seem to be doing much, other than watching the crowd with one eye and the gleaming tower with the other.

The tower looked perfectly normal. Or as normal as a modern skyscraper, with dirt loam hanging over its lower terraces and trees growing up from that, could possibly look. Remo had read somewhere that Randal Rumpp had ordered the trees planted to give the building a friendly, organic look. Instead, it made Remo think of an abandoned temple the jungle was just beginning to reclaim.

The sun was reflected in its upper stories, burnishing it to a bright golden bronze. From the ground, its irregular roof line gave the impression of a mammoth crystal calliope. Remo was still surprised at how thin and unimposing it was. From all the hype about it, he had expected another Empire State Building.

To Remo's trained senses, something was very, very wrong about the Rumpp Tower. He was getting a cool fall breeze directly from the tower. Not swirling around it, as gusts typically do around tall skyscrapers. The wind was blowing *through* the Rumpp Tower. Definitely.

Yet the trees stood still.

Remo looked around the crowd. There was no sign of Chiun. But the cordon had been cast so wide that the Master of Sinanju might be anywhere.

"First things first," Remo muttered.

He pushed through the edges of the crowd to a man in National Guard camos. The crowd gave before Remo without realizing what was happening. He would pinch or prod—once he snapped the wrist of a pickpocket in the act of dipping into a woman's shoulder bag—until he reached the National Guardsman.

The Guardsman wore captain's bars, and was anxiously scanning the skies.

"Captain," Remo began to say.

The captain looked down, frowning. Remo flashed

an ID card that identified him as an agent of the Foreign Technology Department of the U.S. Air Force.

The captain blinked. "FORTEC?"

Remo nodded soberly. "We think this is saucer-related."

The captain made a face.

"Don't believe in them," he snorted.

"Tell that to Randal Rumpp, who's probably brushing up on his Venusian even as we speak," Remo said flatly. "I'm looking for my colleague. He's Korean. Very old. And wears native costume."

"Haven't seen him. He's not here."

"If you haven't seen him," Remo said seriously, "that counts as proof he's probably here. Listen, if he lets you spot him, tell him Remo Gavin is looking for him."

"That's you?"

"Today it is," said Remo, moving on. Remo got on the other side of the barbed wire, flashing his FORTEC card and describing Chiun to each person he encountered. He had read somewhere that over sixty percent of Americans believed in flying saucers. From the response he got to his FORTEC ID, Remo decided the pollsters had severely underestimated their count.

At one point, a Coast Guard helicopter clattered overhead. Everyone stopped to see what it would do. Including Remo.

At first, the chopper—it was a white Sikorsky Sea Stallion—contented itself with buzzing the tower like a plump, noisy pelican.

Evidently, the pilot decided to drop lower to see into the Tower windows. The Sikorsky descended straight down on its wide rotor disk.

It was a smooth descent. At first. But the wind gusts that blew harmlessly through the insubstantial Rumpp Tower were swirling and spiraling around other tall buildings, creating the kind of turbulence that plucks hats off pedestrians.

One eddy pushed the Sikorsky into the south side of the tower.

A collective gasp rose from the crowd. Faces turned away. Others craned eagerly to see.

They all saw what Remo Williams saw.

The rotor blades chopped through the golden panes. They beat wildly, as the pilot attempted to correct his equilibrium.

Not a pane of glass shattered. Other than the rotor whine, no noise came from above.

The chopper pitched and turned. In his effort to clear the tower, the pilot managed to send the tail rotor slipping into the facade. It disappeared as if into still golden water.

"It's being sucked in!" someone screamed.

It looked that way. But only for a moment.

The white Sikorsky veered back into view and, evidently giving up, rattled eastward like a frightened bird.

"Okay," Remo said to himself, "it's not really there."

A screechy voice from somewhere near called, "Rocco!"

"Oh no," moaned Remo. Without looking in the direction of the voice, he ducked down and tried to move as far away from the sound as he could.

The voice called after him. This time it said, "Beppo!"

"Not even warm," Remo muttered.

He slipped back into the crowd at a convenient spot and tried to blend in. He took a moment to break the thumbs of another pickpocket, and to his surprise the moment the man began screaming the area around Remo cleared, as if the people were water and evaporation was taking place.

"The sidewalk's going here, too!" a voice shrieked.

It came from a disheveled man who had been holding a soup can in one hand and a sign that said HELP ME. I AM AN AIDS VICTIM in the other. He was the fifth AIDS panhandler Remo had passed in the crowd, which Remo thought as demographically unlikely as spotting zebra in Central Park. And he ran like a marathon runner.

Since the sudden evacuation had left Remo as exposed as a baby's behind, he moved with the crowd as far as the Rolex Building. There he broke off and slipped into an alley, where he almost stepped on the burning human hand.

Remo stopped. The hand was definitely human. It was shriveled, and a pale, waxy yellow. It was set in a kind of ebony base, with the thumb and fingers pointing skyward.

The tips of each digit glowed with a sick green light.

Before Remo could take it in, a cool voice from the shadows intoned, "You see. You cannot escape your destiny."

Remo hesitated. Before he could reverse himself the screechy voice, sounding very close now, called, "Geno! Oh, Geno!"

Remo groaned like a wounded bear. He had no place to run now.

6

"Harm not ye hand of glory," warned Delpha Rohmer, as she emerged from the shadows, her pale hands making weaving patterns in the air before her. The spidery hem of her long black gown swept the dirty concrete, quickly turning gray with urban grime.

"Glory hand?" Remo asked, one eye on the alley mouth.

"It is potent magic. It will dispel any visitant from the nether realms."

Remo brightened. "Does it work on anchorwomen?" he asked.

"I do not understand."

Cheeta Ching picked that exact moment to burst into the alley, huffing as if from a hard run.

"Guido!"

"Not even close," Remo said.

Cheeta showed her teeth in a smug grin. "I have something to tell you," she said.

"Go ahead."

"I'm pregnant."

"I know. It's on the cover of every magazine in sight."

"And you're not the father."

"Louder. I want there to be no doubt."

"But you could have been," Cheeta said quickly. "You could have been the father to the most famous baby to be born in the nineties. Mine."

"I stand chastised," Remo said sourly. "My life in ruins."

"Good. I wanted you to understand the golden opportunity you lost when you spurned me."

At that point, Cheeta's predatory eye fell on the shadowy figure of Delpha Rohmer.

"Who is this?" she demanded.

Remo decided to go with the flow. "Cheeta, meet Delpha. Delpha, meet Cheeta. Delpha's a witch. Cheeta just rhymes."

Both women looked blank.

"What?"

"What?"

"Never mind," Remo sighed. "I don't suppose you've seen hide nor hair of Chiun?" he asked Cheeta.

"You mean the man responsible for the glorious fulfillment of my womb?" Cheeta returned.

Remo's eyes went wide. On his last assignment, the Master of Sinanju had achieved a long-held ambition: to meet the Korean anchor. Chiun had been carrying a torch for her since he had first beheld her barracuda face on TV. He had had visions of fulfilling the childless anchorwoman and siring Remo's successor in Sinanju with one stroke. But Cheeta had instead fallen for Remo. Remo, for his part, would rather have eaten sand.

By the time it had all been straightened out, Cheeta and the Master of Sinanju had gone off together. Chiun had returned home silent but contented. Cheeta had returned to the airwaves with news of her ovulatory breakthrough.

Still, Remo refused to believe it. Now he could only sputter, "You mean Chiun *is* the father?"

"I didn't say that," Cheeta said tartly. "I'm a married woman. In fact, I categorically deny that my husband isn't the father."

"Please, please," Delpha implored. "You're disturbing the spell. The atmosphere of power must not be dispelled by negativity."

"Spell?" asked Cheeta.

"I told you, Delpha's a witch," Remo said. "She's trying to un-hex the Rumpp Tower."

Cheeta Ching walked up to the smoldering hand of glory.

"Is that real? I mean, a real hand?"

"Sure," Remo said brightly. "In fact, it's probably good enough to eat."

"I resent the implication that I'm a cannibal!" Cheeta flared. "I'm a mother-to-be!" Her bloodred nails flashed and curled before her.

Remo backed away. "Hey, it was just a suggestion." He snapped his fingers loudly. "I know! Now that you two have been introduced, why don't you do an interview? Together. Leave me out of it. I'll find Chiun on my own hook."

A cold voice directly behind Remo said, "Look no further, late one."

Remo whirled.

Chiun, Reigning Master of Sinanju, stood in the alley mouth, his face severe, his long-nailed hands obscured by his joined sleeves.

"There you are," said Remo, relief in his voice.

"You are late," Chiun sniffed, drawing himself to his full height.

"Blame it on the disintegrating infrastructure."

"Grandfather!" Cheeta cried, rushing up to the Master of Sinanju.

Chiun's face stiffened. He froze, as if uncertain how to react.

Then, before Remo's astonished eyes, Cheeta Ching, self-styled supreme anchorwoman in the known universe, bowed before him. Twice.

Regally, the Master of Sinanju returned the bow. Once.

"It is good to see you again, grandfather," Cheeta murmured.

"And you, child. The baby quickens?"

"Only due to your greatness," Cheeta returned.

"Am I hearing this?" Remo shouted. "I'm not hearing this! You're not the father, Chiun—are you?"

The wise hazel eyes of the Master of Sinanju looked over to the face of his pupil opaquely, and tracked beyond him.

His hands emerged from his sleeves. One birdlike claw of a hand lifted and curled, gesturing with a bony yellow finger.

"Remo. Who is this *mudang* I find you with?"

Remo looked over his shoulder. Delpha Rohmer stared back.

"Mudang?" Remo asked Chiun. His Korean was good, but not perfect.

"A white witch," replied Chiun.

"You are very wise to know me for what I am," Delpha intoned.

"He doesn't mean 'white' the way you mean 'white,' " Remo snapped.

"I can see that he is in contact with greater harmonies," Delpha returned. "His aura is perfect."

"Absolutely," Cheeta said. "He helped me unlock my burgeoning womanhood."

"You are both properly respectful," said the Master of Sinanju. His eyes went to Remo's. "Unlike some."

Remo put his hands on his lean hips. "Look. We're here to do a job. Let's do it."

"One moment, Remo. I must examine this artifact." The old Korean strode up to the hand of glory and sniffed the smoke being exuded by its shriveling black fingers.

He looked to Delpha. "The hand of a hanged man?"

Delpha nodded. "I dug it up. It's very old. But there was still enough fat in it to burn."

"That's sick!" Remo said.

"Sick would be to use a woman's hand," Cheeta inserted.

Everyone nodded in agreement except Remo.

"It is potent magic," Delpha said.

"Can it help me get my cameraman back?" Cheeta wondered, circling it. She lifted her minicam to one shoulder and captured the smoking member on tape.

"Don't tell me you nibbled on another one?" Remo asked pointedly.

"Silence, Remo!" Chiun spat. "Do not remind this poor creature of her recent misfortune."

"Misfortune? She's buried alive with her cameraman and she *eats* him."

"I did not *eat* my cameraman!" Cheeta blazed. "Whole . . . I just noshed on a piece he wasn't using."

"His *leg*?"

"He was dead. He wasn't about to jump up and run marathons."

"This is a perfectly reasonable thing, Remo," Chiun inserted. "Now be silent. We must be about our important work."

Delpha lifted welcoming hands. "It is our destiny to work together. The three of us."

Remo told Cheeta, "I guess that leaves you out. Sorry."

"I meant, the three of us who understand the elder wisdom," Delpha added imperiously.

Remo frowned. "What am I—the spear-carrier?"

"No. But you may carry the hand of glory."

"I'm not touching that."

"Remo," Chiun said flatly. "Carry the hand. Come, we will solve this mystery before it blights the entire city."

The three started off, Chiun flanked by the two

women. Remo watched them go. He looked down at the smoldering hand of glory.

"Damn," he muttered, stooping to pick it up. "Why do I always end up with the short end of the stick?"

7

Randal T. Rumpp had not gotten where he was in life by being timid. He had his brashness to thank for his steady rise to the princedom of Manhattan real estate, and just as surely to blame now that he had plummeted to the sad status of paper billionaire in such a stunningly short time.

He did not understand the freaky thing that had befallen the Rumpp Tower. He dimly understood that he was trapped, as was everyone who had had the misfortune to be caught within its narrow confines when the mysterious event occurred.

What Randal Rumpp did understand was that there had to be some way he could turn the situation to his advantage.

The phones shrilled in his ears so loudly he could barely hear himself think. In other rooms on this floor, they also were clamoring for attention.

Hanging up did no good. So Randal Rumpp, because doing something physical always helped his brain to work better, went around his luxurious, self-portrait–dense office and started taking them off the hook, one at a time.

Once in a while, he would check for a dial tone.

The first time he did this he got a weird voice crying plaintively, "Help! I am trapped in telephone!"

"My ass," said Randal Rumpp, going to the next phone.

"Help me! Help me! Help me!" said another phone. It sounded like the same voice, so Randal gave it a shot.

"You say you're trapped?" he demanded.

"Yes! Help me, American! Please help me!"

"How much?"

"How much what?"

"How much would you pay me if I got you out?" demanded Randal Rumpp, getting right to the point.

"I will pay any price. Honestly."

"Okay, I need three billion bucks."

"Billion with a b?"

"Yes."

"Okay, I do this for you. Three billion."

"Up front."

"I cannot advance any money while I am in telephone," the weird, tinny voice said, reasonably enough.

"I'll settle for half up front," countered Randal Rumpp, who, had he not been so hard-up, would never have wasted time talking to the disembodied voice. But the man sounded hard-up. And vaguely foreign. The real money today was in foreign hands. Maybe this was some wealthy Japanese industrialist, and Randal Rumpp would luck into a killing. It had happened before.

"I am sorry. You must release me first."

"What are you, some kind of telephone genie? I pop the cork, and you give me three wishes?"

"Three billions. That is our agreement."

"Get lost," said Randal Rumpp, knowing a scam when he smelled one.

The cacophony of office phones having fallen silent, he moved on to his executive assistant's office.

"Dorma, I want every phone on this floor off the hook. Now."

The woman sat frozen at her desk, eyes staring straight ahead in the classic thousand-yard stare. They were misting over. She held a white linen handkerchief before her, as if it were too heavy to raise to her eyes or let fall to her lap.

"Did you hear me?"

"They . . . sank . . . without a trace. . . ." she moaned.

"How would *you* like to sink without a trace?" suggested Randal Rumpp, who boasted in his autobiography that he hired women to staff his empire because he felt they were just as capable as men. He neglected to mention that they also worked a third more cheaply and were twice as easy to intimidate as men.

"I . . . don't . . . care. . . ." Dorma whispered eerily.

"Then I'll do it myself," Rumpp snapped.

It took a while. Every so often he heard the weird foreign voice crying out from the receiver's diaphragm, like a lost soul. He slammed those phones harder than the others.

By the time the floor had fallen silent, the sun was setting. It was then and only then that Randal Rumpp realized the electricity was off. It had not been off before. The computers had been running. Now their screens were dim to the point of grayness.

Whatever had happened, the electricity was no longer flowing through the building's wiring.

He made a mental note to sue the contractor who had put in the wiring, and Con Ed as well. If he sued enough people, he was bound to recoup enough of his losses to bounce back.

Randal Rumpp brushed past his executive assistant and plunked himself down behind his massive desk. He decided to play a hunch.

There was one cellular phone in the office. It had not gone crazy like the others. He picked it up, extended the antenna, and stabbed out the number of the President of Chemical Percolators Hoboken, his chief creditor.

"Mr. Longstreet's office," a crisp voice announced.

"Randal Rumpp calling."

He was put through without another word.

"Alan? Randal here. By any chance have you heard about what's going on up here in the Rumpp Tower?"

"The TV is full of it. I don't understand. What *is* going on? Are you all right?"

"Never felt better. Listen, I don't appreciate being foreclosed on."

"The Tower was our collateral on the Shangri-Rumpp deal, and we had to call in the note. We had no choice."

"And neither did I."

"Beg pardon?"

"You can't seize a building you can't touch," Randal Rumpp said flatly, looking at his face reflected in his buffed and polished fingernails.

"Are you saying you're responsible for this . . . this Halloween prank?"

"No prank, Chuck. The Rumpp Tower is Randal Rumpp's top tangible asset. Now it's been converted into an intangible asset. Never play against a born winner. Chumps like you always lose."

At that Randal Rumpp hung up, smiling a simpering smile that could have belonged to a turn-of-the-century chorus girl.

"That ought to tangle up their balance sheets while I formulate my next move."

The trouble was, Randal Rumpp didn't have a next move. In fact, he still didn't know what the heck was going on. But in the game of life, he knew, he who talks big and bluffs high usually walks away with the jackpot.

And since he was a virtual untouchable in his own tower, he might as well pull on people's chains a little more.

"Get me BCN," he called into the next room.

"How? The phone's are all dead."

"Never mind. I'll do it myself." He stabbed out a

number on his cellular and identified himself to the BCN switchboard. He was put through to the news director at once.

"Let me speak with Don Cooder."

"He's covering the Lincoln Tunnel collapse."

"Really?" said Randal. "It collapsed, huh? Maybe I'll rebuild it. How about the baby-maker—what's her name?"

"Cheeta Ching?"

"That's the one. Put her on. Tell her Randal Rumpp is offering her an exclusive in the Rumpp Tower spectacular."

"Spectacular?"

"You *are* covering this story, aren't you?"

"As a matter of fact, Miss Ching is down on Fifth Avenue now."

"Great. Tell her to meet me in the lobby in five minutes."

"But—"

Randal Rumpp hung up. He went to a wall mirror and primped his hair, straightening his fire-engine-red Hermes tie. He had to duck and twist to see himself clearly, inasmuch as he had had his last name etched vertically into the mirror surface. It was an antique, for which he had overpaid. But with his name on it, it was sure to fetch a princely sum when he got around to selling it.

"I look great," he said. "A winner."

As he walked past his secretary he said, "If anyone wants me I'll be down in the lobby, schmoozing with the media."

The woman looked up, pale and drawn. "There are no media in the lobby."

"There will be by the time I get down there," Randal Rumpp said confidently.

It was a prediction that proved true only because the elevators had gone dead. Randal Rumpp began the slow, tortuous stairwell descent to the lobby, vowing that when things got back to normal he would have a greased brass firepole installed in a masonry column, so if this ever happened again he could zip down to the lobby, just like Adam West.

8

Up close, the Rumpp Tower looked more charcoal than bronze. Dying sunlight made it smolder, as if fires lurked beneath its opaque surface.

Remo looked around. Fifth Avenue was deserted in both directions for several blocks. It was a strange sight. But it enabled them to work unchallenged.

"He stepped into the lobby and just fell out of sight," Cheeta was explaining.

"Ridiculous," snorted Remo.

"Supernatural," said Delpha.

"I saw it all," added Chiun. "From my place of vantage. Before him, a lowly fireman was pulled down to a like fate."

Cheeta Ching looked startled. "You were here before, Grandfather?"

"In my secret capacity, I was studying the fate that has befallen this mighty but hideous structure."

"Was there nothing you could have done?" Cheeta asked, to Remo's relief. She hadn't seemed to pick up on Chiun's broad hint that he worked for someone important.

"Alas, no," said Chiun. "For when confronted with the unknown, the first rule of Sinanju is to observe, lest one become ensnared along with lesser mortals."

"Very wise," said Delpha.

"That's why I made my cameraman go in ahead of me," Cheeta said.

"You sent your cameraman in to his death?" Remo blurted.

"He is not dead," Delpha intoned, snatching the hand of glory from Remo. "He has merely gone to another realm."

"Bull! There's gotta be a scientific explanation for what's happening here."

"Self-blind science cannot explain all," Delpha insisted.

"Sure it can."

"Then why do men have nipples?"

That stumped Remo. While he was pondering the imponderable mystery, Cheeta snapped her fingers and offered a theory of her own.

"I know! It's a dimensional rift opening up."

"Huh?"

"Our planet is intersecting with a parallel dimension, causing an exchange of realities."

"Bull!" Remo exploded.

Chiun cut in. "Silence! Speak, child. Tell us more."

"It's just a theory," Cheeta said slowly, "but I think the tower is slowly entering the Fifth Dimension, or a parallel reality."

"Why?"

"Maybe it's a cultural exchange."

"With who?" Remo snorted. "Rod Serling?"

"Remo!"

Remo subsided. Cheeta went on.

"With any luck," Cheeta said smugly, "we'll get a skyscraper of theirs in exchange."

"What if they don't have skyscrapers in Dimension X?" Remo asked dryly.

"Then we'll probably get a pyramid, or something just as cosmic," Cheeta said flatly.

"This is not what my inmost eye tells me," Delpha warned.

"My ass," Remo said.

* * *

A crowd was collecting behind the ground-floor display windows of the skyscraper, where the boutiques and high-priced antique stores were. Others milled about the atrium lobby aimlessly.

Remo had never seen such forlorn faces. Some were calling out, but Remo couldn't hear the words.

He walked up to the glass of a window display.

"Remo," Chiun admonished. "Be careful. . . ."

"Relax, I'm just going to check this out."

Approaching, Remo lifted both hands to the glass. He set himself in case his highly attuned nervous system encountered something it could not handle, and he had to retreat fast.

His fingers were reflected in the glass. They approached one another's mirror image. At the point when they should have touched, both sets kept going. His fingers seemed to be swallowing each other.

Despite himself, Remo felt the hairs on the back of his neck lift and stiffen.

More incredibly, a part of the crowd inside, seeing how easily Remo's hand had passed through the seemingly solid glass, began beating their fists against the inner glass walls.

Their hands did not go through. In fact, the glass clearly wobbled in its frame from the strong blows.

"This is weird," Remo said, withdrawing his hands. They looked okay. He returned to the others.

"Do you still doubt that dark forces are at work?" Delpha inquired coolly.

"There's a scientific explanation," Remo insisted, frowning at the tower.

"No science of man can account for this."

"It's like a two-way mirror," Remo decided aloud. "You know, where the light goes through one way but not the other, so it's a mirror on one side and clear glass on the other."

"That makes no sense whatsoever," Cheeta Ching said snippily.

Remo frowned. "It's just a working theory. The light bulb wasn't invented in a day, you know."

Delpha lifted her hand of glory to the sky and waved it back and forth, getting oily smoke into their nostrils.

"Ia! Ia! Shub-Niggurath!" she howled. "Oh, All-Mother, we wish to communicate with the cameraman who disappeared into your nurturing earth."

"What is this crap?" Remo demanded.

"Shh, Remo!" Chiun hissed. "It is a *kut*."

Remo understood *kut*. It was Korean for "seance."

"This is loopy," he growled.

Chiun whispered, "Some matters must be dealt with in the traditional manner. Let the *mudang* work her white magic. It may not be Korean, but there may be some usefulness in it."

"How do you know it's not black magic, Little Father?"

Chiun shrugged. "She is white. What other kind of magic can she work?"

Delpha closed her eyes. Her face began to contort.

"She's in touch with higher forces," Cheeta said breathlessly.

"Looks like she's having a standing orgasm to me," Remo muttered.

Delpha's next words were incomprehensible. They weren't English or Korean. Remo decided they were probably witch, and therefore not important.

Delpha swayed like a palm tree that had been dipped in tar. Her face warped and twitched as her mouth chanted inarticulate phrases.

Then her eyes jumped open.

"I have seen! I have communed with the greater wisdom."

"What? What?" Cheeta demanded.

Delpha turned to Cheeta. "I have seen inside your womb."

"No!"

"Yes! It is a boy!"

Hearing this, Chiun turned to Remo, smiling happily. "Did you hear, Remo? A boy! A strapping Korean boy. I have always wanted a male child."

"The skyscraper!" Remo snapped. "Remember the skyscraper? We're here to figure out what the dingdong hell is going on with this stupid skyscraper."

Joyous faces collected themselves, sobered, and the three celebrants reluctantly returned to the matter at hand.

"Did you communicate with anyone about the mystery?" Cheeta wanted to know.

"I have heard a name spoken by the winds that whistle through this Tower of Babel."

"What name?"

"It begins with an R."

"R?"

"The second name begins with an R," Delpha added.

"R . . . R . . ." Cheeta repeated, frowning. "A name that begins with an R . . ." Her smooth brow furrowed. "It's on the tip of my tongue."

"Try Randal Rumpp," Remo offered acidly.

"That's it!" Cheeta howled. "Randal Rumpp! Of course. Randal Rumpp. Is he responsible for this?" she asked Delpha.

"So the Great Goddess whispers in my third ear."

"Oh, brother," Remo groaned.

Chiun tugged on Remo's T-shirt and drew him aside. "Remo, what is wrong with you this night? Respect the powers that reveal hidden knowledge to that woman."

" 'Hidden knowledge'? She didn't exactly pull the name Randal Rumpp out of a hat, now did she?"

"I do not know if her white demons wear hats," Chiun said vaguely.

Remo pointed out the bronze lintel over the main entrance. It read: RUMPP TOWER.

"Maybe she got a major clue from that," he snapped.

Chiun looked, sniffed delicately, and said, "Coincidence."

Remo threw up his hands and groaned, "Oh, I give up!"

"Look!" Cheeta screeched. "There he is!"

"Who?" Remo said, turning.

"There he is! Randal Rumpp himself!"

"It is just as the All-Mother told me," Delpha called.

Chiun squeaked, "There, Remo! Proof!"

"Oh, blow it out your backside. Of course that's Randal Rumpp. It's his building, isn't it?"

In the main doorway of the Rumpp Tower Randal Rumpp had appeared, his hair slicked down with sweat and obviously breathing hard from exertion.

He was holding up a sign. It said: HALF PRICE.

"Don't tell me this is a cheap retail promotion," Remo growled.

Under the HALF PRICE were words scrawled by a blue felt pen: *Wanna interview me about this?*

Cheeta Ching read those words. Their full meaning hit her like an anvil dropped on her head from the thirteenth floor. She shouldered her camcorder and without another thought—or any thought in the first place—she sprinted for the main door.

Remo and Chiun were caught by surprise. Never in their wildest dreams would they have imagined that Cheeta Ching would go plunging into the building, knowing what she did.

But an unbroadcast story was like blood in the water to the Korean Shark, and she plunged in. Through the immovable door, through the unresisting glass, through the startled figure of Randal Rumpp.

And promptly began sinking into the floor.

"Cheeta!" Chiun shrieked. He started in.

Remo got in front of him. "Wait, Little Father. You can't go in there!"

"Cheeta!" he squeaked. "She must be saved!"

"Forget her," Remo said, moving to block the Master of Sinanju. "She's gone."

"But the baby!"

"I'm sorry, Chiun, I don't care what you do or say, I can't let you go there. It's crazy."

The wispy head of the Master of Sinanju darted this way and that, attempting to see around Remo. His eye were frantic, his mouth a round hole of anguish.

"Look!" he shrieked.

Remo turned. And the instant he did so, his legs seemed to turn to water.

For a wild moment, Remo thought he was sinking into the pavement under his feet. No such thing. The Master of Sinanju had, with a sandaled toe, separated his ankles with such speed that Remo never felt the twin blows.

He went down on his knees, his stricken eyes following the blue-and-golden specter that was Chiun.

The Master of Sinanju bounded through the glass doors.

"No, Little Father!"

And before Remo's horrified eyes, he too began sinking into the lobby floor.

9

Remo tried to get up. His legs refused to obey him. He was on his knees and helpless.

"Chiun! *Chiun!*"

"O Shub-Niggurath, hear our plea," moaned Delpha. "Smite the clutching hands of the Great Horned One, who pulls your children down into his fiery domain."

"If there's anything constructive you can do," Remo said, struggling to get his legs to work, "do it now."

Delpha closed her eyes. Her green eye shadow made it seem like they had been replaced by dull glass orbs. "It is in the lap of the All-Mother," she murmured.

His face twisting with fear and anger, Remo watched as Cheeta and then Chiun sank into the seemingly solid lobby floor. Randal Rumpp stuck around only long enough to acquire a dark stain in the crotch of his sharply creased pants. Then he fled in the direction of a fire door. He was followed by a knot of people shaking their fists at him.

Remo closed his eyes. He couldn't bear to watch. He willed the blood to return to his legs. He got the pins-and-needles sensation that told of returning function. Still, his legs were slow to respond. Whatever it was Chiun had done, it certainly had been effective. Remo was almost an invalid.

He blocked out Cheeta's frantic cries of, "This can't

happen to me! I'm the perfect anchorperson! Somebody do something!"

There was no sound from the Master of Sinanju. Of course, Remo realized, Cheeta's screechy caterwauling may have been drowning him out.

Finally, when his circulation was again flowing normally, Remo regained control over his lower body. He ignored the tingling residual pain and found his feet.

Remo ran to the main entrance. There he found a yellow hump on the pink marble floor that looked like half a grapefruit fringed with cotton. As he watched helplessly it sank from sight, silently, soundlessly, and completely.

"Chiun!"

Remo was swatting at the glass door. It might as well have been a hologram.

Carefully, he put one leg in. It went through without sensation. He let the toe of his Italian leather loafer touch the lobby floor. It dropped down and out of sight. He felt nothing. Not warm, not cold. Simply . . . not there.

Remo withdrew the leg. He moved back and looked around frantically. The biggest thing in sight was a light pole. He went to it and began kicking the concrete base with controlled fury.

The pole shattered and began to tip. Remo raced to meet the descending light housings. There were two. The streetlights along this stretch of Fifth Avenue resembled two-headed serpents. He caught one, laid it down on the ground. Going to the base, he chopped away at the cables and copper wiring until they came loose.

Then, using both hands, he levered the base of the pole in a line with the main entrance and began to shove it in.

Remo kept pushing until he felt the other end beginning to tip. He pulled back about a foot of the pole and, certain of its balance, jumped on.

Hands held out to his sides, Remo began to walk the pole like a log bridge. He passed through the glass entrance and found himself balanced over what looked like solid marble flooring, although he knew it wasn't.

His dark eyes said it was solid. His other senses told him otherwise. If he fell, he knew he would be in deep trouble.

While people gathered around, shouting with their mouths but emitting no audible sounds, Remo got down on his knees. He dropped a hand into the flooring.

His hand vanished up to his thick wrist. He felt around experimentally. Nothing.

Remo shouted, "Little Father! Chiun! Can you hear me?"

No sound came back.

He brought his hand back and cupped it over his mouth.

"Chiun!"

Then he heard something. Faint. A voice. Thin. He couldn't make out the words.

"What?"

A single word was repeated. It sounded like "fetch."

"Fetch?"

A "no" came back. It was clear enough. The far-away voice was saying "no."

"Not 'fetch'?" Remo called down.

The word that sounded like "fetch" was repeated.

"Louder!" Remo yelled at the marble. "I can't make it out!"

Then, something jumped out of the floor.

It happened so fast and was so unexpected that Remo's reflexes barely warned him to get out of the way in time.

A man came sailing up in a long arc. The parabola

of the arc carried him through the second-level atrium floor and out into the street.

He began to fall.

Remo moved then. He flashed along the fallen lamp pole and out onto Fifth Avenue. Getting under the man, he raised his arms.

Remo had no idea if he could catch him. There was no question he'd be in the right place at the right time, but there was no way of knowing if the man would land in the upraised cushion of his arms . . . or fall through them and into the unforgiving pavement.

Remo set himself for the worst.

The man struck his hands like a bony sack of potatoes. Remo felt the impact bring him to his knees. It knocked the breath out of the man, but Remo's arm bones survived without shattering. He laid the man out.

"Who are you, pal?" Remo asked.

The man who had been ejected from the phantom skyscraper seemed to be staring through Remo, as if he had beheld sights that had dazzled his senses. "Never mind me," he gasped. "The others."

"Others?"

"Catch."

" 'Catch'? Was that the word? 'Catch,' not 'fetch'?"

"Hurry," the man gasped.

Remo moved back, his arms lifted. There was no time to figure out what was happening. He had to be ready.

Cheeta Ching came next. Remo heard her shriek of fright seconds before she popped—literally popped—out from the golden facade of the Rumpp Tower in a shallow arc.

Remo called up. "Don't worry! I'll catch you."

Like an infielder, Remo positioned himself for the catch.

Cheeta Ching, still shrieking, landed across his arms. Her arms flung out and took hold of his neck,

her nails gouging red streaks in the vicinity of his jugu-
lar. She buried her sticky-haired head in Remo's
shoulder.

"You can let go now," Remo said. "It's me.
Rocco."

Cheeta Ching looked up dazedly.

Her voice sounding surprised, Cheeta said, "I'm
alive."

"And clawing," Remo pointed out. "I'd like my
neck back. If you don't mind."

Cheeta's manicured talons disengaged, like a gross
of hypodermics withdrawing from flesh.

Remo set her on her feet.

"Thank you, Renko," she said. This time, her voice
sounded subdued.

"That's—" Remo caught himself. "Never mind. Did
you see Chiun?"

"No."

"No? Then how'd you get out of there?"

"I have no idea. It was all dark. I thought I was
dead. I was caught in traffic. But the cars weren't
moving. They weren't there. I mean, they were there,
but they weren't. It was just like a 'Far Side' cartoon.
'Traffic Jam of the Damned.' I think one of them
struck me. Because I was flying through space."

Cheeta Ching squeezed her almond eyes shut and
her whole body shuddered so violently that matte finish, like old paint, flaked off her smooth features.

"Never mind." Remo moved back into position.
With any luck Chiun would be along any second now.
But several seconds passed. Then a minute. And the
minute became three.

Delpha had gone to Cheeta's side to offer comfort.
She called to Remo.

"I sense great conflict below. The wise old one has
joined in mortal battle with Baphomet. He has made
the Great Horned One vomit up his victims. Now he
must become demon vomit himself if he is to live."

"Crap and double-crap," Remo muttered.

Delpha's deep voice rose. "Beware! The fiends below grow in power. They will demand payment for your blaspheming them."

Disgust on his face, Remo returned to the fallen light pole and walked along it back into the lobby.

He called down, "Chiun!"

There was no answer. His eyes were hot and dry, as if the tears of remorse had evaporated before they could escape his tear ducts.

Remo looked up. On either side of the brass-and-marble atrium lobby, potted trees formed a sentinel row. At the far end, water drooled down the wall. The water made no sound. Remo realized it must be the famous eight-million-dollar waterfall. It looked more like a main break.

There was a magnificent brass clock on one wall. It read three minutes past seven. Remo decided that if he got no sign from Chiun by five past, then he would jump in himself.

No matter what the consequences were.

The Master of Sinanju grew tired of waiting for his pupil.

There was darkness all around him. Darkness and shadows. Vehicles. They were as insubstantial as smoke, for when he moved near one, no vibrations were given back.

Chiun found that he could walk through these shadowy machines. His face was screwed up in unhappiness as he did so. He could not wait forever.

His path took him finally to a solid form. In the darkness it was impossible to tell what the form was. It gave back coldness and the dank smell of the tomb.

Earth. It was the earth.

He put his hands into the wall and he felt dirt, closely packed and firm. He inserted a forefinger deep into it. The dirt crumbled, surrendered, and tumbled loosely out of the wall.

Using both hands, the Master of Sinanju began to dig a horizontal hole.

He could only imagine where it might lead. But any other hell was to be preferred to this hell of ghost machinery.

The lobby clock read five past.

Remo set himself.

Then, through the intangible lobby glass, Delpha's voice came.

"I am warned of an approaching presence."

Remo whirled.

"Where?"

"It is near, and drawing nearer."

Delpha's eyes were closed. She held the hand of glory high. Its fingertips each burned a sickly green. Remo could see them tremble. Delpha's drooping, cobwebby sleeves trembled too.

"It is very near!" she cried.

Without warning, the pavement under the opposite end of the lamp pole on which Remo stood cracked. It heaved up. The lamp pole, balanced precariously, began to tilt downward.

Remo hesitated, his brain thinking furiously.

Then the lamp fell into the lobby floor, taking him with it.

He had a momentary sensation of falling through darkness and shadow. The disorientation was sudden and absolute. But his racing brain repeated only one thought: There's gotta be a rational explanation for all this.

10

Randal T. Rumpp lost the pursuing pack at the tenth floor.

It had all happened so fast, his brain was still trying to process everything. He had walked all twenty-four floors to the lobby, confident that he was about to give the greatest interview of his business career.

He had been smiling as he stepped into the stunning wonder of the Rumpp Tower's six-story atrium. It was a concession he had been forced to make to the city, in order to get the zoning variance that would enable the tower to go up in the first place. In private, he complained bitterly to his architects that it was costing him a fortune of retail footage, and instructed them to make it as small and narrow as possible. Every optical trick was employed to create the illusion of space that wasn't there. And to dazzle the smart ones, a garish, eye-repelling Italian marble was layered over every exposed surface.

In public, Randal Rumpp hyped it as the greatest thing to hit New York since the toasted bagel.

It had been one of his favorite scams, and he always smiled when he entered the arcade.

His smile had collapsed to a surprised pout when he turned a corner and came upon his would-be interviewer, silently sinking into the marble he had personally scoured Italy for.

Randal Rumpp had only had time to wet his pants

in fear before he'd doubled back for the safety of the stairwell. It was too late. He had been spotted by a group of shoppers, tourists, and Tower residents.

"That's him!" they shouted. "It's his fault! He built this monstrosity!"

They had pursued him like the villagers from *Frankenstein*, shouting that he was to blame for their plight.

Randy Rumpp didn't exactly disabuse them of that notion. He knew that if he survived the sprint to his office, word would spread. He wanted credit for the whole crazy mess. It would help him pull off the greatest deal of his life.

Or it would land him smack in a federal penitentiary.

Eventually, the stamina he had gained from endless games of tennis paid off. The pack thinned, fell back. By the eighteenth floor, he had outlasted them. And he was barely winded.

Randy Rumpp burst in on his executive assistant.

"Let nobody in," he huffed. "No matter what."

"Yes, Mr. Rumpp."

"Any calls?"

"No, Mr. Rumpp. The phones are dead."

"For Randal Tiberius Rumpp, the phones are never dead." He strode into his inner office, grabbed up the cellular phone, and gave it a flick. The antenna snaked out to its full length.

He dialed a local number as he stepped out of his wet pants, then laid them on the double-R monogrammed rug to dry.

"Office of Grimspoon & Laughinghouse, Attorneys at Law," a professional voice said.

"Put Dunbar Grimspoon on. This is Randal Rumpp."

"Go ahead, Rumppster," said a firm male voice a moment later.

"I've moved up in the world. I'm called the Rumppmeister now."

"I'll write it down."

"Dun, I got a legal hypothetical for you."

"Shoot."

"Let's say the bank forecloses on the Rumpp Tower."

"Yes?"

"Let's say before they can serve papers, the building goes away."

"What exactly do you mean by 'goes way?' "

"It no longer occupies the block."

"Randal, what are you up to now?"

"It's a hypothetical," Randal Rumpp said quickly. "The Tower's not there. So. Who owns the air rights?"

"Air rights? Since the building itself is the collateral, I guess you do. The lot, too."

Randal Rumpp's brisk voice brightened. "Are you sure?"

"Not without a week's worth of intense research at six hundred per hour."

"If I made use of the lot and air rights, it would hold up in court, wouldn't it?"

"Maybe. Probably. It sounds like a precedent-setter. I think we could litigate it in your favor. Hypothetically."

"Thanks, Dun. You're a classy guy."

"I'll send you a bill."

Smiling, Randal Rumpp hit the disconnect. "Send me a bill. What a kidder." He dialed again.

"Office of Der Skumm & Associates, Architects."

"Randal Rumpp here. Let me speak with Derr."

A flavorful Swedish voice came on the line, saying, "Der Rumppster! How's der boy?"

"Couldn't be better. Listen. I may have a deal for you."

"Dot so?"

"Don't sound so surprised. The stories that I'm on the ropes are highly exaggerated, Der. Tell you why

I called. I want you to draw up plans for another Rumpp Tower."

"Anodder Rumpp Tower?"

"Only bigger, bolder, and brassier than the original."

"Dot vill take some doing."

"But you can do it, right?"

"It will have to be der same height as der first."

"No. Higher. I want it twenty stories higher."

"But der zoning laws . . ."

"Screw the Zoning Commission. With the deal I'm gonna offer them, they'll be happy to let me build this thing in Central Park."

"Okay. Dis I can do. But first, where do you intend to build dis new Tower of yours?"

As Randal Rumpp leaned into the telephone, his voice deepened and grew conspiratorial.

"Exactly," he said, "where the old one was."

"Vas?"

"Er, I hate to break this to you, Der, since you built the first one, but we lost it."

"Der bank foreclose?"

"They tried to. They were too late. I beat them to the punch."

"I do not understand what happen to my magnificent building. My pride and joy?"

"It suffered a business reversal," said Randal Rumpp unconcernedly. He reached down to test the crotch of his discarded pants. Definitely drying. He wiped his fingers on his tie.

"You are talking riddles. Speak plain English."

"Look, I'm in the middle of three different deals here," Randal Rumpp said, checking an imitation Rolex watch he had purchased off a street vendor when he'd had to pawn his original. "Instead of me explaining it to you, why don't you turn on the TV? The news boys can fill you in."

"But—"

When Randal Rumpp disconnected, he was grinning from ear to ear.

"Now," he proclaimed happily, "all I have to do is convince the city to fund the project, and I'm back on top!"

11

The human eye contains a chemical substance commonly known as "visual purple." It increases night-vision capabilities whenever the retina is exposed to dark conditions. Normally, it takes a few minutes for the night vision to reach optimum sensitivity.

Remo Williams willed his visual purple to compensate for the complete lack of light that surrounded him, and got almost instant results.

It helped. Enough to see shadows and outlines.

He was, Remo was surprised to discover, in a garage of some kind. There were cars set in rows. Most very expensive. Mercedes. Bentleys. Rolls. Even a Porsche.

Okay, Remo thought. I'm not in Hell or China. That's a start.

He began to move about in a circle. It was actually a widening spiral—an old trick. The quickest and most efficient method of reconnoitering an unknown area is to move in a widening spiral, taking in as much territory as possible without losing one's starting point.

Remo found himself confronting a solid wall. At least, it looked solid. He went through it without resistance or tactile sensation.

He was forced to close his eyes, even in the dark. The optic nerve screamed back at him when it connected with the wall.

99

Remo realized he was in the basement garage of the Rumpp Tower. He had fallen two floors, so this must be the subbasement. It was too high to jump back, even if there had been anything to jump back to. The lobby floor wouldn't exactly catch him.

He cupped his hands over his mouth. "Chiun!"

No answer.

Remo continued his circuit. He noticed that, while there was a concrete flooring beneath him, his feet sank into it like a deep-pile rug. He was actually walking on a surface immediately under the floor. Probably the hard-packed dirt foundation, he figured.

It was eerily still in the subbasement. Ordinarily, there would be air flow from ventilation ducts. Not here. Just an uncanny stillness and absolutely no sound.

Remo kept moving. Soon, his sensitive nostrils picked up a faint scent. Human. Smelling faintly of chrysanthemums. A personal scent he knew only too well.

"Chiun," Remo whispered. He lined up with the odor trail, and moved along it.

It brought him, with almost no deviation, to a blank wall, from which spilled fresh earth that might have been excavated by a very tidy steam shovel. The earth seemed to be spilling from the solid wall. Not a crack showed. Yet a fetid breath of air seemed to be coming out of the wall at the precise point where the dirt lay in piles.

Remo ignored the evidence of his eyes and moved into the wall. He discovered himself, after a moment of darkness even his visual purple couldn't dispel, in a tunnel. It sloped up, and Remo saw daylight.

Before Remo could move toward the light, he heard a sound behind him.

It was a low moaning, a kind of mew mixed with a barely human sobbing. It made Remo, in spite of himself, think of a sound that might have filtered out of a primordial forest.

Hesitating, he muttered, "What the heck," and moved back toward the sound.

The subbasement was as large as the foundation, so there was quite a bit of area to search. The walls were a problem. Remo could pass through them, but not see through them. Once, he lost his orientation and started into a wall, only to encounter a stubborn solidness. Remo literally bounced off the wall, and almost lost his balance.

Remo realized then that he had tried to go through an outside wall. The wall itself was no problem, but the earth beyond was as solid as earth should be.

The sound came again. This time, it blubbered.

Remo got a fix and swept toward it. This time, he simply closed his eyes and moved in a direct line. It was easier that way. The seemingly solid walls and cars only confused his eyes. But his hearing could not be fooled.

When Remo picked up human lung action and an accelerated heartbeat, he opened his eyes.

The gloom quickly lifted as his visual purple kicked in.

There was a man almost at his feet. He was on his hands and knees—actually, on his knees only. He was using his hands to try to climb the set of concrete steps that led to the upper basement. His hands were going through the hard-looking steps. As if he refused to accept his inability to make contact, he kept trying.

A sob broke from his lips.

Gently, Remo said, "Hey, buddy. Let me give you a hand."

"Help me. Help me. The steps won't let me touch them. I don't know where I am. I don't know what's going on."

The man sounded as if on the verge of nervous

collapse. Remo decided to deal with him in the most expedient way. He reached down, got the back of the man's neck vertebrae, and found a responsive nerve. The man simply fell into the steps, as all volition left him.

Remo gathered him up, realizing only then that he had a fireman. The black-and-yellow slicker told him that.

Once more closing his eyes, Remo retraced his steps. This time, he zeroed in on the breath of cool night air that was coming from the earthen tunnel.

When he saw pink light through his lids, he opened his eyes.

Remo, the limp fireman in hand, emerged onto deserted Fifth Avenue. He laid the fireman out on the sidewalk. The man kissed the solid pavement and began to crawl toward the distant police lines, as if fearing that to stand up would cause him to lose all support.

"Remo! Come quickly!" Chiun's excited voice squeaked.

It was coming from around the corner. Remo moved in the direction of the summons, thinking, "What now?"

He came around the corner to find the Master of Sinanju, Delpha Rohmer, Cheeta Ching, and the man who could only be Cheeta's missing cameraman, staring at an antique store's display. The cameraman was capturing it on film. He looked as steady as a three-legged chair.

As Remo came up, Chiun said, "We have found the zone of disturbance."

"We have?" Remo asked, looking over their shoulders.

"Lo!" announced Delpha Rohmer, pointing to the display. Around her, the faces of the others were grim and drawn.

It was a Halloween display. Centered around a

black velvet surface were assorted ikons, chief among them a goat's head set in the middle of a silver pentagram.

"I see the head of a goat and the Star of David," Remo said tightly. "So what?"

"It is the symbol of Baphomet, the Horned One," Delpha intoned in a chilly, distant voice. "Some ignorant window decorator, unaware of the forces he was unleashing, made this display and brought ruin down on his head."

" 'He'? What makes you say 'he'?"

"No woman would do this," Delpha snapped. "Women are naturally intuitive. A woman would know better than to create such a potent configuration. Besides, those horns are so phallic."

"I give up," Remo said.

"No. We must not surrender to the dark forces. There are countermagics we can summon up."

"That's not what I—"

Delpha cried, "Back! I must unleash my full charms!"

"Everybody step back thirty or forty miles," Remo growled. "This could be serious."

"What did I ever see in you?" Cheeta sniffed, pulling her cameraman back and pointing first him, and then his lens, in the direction of Delpha Rohmer.

"A snack."

Chiun's wizened cheeks puffed out in indignation. "Remo!"

"Sorry, Little Father."

As Remo watched, Delpha squared her wan shoulders and began to chant, "Max Pax Fax. Spirits of darkness, dispel before my feminine talismans."

She threw up her arms. Nothing happened, except that Remo reached up to pinch his nose. The toadstool odor was there again. He realized it was coming from under Delpha's armpits.

"Is it working?" Cheeta breathed.

Remo looked up. He saw a gray-streaked pigeon attempt to land on one of the trees that decorated the lower setbacks of the Tower and fall through, only to jump out of the trunk in a scattering of frantic wings. "No."

Delpha frowned. "My female powers are not strong enough."

"Tell that to my aching nose," Remo muttered.

"Is there anything *I* can do, as a female?" Cheeta called.

Delpha looked back over her shoulder.

"Do you shave your armpits?"

"What kind of question is that?" Cheeta wondered.

"Do you?"

"Of course."

"Then you are powerless," Delpha said flatly.

Remo looked at Chiun. "Anything about this you care to explain to a skeptic?"

Chiun sniffed. "It is white magic. It may not be as good as yellow."

"Yellow couldn't smell as bad, that's for sure."

Delpha continued to hold her pose. She stood rigid and unmoving. In the distance, the cacophony of New York traffic noise came and went. It was quieter than usual, and had an almost frightened quality.

Remo noticed that the crawling fireman had finally reached police lines, and was being lifted over the barbed-wire barrier by helpful hands.

His "Thank God!" was probably audible in Hoboken.

When Remo's attention returned to Delpha Rohmer, he saw nothing that made any more sense than before.

Curious, he moved to a better angle.

He saw that under Delpha's armpits were two clots of black hair, thick enough to pass for twin muskrats.

"Is there a name for what you're trying to do?" Remo called. "Or are you just imitating Elsa Lancaster?"

"It is hair magic."

"Hair magic?"

"A potent talisman," Delpha explained, straining to keep her arms high. "Modern women have been brainwashed into shaving their bodily hair."

"I heard it had something to do with good hygiene."

"It is a scheme by men to deprive them of their most attractive lures, their greatest power, before which most gods and male demons are powerless. Delilah understood this."

"Yours aren't exactly raising the dead here," Remo pointed out.

"You are right. I must unveil my most fearsome talisman." Her hands dropped to her shoulder straps.

Remo's eyes went surprised. "Not—"

"I must be skyclad!"

At that, Delpha shrugged her shoulders and her black spidery gown slipped to the sidewalk, revealing a third muskrat.

Remo looked to Chiun. The Master of Sinanju brought one sleeve of his kimono up to his eyes to shield them from the white woman's shameful nakedness. Cheeta was positioning the cameraman and hitting the zoom button.

Remo decided to withdraw.

"Nice show, huh, Little Father?" he asked dryly.

"Why is she naked?" Chiun asked.

"She's trying to flash the goat's head into surrendering."

"Ah, Flash Magic. I have heard of this. Is it working?"

"Well, she *is* turning bluer."

The Master of Sinanju stole a peek, then quickly looked away again. "Remo, this is embarrassing."

"Glad you've come around to my way of thinking. How about we ditch the two dips and get down to work?"

"Cheeta is not a dip," Chiun sniffed.

"Okay. She's a dipette. My offer stands."

"Quiet," Cheeta hissed. "You'll ruin the magic spell."

"Perish the thought," Remo said. To Chiun he added, "I rest my case."

Remo folded his arms. "Then I wait here until the moon turns blue."

Chiun looked up. The moon was high overhead, very full and not at all blue.

"It is no such color," he sniffed.

"That isn't the moon I meant," Remo said, pointing to Delpha's pale, goosebumpy backside.

Chiun hid his face anew.

Remo was saying, "Give it up, Delpha," when the helicopter arrived with a noisy clattering.

"Get a shot of that!" Cheeta told her cameraman, slapping him on his head like a spotter signaling a mortar man to fire.

The cameraman pointed his videocam up at the descending helicopter, an eggshell-colored Bell Ranger with a red stripe.

It settled into the middle of Fifth Avenue, revealing the world-famous BCN logo.

Cheeta screeched, "You idiot! That's us!"

"But you said—"

"Never mind," Cheeta said, rushing to meet the pilot, who was braving the prop wash to come in her direction. He actually saluted before speaking.

"Miss Ching. The station just received a call from Randal Rumpp. He's offering you an exclusive if you'll meet with him."

"But we can't get in!" Cheeta fumed. "We tried."

"The news director said to do whatever you had to."

Cheeta looked at the pilot, at the helicopter, and back at the streaked-by-sunset Rumpp Tower.

She wrapped her bloodred fingernails about the pilot's tie. "How do you feel about flying into Randal Rumpp's office?"

"Miss Ching?"

Cheeta grinned like a happy moray eel.

"I promise you the ride of your life," she said.

12

Randal Rumpp was explaining to the mayor of New York City the facts of life.

"Look, you can't collect property taxes on it, you can't move it, you can't sell it, and let's face it, Mr. Mayor, you run the greatest city on the face of the earth. Do you want an embarrassment like a sixty-eight-story skyscraper that no one can enter on your hands?"

The mayor's voice was suspicious and taken aback at the same time. A unique combination.

"What do you . . . propose?" the mayor asked.

"You waive all property taxes for the next hundred years, provide the manpower and the material, and I'll build a new, bigger, and brassier Rumpp Tower on this exact spot," Randal Rumpp said quickly.

"Can you . . . do that?"

"Why not? You can't touch, taste, or feel the current one. It's as useless as tits on an avocado. So we build up from the current foundation, and through it. Make it taller. Of course, I'll need a piece of all frontages."

"Why?"

"We gotta bury the old facade, don't we? You don't want it to show through. It'll ruin the effect. I think the new one should be green. Like glass money."

While the mayor was digesting all this, Randal Rumpp took a sip of Marquis Louis Roederer Cristal champagne from a Baccarat crystal goblet with the name "Rumpp" carved into the base. It was the only one of its kind. Rumpp had had two made, but upon delivery smashed one, in order to make the survivor more valuable. In another year, Randal Rumpp figured, it would be a collector's item and he had plans to move it through Sotheby's.

The mayor's voice came again.

"What about the people trapped inside? What about you?"

"I'm working on that, Mr. Mayor. It took a lot to pull this off. It's going to take a lot to undo it."

"This is insane, Rumpp. You can't get away with something this big."

"Everything I ever got away with in my life was big," said Randal Rumpp coolly, draining the goblet. "Get back to me when you have something I can work with."

He hit the OFF button on the cellular, then bounced out of his seat, humming.

"It's working!" he chortled. "It's really, truly working! I'm going to get a higher tower, and I won't even have to pay for it. This will be the deal of the century!"

In the outer reception room, a phone rang. Rumpp marched in and confronted his executive assistant.

"I thought I told you to leave every phone off the hook!" he snapped.

The woman was shaking. "I couldn't help it. I wanted to see if it worked."

"Try it."

She picked up her receiver and said, "Hello?" A notch appeared between her brows. After listening a moment, she handed the receiver to Randal Rumpp, saying, "I . . . think it's for you."

"Who is this?" Rumpp demanded.

"I am Grandfather Frost," said a strange voice.

"Never heard of you."

"I am like your Santa Claus. I bring presents to those who are good."

"Yeah? How come I never heard of you?"

"I am secret. You understand?"

"No."

"Let me out and you will understand."

"Are you that crazy guy?"

"No, I am not crazy," the voice insisted. "I am Grandfather Frost. I am able to do amazing things. Remarkable things. Set me free, and you will see with your own eyes."

There was something about the voice—Randal Rumpp realized it was the same voice as before—that intrigued him.

"Amazing things, huh?"

"Yes," said the confident voice. Randal Rumpp was beginning to like this voice. Its smooth tone reminded him of his own.

"Listen, do you know who you are talking to?" he asked.

"No."

"I am Randal Tiberius Rumpp."

"I have heard of you," the voice said instantly. "You are very famous and very, very rich."

Rumpp smiled. "That's me. Impressed?"

"Very. You are exactly the man I have been seeking. You are powerful."

"Right. Good," said Randal Rumpp, growing bored with the conversation. He had the attention span of a flea. And suddenly, he got the idea that the weird voice was about to put the arm on him.

"Listen, pal," he said, his tone becoming brittle, "I have my own problems."

"Which I alone can solve."

"Is that so? Well, right now I'm in my office in the Rumpp Tower and the whole place has gone crazy. The people inside can't get out without falling into the ground. And nobody can touch this place. It's like

Spook Central here. I'm inhabiting a haunted sky-scraper. How are you going to help me with that?"

"It is not I who can solve your problem," the voice said.

"I thought so."

"You can solve your own problem."

"Yeah? How?"

"Set me free."

"How will that help me?"

"I am cause of problem," the voice said. "I am making your Tower like ghost. You set me free, and your building will return to normal once more."

"Why should I believe you?" asked Randal Rumpp.

"What have you to lose?"

"Okay, I'll bite. How do I set you free?"

"I do not know. I am trapped in telephone. Usually, I come out without any trouble. I think maybe you must pick up correct telephone receiver to release me."

"Do you have any idea how many individual phones there are in the Rumpp Tower, on this floor alone?" Rumpp said hotly.

"I do not care. One of them will release me. You must try, if you desire normalcy again."

Randal Rumpp slapped his hand over the receiver and muttered to his assistant, "This guy doesn't know what he's asking. Wants me to answer every phone in the building."

The secretary simply looked blank. The side of the conversation she was privy to wasn't exactly balanced. And Randal Rumpp was standing there in his mono-grammed argyle socks and boxer shorts.

Rumpp pursed his mouth thoughtfully. "Okay. Tell you what. I'll give it a shot, see how far we can take it. No promises."

"Thank you."

"There's one other thing."

"Anything."

"A while ago, you said something about three billion."

"I did."

"I still want it."

"It is yours."

And the weird voice was so smooth and confident that Randal Rumpp, for a wild moment, actually believed it to be sincere.

"I'll be in touch," he said breezily.

"I will be here. In telephone."

Randal Rumpp hung up, and told his secretary, "Hold all my calls. Especially if that loser calls back."

"But . . . what about the promise you made to that man?"

"In my own sweet time. If that chump can un-jinx the Rumpp Tower, I don't want it to happen until after I close my deal with the mayor."

Randal Rumpp closed the door to his office.

His executive assistant stared at the oaken panel for several long moments. Her oval face was stone. Then, without a word, she moved out into the corridor. She began going from office to office, lifting every receiver and whispering "Hello?" into each one.

13

Delpha Rohmer was saying, "Shaving your armpit was the absolutely worst thing you could do."

"Really?" shouted Cheeta Ching over the rotor churn. The BCN news helicopter was rising into the Halloween sky. It was very dark now. The hunter's moon hung in the black sky like a sphere of shaven ice.

"Without doubt," said Delpha, arranging her gown. "This hair is called shade. In the old days, those who persecuted my Craft depowered witches simply by shaving their armpits."

"No!"

Delpha nodded. "Yes, Shade has many uses. Tied in a silken bag, it makes an infallible love potion. Thus, if you wish to succeed in love and in life you must let your natural hair grow."

Cheeta Ching was looking at Remo when she asked, "Would that explain why certain people don't succumb to my obvious charms?"

Remo avoided Cheeta's pointed glance. He watched the darkened Rumpp Tower floors drop away, frowning.

"Yes," returned Delpha. "In ancient days females went bare-breasted. It wasn't until men made them cover their natural breasts that the breast became an erotic icon. However, underarm hair has always been one of the most erotic sights a man can see. And one of the most intimidating."

"Is that why they made us shave them?" Cheeta asked.

"Yes."

"The beasts!" Cheeta huffed.

Seated in the rear, Remo turned to the Master of Sinanju. "Is it just me, or are those two making even less sense than usual?"

"It is you," Chiun sniffed, arranging his kimono skirts absently.

"Did I ask you how the current contract negotiations are going?" Remo asked the Master of Sinanju, knowing the rotor noise would prevent their conversation from being overheard. Even by the cameraman seated beside them.

"You have not."

"So, how are they going?"

"Slowly. Smith is holding my most recent bargaining ploy against me."

"You mean the time when you were going to quit to become Lord Treasurer of California, but your candidate turned out to be a Central American dictator in disguise?"

Chiun made a face. "You are just like Smith. Distorting the truth to further your own designs."

"How else do you explain what happened?"

"I was duped. I would never have allied myself with that villain's court had not Smith exiled us to California in the first place."

"We were not exiled," Remo pointed out. "We were on an assignment. How was Smith to know that the guy we were supposed to protect turned out to be a potential hit?"

"He is emperor," Chiun squeaked. "He is supposed to know these things. And none of this would have happened except for your own negligence."

"Old news," Remo said, changing the subject fast. "When you go round again, put in my request for a new permanent residence. I'm tired of living out a suitcase."

"Do not worry, Remo," Chiun said frostily. "I intend to hold the loss of our precious home against Smith during the final discussions."

Remo folded his bare arms. "Good. I want to settle down again,"

"Too late," Cheeta called back. "I'm already married. And pregnant."

"My hopes are dashed forever," Remo said sourly. "Guess I'll junk my hope chest."

The helicopter reached the serrated roof of the Rumpp Tower. Here, the top-floor apartments had unique, two-sided views of the city. Randal Rumpp had sacrificed floor space for the dual windows. It was considered a bad move, but Rumpp had the last laugh. He simply hyped the view and charged triple rent. Tenants gladly paid extra for an improved view, even with their square footage reduced. Once again, the fantasy had sold.

The lights were out all over the Tower. Still, in the dying light of the sun, they could see people in their apartments, some apparently oblivious to their situation as cosmic prisoners.

"Rumpp's office is on the twenty-fourth floor," Cheeta was telling the pilot.

"So?"

"Take us to that floor."

They began counting down from sixty-eight. When they reached twenty-four Cheeta said, "Go to the south side."

The pilot sent the chopper canting around. It twirled like a yo-yo in expert hands, then hovered in place. He said, "I don't see him."

"Who cares? Just fly in."

"Miss Ching?"

"Did you leave your balls at home? I said, 'Fly in'!"

"But we'll crash!"

"Like hell, we will," Cheeta said, grabbing the joystick. She sent the helicopter diving into the side of the Rumpp Tower like a flying buzzsaw.

The pilot's scream was no louder than the rotor noise. It just sounded that way.

Randal Rumpp was sitting with his back to the south facade, trying to put his pants on both legs at a time. Too many people had taken to saying that Randal Rumpp put his trousers on one leg at a time, like everybody else. Rumpp couldn't stand being compared to what he called "the chump in the street." As soon as he had mastered the trick, he would call in a news crew to film the myth-making technique.

Then it happened.

There was no sound. No warning. No nothing.

His first impression was of being swallowed by a monster bird with furiously whirling wings.

One second he was sitting at his desk, trying to draw his five-hundred-dollar button-fly pants over his monogrammed socks, the next he was enveloped in a fast-moving cocoon filled with people.

It happened in an instant. Enough time for him to dive to the floor. He rolled and rolled, wreaking minor havoc on his high-maintenance haircut. Only when he had gotten disentangled from his pants did he get a glimpse of something that made sense. Or almost made sense.

The sight of a helicopter's tail rotors, slipping into the wall separating his office from his assistant's, caused Randal Rumpp's eyes to go very round.

"Are they crazy?" he shouted. "I could have had a heart attack!"

He picked himself up off the floor, calling, "Dorma! Did you get the number of that chopper? I want to sue those jerks!"

There was no answer from the adjoining room.

When he went to look, Randal Rumpp found the room deserted.

"I think that was him!" Cheeta was shouting.

"The guy we ran through?" the wide-eyed pilot demanded.

"Yes. Turn around. And turn on your lights."

The pilot obliged. Chin-mounted floodlamps kicked in, painting the corridors and rooms of the Rumpp Tower in blazing light as they passed through them.

"I don't understand this," the pilot was saying, in a voice that could have been coming through a tea strainer.

"Don't try," Cheeta said. "Just go with the flow."

"I gotta get my bearings."

"Get them fast."

The pilot brought the chopper to a hovering point, half in and half out of the main corridors. He was having trouble dealing with the situation, inasmuch as he couldn't see his own tail rotor and there was a potted rubber plant growing out of his crotch.

He sent the chopper spinning in place, until the nose was pointed back in the direction of Randal Rumpp's office. Cheeta Ching's screechy voice was in his ear again.

"Now, go slowly! I'll tell you when to stop!"

The pilot pushed the cyclic ahead. The wall came toward them, and every sense screamed danger. He forced his eyes to stay open as the wall pushed up against his pupils and he entered the wall.

There was a short interval of subatomic darkness, and they were in an anteroom.

"There he is!" Cheeta howled.

Randal Rumpp did not hear the helicopter approach. So when it emerged from the wall like a red-and-cream soap bubble, it took him by surprise.

"I'll sue!" he shouted, shaking his fists at the people in the bubble.

Then he recognized Cheeta Ching, superanchorwoman. The hottest media celebrity of the month, by virtue of the fact that a lucky sperm had penetrated last month's egg.

Rumpp forced his prim lips into a broad grin. He opened his fist and waved, in as friendly a manner as his ragged nerves would allow.

"Hi!" he said gamely.

Cheeta was waving back, all thirty-two teeth seemingly bared.

Randal Rumpp made an all-encompassing gesture with spread arms. "Ask me how I did it!" he shouted.

Cheeta's mouth made a *What?* shape.

"I said, ask me how I pulled off the greatest magic act since David Copperfield!"

Cheeta stuck her head out of the bubble. She was definitely talking, but there was no sound coming out of her red mouth. It was obvious to Rumpp that she couldn't hear him, either. No more than he could hear the helicopter blades as they slashed the still air of his office. Weren't those things supposed to kick up a little dust? There wasn't even a breeze.

Randal grabbed a pen and stationery off his assistant's desk and wrote ANOTHER RANDAL RUMPP TRIUMPH.

Cheeta ducked inside, scribbled on a notebook, then pressed the open page to the inside of the Plexiglass bubble. One word was visible: HOW?

Rumpp wrote in return: A MAGICIAN NEVER TELLS. He smiled as he held up the answer, because a video camera suddenly poked out of the side and was staring in his direction. He made sure his tie was on straight and the hair was over his ears evenly. Image was everything.

Then he remembered his pants. Rumpp looked down.

"Oh, shit!" He stepped behind his assistant's desk so the camera wouldn't pick up his hairy, exposed legs.

He wrote on the pad, I CALL THIS TRICK SPECTRALIZATION.

The pilot was saying, "I can't hover like this forever."

"Hold your pecker," Cheeta said. "I almost have my story."

"But you don't have any sound."

"For once, this is a time where no sound makes the footage. This is going to look *sooo* spooky on the air."

"It's pretty freaking weird right now," said Remo, who was feeling like a mere hitchhiker. He and Chiun were absorbing the unique experience of being in a helicopter hovering inside a skyscraper. After they had gotten used to the disorienting effects, Remo decided it felt stupid. Like being inside a video game. He wanted to step out, but even though his eye told him there was solid floor under the skids, everything he had witnessed indicated that to step out would be to fall twenty-four stories to the subbasement, and his death.

"Can you figure this out, Little Father?" he whispered. "He can't hear us and we can't hear him. But we're both making noise."

The Master of Sinanju was silent. His keen hazel eyes were darting this way and that, and Remo could tell by the set expression on his wrinkled face that he had no more idea what had happened to the Rumpp Tower than he did.

Eventually, the pilot could stand it no more.

"I'm outta here!"

He spared Randal Rumpp the novelty of being run through by a helicopter and sidled out through the eastern wall.

Once they had emerged into the night, their floodlamps making hot spots on adjacent buildings, Remo said, "Well, that was an experience we won't soon forget."

Cheeta smacked the pilot on the head and snapped, "You idiot! I wasn't through yet! Go back in there!"

"I vote we land," Remo said.

"This is a news helicopter, not a democracy!" Cheeta snarled, slapping the pilot again. "I order you to go back in there!"

The pilot, holding his head in one hand, sent the helicopter back toward the gleaming pinnacle that was the Rumpp Tower. He looked as scared as if he were about to jump into a bottomless hole in the earth itself.

The chopper raced to meet its own reflection in the Tower.

They all watched themselves in a disorientation of reality that was perfect for the occasion.

Then, from one corner of the twenty-fourth floor, there came a burst of white light.

And the Master of Sinanju, his voice a shrill squeak, cried out.

"Turn away! Turn away! We will all be killed!"

14

Dorma Wormser, executive assistant to Randal Rumpp, had gone through most of the twenty-fourth floor, picking up telephone receivers and speaking into them without success.

She wasn't quite sure what she was going to accomplish. But she would do anything to rectify the terrible thing that had happened to her place of work. If for no other reason, than it meant she could go home. After over a dozen years as Randal Rumpp's glorified secretary, being traffic manager to every conceivable hype and scam, going home every night was her favorite part of the working day.

It had been different in the beginning, when Randal Rumpp was a cocky young developer trying—Dorma was convinced—to outdo his old man, developer Ronald F. Rumpp. Every new deal was a challenge. Every success a cause for celebration.

Somewhere along the line Randal Rumpp had peaked financially. Unfortunately, by that time his ego had gone ballistic. His eye was always on the next deal, a bigger score. The publicity rush he invariably got kept him from tying up the loose ends of the previous deal. He talked openly of running for president, while overpaying for every gaudy object that caught his eye, like some overcapitalized raccoon.

It had all come undone with the fiasco Rumpp had dubbed "Shangri-Rumpp." He had already bought into three other Atlantic City casinos. All successful. But he wanted to build one that would go down in gambling history.

Shangri-Rumpp was designed to be the biggest thing on the boardwalk.

And it was. The first night it pulled in six million dollars. Investors predicted that within a month Shangri-Rumpp—with its gilt domes, faux-gem trimmings, and neon fountains—would be synonymous with Atlantic City.

Unfortunately for Randal Rumpp, he had cut costs in a foolish area. The chips. Each one was emblazed with an RR on one side and Randal Rumpp's simpering profile on the other. Rumpp had insisted on it.

So when the manufacturer could not deliver a sufficient quantity by opening night, Randal Rumpp faced a difficult choice: Go with blanks, or postpone opening night.

He did neither. Instead, he had had an emergency order placed with a manufacturer of plastic fast-food drink cup lids. They were cheap, they were inexpensive, and they would retain the sharpness of his profile in the stamping process.

They were also, Randal Rumpp discovered to his eternal regret, as easily counterfeited as cornflakes.

On his second day of business, more chips were cashed in than had been delivered. The record six-million-dollar opening turned, overnight, into a nearly twenty-million-dollar sinkhole.

When he realized the magnitude of the financial hemorrhaging, Randal Rumpp faced another difficult choice: Close down until the original chips came in, or keep playing.

As always, Randal T. Rumpp led with his ego. He ordered the roulette wheels to keep spinning, the blackjack dealers to keep dealing, and the baccarat tables to remain open, boasting, "The slot machines will keep us going until the chips are down. I mean, in."

When he lost over twenty-five million to counterfeit chips on the third night, Randal Rumpp issued a statement that Shangri-Rumpp was setting new records for payouts and quietly talked his father into buying forty million dollars' worth of twenty-dollar Shangri-Rumpp chips to bail him out for the first operating week.

It was a disaster from which the Rumpp Organization had never recovered. Not even when Randal Rumpp refused to allow his father to cash in his chips, claiming they were "shoddy counterfeits."

The entire house of cards began to collapse then. Loans were called due. Assets were seized. Staff was fired. Dorma Wormser, like most Rumpp employees, was forced to accept a fifty-percent pay cut. The only reason she stayed on was because jobs in corporate America in the early nineties were scarce. Especially if a job-seeker was in the position of having to list Randal Rumpp as a reference.

And now this. She was trapped, with an angry mob roaming the building. A mob that blamed Randal Rumpp for their plight.

If there was anyone who could help, Dorma Wormser wanted to talk to him.

She was beginning to think she would have to test every phone in the Tower, when she tried a desk phone in the executive trophy room. It was off-limits to everyone except Randal Rumpp. It was the place where he kept his favorite trophies—from his childhood Monopoly game and photographs of former girlfriends, to the more modest business acquisitions, such as the solid-gold stapler that never worked but was brought out for office photo opportunities.

The desk phone was a simple AT&T ROLM phone. But it had been Randal Rumpp's first business phone, and he treasured it. The bell had been disabled, but a red light winked on and off, indicating an incoming call.

She lifted the receiver.

Dorma Wormser had answered telephones both personally and professionally for most of her life. She was good at it. Her voice was clear and crisp. Her manner smooth and businesslike. It was the perfect executive assistant's telephone voice.

This time, she whispered a timid, "Hello?"

There was no answer. Just a rushing, like a comet composed of static coming in her direction. It grew louder very fast. Soon it was a wooshing roar. It was coming from the earpiece. Definitely.

Then came the flash of blinding white light that changed everything.

After she had regained her sight and other senses, Dorma Wormser knew she would look back upon her life in entirely different terms. She would never regain the normal, ordinary existence that had been hers before she'd picked up that ordinary telephone handset, as she began the long slide into nervous collapse that would haunt her for the rest of her days.

The stunningly bright light was all around her. It was soundless. It was not an explosion, but the suddenness of it was enough to knock her on her back. How long she was out, Dorma Wormser had no idea. Her eyes fluttered open and there it was, floating directly above her.

"Oh, God," she moaned.

It might have been a man.

Her initial impression was that it was white. It was white from the hairless bald top of its bloated head to the tips of its very white feet. But it was not all white. Some of it was golden. There were golden veins on its smooth white skin. Not in, but on. They lay along the skin like printed circuits, except that they pulsed and ran with fleet golden lights.

That was weird enough. But the thing that shocked

Dorma Wormser, that sent her scrambling to her feet and running for help, was the dead way the manlike thing floated just under the high ceiling. It was like a white, lifeless corpse filled with helium.

Worst of all, it had no face.

15

The pilot of the BCN news helicopter heard the voice of the old Korean warn him against flying into the Rumpp Tower. His brain told him that the shrill voice was serious. His brain also screamed that he was flying into a solid object and should swerve to avoid it.

He had been with BCN for over six years, half of them working for Cheeta Ching. Before that he had been a bush pilot in Alaska. And before that he had seen action in Grenada. He was used to risk. Even though every fiber in his high-strung being told him to swerve, he stayed on course.

If I die, he reasoned, I die. If I disobey the Korean Shark, I'm worse than dead.

He closed his eyes, not bothering to hope for any particular result.

So it came as a total shock to him when Cheeta Ching dug her bloodred claws into his shoulder and screamed, "You heard Grandfather Chiun! Swerve, you testosterone-drunk fool!"

The pilot's eyes flew open. He pulled back on the collective. Just in time. The helicopter swooped up and over the Rumpp Tower, a fly's-eye panorama of repeated helicopter reflections chasing it along every mirrored surface.

When the chopper had flattened out into a lazy circle and everyone's stomach had climbed down out of their throat, Remo asked the Master of Sinanju a question.

"What is it, Little Father? What did you see?"

"The building has found its proper vibration."

"Huh?"

"He means it's solid again," Cheeta offered. "Right, Grandfather?"

Chiun nodded somberly. "I do."

Everyone looked. The Rumpp Tower looked no different. The last hot, purplish-orange rays of the sun were streaking its sawtooth top, but otherwise it had become a kind of stalagmite of obsidian, with a subtle bronze underhue.

"Looks the same to me," Remo muttered.

"Now look with your eyes," spat Chiun, pointing down with one spindly finger.

Everyone looked downward.

Several floors up from the RUMPP TOWER sign over the Fifth Avenue entrance, a balloon was swirling in the eddies and currents surrounding the Tower. It was Halloween-orange and had a pumpkin face. Evidently, someone from the crowd behind the distant barbed wire had released it.

As they watched, a gust of wind swept it up. It skidded close to the Tower facade and, as it rose, bounced off.

"It bounced!" Cheeta breathed.

"I saw this happen before," Chiun offered.

"Praise Diana, Goddess of the Moon!" Delpha cried, closing her eyes and lifting empty palms to the moon. "My womanly magic proved true."

"My ass," said Remo, quickly pinching his nose shut.

"You did this?" Cheeta asked, dumbfounded.

"Indeed," said Delpha calmly. "You may interview me now. I suggest a two-shot."

"And I suggest we land before I throw up," Remo said.

Cheeta said, "Later. I want to see what's going on in the Tower. You! Cameraman! Let's get some footage."

The cameraman got his video up and running.

"Make a circle of the building," Cheeta told the pilot.

Delpha chimed in. "Good. Circles are good. They represent femaleness. If we create enough of them, they will dispel the Horned One forever."

"Shouldn't we be landing, to let the people know it's okay to come out now?" Remo suggested.

"No," Cheeta said sharply, "Later. If we set them free now, we can't interview them."

"Since when does a story come before people?"

"Since before Edward R. Murrow," said Cheeta solemnly.

"Can I quote you on that?" Remo asked.

Before Cheeta could answer, Delpha cried, "Look, I see an otherworldly apparition!"

Cheeta's glossy head snapped about, like that of a confused Mako shark. "Where? Where?"

Delpha pointed. "There! In that corner office."

The cameraman was trying to position his lens, saying, "Where? Which corner? I don't see anything."

Delpha reached back and yanked the camcorder lens toward the southwestern corner of the building and held it.

"Do you see it now?" she asked.

"I don't know," the cameraman said. "I think you bruised my eye."

"Just keep taping," Cheeta said. "The network will gladly buy you a glass eye."

They swept past the corner and around to the other side, where the Spiffany Building, as solid as the granite it was built of, lay bathed in cold moonlight.

Cheeta asked, "What did you see?"

"It looked like an evil spirit," Delpha said, more pale-faced than usual. "I think it was a night-gaunt."

"What's a 'night-gaunt'?" Remo asked.

"It is a creature normally seen only in dreams," Delpha explained. "They have rubbery skin, long forked tails, and no face at all."

"This thing you saw had no face?"

Delpha nodded. "No more than an egg does."

"Sounds like a night-gaunt to me," Remo said dryly.

"If night-gaunts are breaking into the waking world, I fear for humanity. *None* are female."

Cheeta frowned. "God. What is this world coming to?"

"There is only one odd thing," Delpha said slowly.

"What's that?" asked Cheeta.

"Night-gaunts are usually black-skinned. This one was completely white. I will have to consult the *Necronomicon* about them."

To Remo's surprise, she pulled a dog-eared paperback book from under her skirt and consulted it.

"This is strange," she said thoughtfully. "There's no mention of white night-gaunts. Not even in the demonology concordance."

"It doesn't matter," Cheeta put in. "We got it on tape, whatever it was." She glared back at her wincing cameraman. "At least, we'd *better* have gotten it on tape."

"But the *Necronomicon* should list it if it exists," Delpha said worriedly.

"Maybe you got the abridged edition by mistake," Remo suggested helpfully.

"Remo," Chiun flared, "you are behaving like an idiot."

"I've been dragged down by the company I'm forced to keep. Look, can we just land this thing?"

"An excellent idea," Chiun said sternly. "We will land and rescue the persons formerly trapped within this glittering monstrosity, thus earning the eternal gratitude of this country and whoever may rule it."

"Why would we do that?" Remo wanted to know.

"Contract negotiations," Chiun whispered.

"Oh."

This half-overheard conversation made Cheeta Ching think of something.

"You know, it's quite a coincidence."

Remo made his face blank. "What is?"

"Bumping into you two again like this. Clear across the country."

Remo looked away. "It's a free country. We travel a lot."

"Whose campaign are you with this time?"

"Nobody's. We're in a new line of work," Remo explained, blank-voiced. "We're insurance adjusters. We're out here because Randal Rumpp needed extra fire insurance."

"That's ridiculous!"

To which, Remo offered a business card that identified him as Remo Wausau, with Apolitical Life and Casualty.

"This is awfully unlikely," Cheeta said.

"Tell her, Little Father."

Chiun thinned papery lips. "It is as Remo says," he said with obvious distaste. "We are adjusters of insurance. Temporarily."

"Okay, I believe you," Cheeta said, returning Remo's card.

Remo blinked. He had to will his face still to keep it from dissolving into incredulous lines. The blunt-faced barracuda had bought his lame story on no more strength than Chiun's word. What the hell? he thought. Anything to get us through the night.

Remo settled back as the helicopter pilot wrestled his craft into a soft landing on Fifth Avenue. Maybe when they got into the building, he and Chiun could figure out what was really going on, waste anyone who needed wasting, and split before Delpha decided to flash somebody into asphyxiation.

Remo didn't think his sinuses could stand another high-speed scouring.

16

At first, Randal T. Rumpp thought his executive assistant had broken down. She was babbling again. Worse, she was raving.

"It—it's a ghost! A real ghost!" Dorma Wormser cried.

"What's a ghost?" Rumpp asked calmly. It was important to be calm when dealing with the unstable.

Dorma grabbed his arm. "The thing in the trophy room. Come see, come see. You'll see. It's real."

Randal Rumpp looked out the window. The BCN helicopter was fluttering around aimlessly. He wasn't finished being quoted yet, but the chopper didn't seem interested in coming back for more pearls of Rumpp wisdom.

He let his executive secretary tug him to the trophy room, thinking this had better be worth his time.

Randal Rumpp saw right away that it wasn't a ghost. Even though it was white and floated just under the ceiling like a ghost probably would float, it was no ghost.

It looked vaguely humanoid. There were two arms, two legs, a trunk, and a head. The head was not like a human head. It was too big, too smooth, too white, and too hairless, and where its face should have been there was a kind of puffy balloon.

In the dim light, the thing shone. Its edges were misty.

Dorma whispered, "See, Mr. Rumpp? A ghost."

"It's no ghost," said Randal Rumpp, grabbing an original Frank Lloyd Wright chair. He lifted it up over his head and poked at the floating apparition with the chair's hard legs.

The legs went right through the floating white being.

"See? It's unreal," Dorma said.

"It's no ghost," repeated Randal Rumpp sternly. "Get a grip on yourself."

"How can it not be a ghost?"

"Because," Randal Rumpp pointed out reasonably. "It's got two cables sticking out of its shoulders. They look like coaxial cables. Coaxials mean electricity. Ghosts aren't electric."

"How . . . how do we know that?"

"Because we have a grip on ourselves," said Randal Rumpp, moving around to get a better look at the floating thing.

The thing was emitting a kind of soft shine, like a low-energy light bulb. Through it, certain details could be made out. The pulsing golden veinwork. The fact that it wore boots and gloves, and there were straps that snugged at his shoulders.

Randal Rumpp was trying to see what the straps were holding on to when he noticed the thing's belt. The buckle—it was round and white—suddenly blinked red. It was a very angry red color. It made Dorma shrink in fear. Then it turned white again. Then red. It was like something short-circuiting.

Randal Rumpp took this as further proof that the thing was electrical. Randal Rumpp feared nothing electrical. Not even the electrician's union, which could make or break a construction project.

"What does the red light mean?" Dorma wondered from the safety of the open door. She looked ready to bolt.

"It means," Randal Rumpp said, pointing to the

Sears DieHard battery clearly strapped to the floating thing's back, "that its power is running low."

"I don't understand."

"That makes two of us. Where did it come from?"

"I think . . . I think it came from the telephone. . . ."

Rumpp scowled. "Telephone?"

For the first time, Rumpp noticed the phone off its hook.

He turned to his cowering assistant. "I told you not to touch the phones!" he shouted.

Without warning, the glowing thing came to life. It grabbed at its belt buckle, then went dim and fell to the floor with a thud.

Dorma screamed and fled. Randal Rumpp knelt beside the thing. He reached out to touch it and, to his surprise, he got the slick, plasticky sensation of touching something like vinyl. His fingers recoiled. He hated vinyl. Especially vinyl siding. It offended his sensibilities. His first home had had vinyl siding. The day he'd traded up to his first condo, he'd had it torched so no one could throw it back in his face when he became famous.

The thing lay supine for only a minute. Then, with a sound like a respirator, the white bubble that was the thing's face crinkled inward. It expanded. Contracted again, crinkling. The crinkling was something seen, but not heard.

"It's still breathing," Randal Rumpp muttered. "Whatever the heck it is."

He tried to shake it.

"Hey, pal. Wake up. You're on my time now."

The thing struggled into an upright position. Its featureless face swiveled in his direction. Even though there were no eyes, Randal Rumpp had the distinct feeling he was being stared at. It gave him the creeps. Worse than cost overruns.

Then, even though the thing had no discernible mouth, it spoke.

It said, "Ho ho ho."

"Hello. Do you speak English?"

"*Da.*"

Too bad, Rumpp thought. Maybe I can communicate with it some other way.

"Me Rumpp," he said, pointing to his own chest. "Rumpp? *Comprende?*" He pointed to the thing's chest. "You name?"

To his surprise, the thing stabbed its own chest with its thumb and said in perfectly understandable English, "I am Grandfather Frost. Ho ho ho."

"You speak English?"

"*Da.*"

Scowling, Rumpp said, "*Da* isn't English. It's baby talk."

"*Da* mean 'yes.' You understand 'yes'?"

"Yeah. I've been hearing it all my life. Listen, where did you come from?"

"Telephone."

"That so? How'd you get into the telephone in the first place?"

The creature struggled to its feet. It grabbed at its right shoulder, as if in pain. "It is long story," it said, moving about the room and examining the objects kept on display tables and open shelves. "I am thinking we do not have time for long story now."

"Yeah? Why not?"

"I must escape."

"What about the three billion we were talking about?"

"Take a check?"

"You have one on you?"

"*Nyet.* I mean, 'no.' "

Rumpp frowned. "*Nyet.* Where have I heard that word before?"

"I do not know, but I must be escaping now. Thank you for your time."

Randal Rumpp grabbed the thing's arm. Standing,

the thing was shorter than he. And that was saying something, considering that its boot heels were as thick as a stack of waffles.

Randal Rumpp expected no fight. And he was right. The creature didn't struggle at all.

But Randal Rumpp was suddenly on his back, trying to get the air the floor had knocked out of his lungs back where it belonged.

"Ghosts," he gasped, "don't use judo."

Then the creature spoke another unfamiliar word. *"Krahseevah,"* it said. Its voice sounded very pleased.

Gasping, Rumpp got to his feet. The creature was examining a gold-filled Colibri cigarette lighter with the initials "RR" set in diamonds. Rumpp noticed it no longer shone. And its face, which was a bladder that kept expanding and contracting as if in rhythm with its measured breathing, crinkled audibly now.

Somehow, it was able to see through that featureless membrane.

While it was distracted, Rumpp leaped in front of the only exit.

"You go out over my dead body!" he warned.

"There is no need for dead bodies," said the faceless thing, retreating to the telephone receiver. He dialed directory assistance and asked, "Give me number of Soviet Embassy, please."

The operator's response came loudly enough for Randal Rumpp to hear it clearly.

"I'm sorry. There is no listing for a Soviet Embassy in this city."

"What! Then provide me number of Soviet Embassy in Washington."

"What do you want with the Soviet Embassy?" Rumpp asked suspiciously.

"I must give them present," the thing said flatly. "Grandfather Frost forgot them this year."

"Christmas hasn't happened yet. In fact, it's only Halloween."

The thing started. "Excuse, please. What month this?"

"October."

"What year this?"

Before Randal Rumpp could answer the insane question, the operator was saying, "I'm sorry. There is no listing for a Soviet Embassy in Washington, D.C. Would you like me to try Washington state?"

"No Soviet Embassy? What happened to Soviet Union?"

"It dissolved," Randal Rumpp said flatly, just to see what response he'd get.

A dramatic one, as it turned out.

The blank-faced white creature dropped the telephone and began to moan.

"Soviet Union dissolve in nuclear fire! What about Georgia?"

"It's still down there between South Carolina and Alabama," Randal Rumpp said.

"I am not meaning U.S. Georgia. I am meaning Georgia in Soviet Union."

"Search me. I can't keep track of what's left of Russia."

The thing's bladder-like face regarded him. "It is gone completely?"

"Yeah. Yeah. Completely. And good riddance."

"I am homeless expatriate," it said, cabled shoulders falling. "Without family."

"Look," Rumpp said sharply, "we have some business to conduct here. Let's leave sentiment out of it."

"I am man without country, and you are without human feelings," the thing blubbered. "After all I have done for you."

"What have you done for me?"

"I have restored your building."

It was Randal Rumpp's turn to appear startled. "You have? Are you sure?"

"Am positive. If building were no more, I could not

be standing on floor as I am now. Would fall through to death."

"Why not?"

"I am vibrating normally. Therefore, floor is vibrating normally."

Randal Rumpp raced to a window. He took up the Frank Lloyd Wright chair and started banging it against a big bronze solar panel, splintering the legs of the eighty-thousand-dollar original. But Rumpp didn't care.

The glass cracked and shattered, and pieces fell out.

He stuck his head out and watched them fall.

The largest pieces shattered into a million golden shards when they hit the pavement below.

At that moment, the electricity returned.

"It's true! It's true!" Rumpp said distractedly. "Not now! I haven't closed the megadeal of the century yet!"

He grabbed the slick creature and said, "Make it go back to the way it was."

"I cannot."

"Then tell me how it got that way in the first place."

"I am not sure. Was sucked into telephone, but number I dial did not pick up. I think I was tricked by American agents. I have been trapped in telephone system since I do not know how long ago. I think I became trapped in your building, and somehow it became as I was. A ghost."

"You're no more a ghost than I am," Rumpp insisted, giving the thing's arm a hard squeeze.

"True," it gasped, grabbing it shoulder.

"Explain it again. You got sucked into the phone?"

"*Da.* I mean, yes."

"Show me."

"Why should I?"

"I'll give you this Rolex if you show me."

The faceless thing hesitated. He accepted the watch, put it to the side of his head where his left ear should have been, and listened curiously. He brought the watch face up to what passed for his own.

"Is fake," he said, returning it disdainfully.

"How do you know?"

"True Rolex has smooth secondhand movement. This jerks. Is no good. Cheap copy."

"Show me how you did it," Randal Rumpp said quickly, pulling out his ace in the hole, "and I'll let you have this entire building."

The thing moved its smooth head around like a curious radar dish. "Worth how much?"

"A quarter billion."

"Is deal. But I must have safe number to call."

"I got one. Dial 555-9460."

"Where is that?"

"My Florida summer home. The weather's great right now."

"Hokay. I go there," said the thing, picking up the receiver and stabbing the key pad with a flexible white finger. As he dialed the number with one hand, he squeezed the handset between his lifted shoulder and his head, and reached down to his circular belt buckle.

He gave it a twist. Instantly, his outline became a kind of fuzzy nimbus of light. Randal Rumpp blinked as the details of the creature's outer skin grew indistinct.

Then, like a cloud that was being sucked into a cave, the creature collapsed into the mouthpiece.

There was no sound. Just a quick inhalation of glowing white smoke. The deformed head was the last to go. It was drawn into the receiver, which hung in the air a brief moment, then hit the hardwood floor.

"Damn!" said Randal Rumpp, racing back to his office, yelling, "Don't answer that phone! Don't answer that phone if you value your fucking job!"

The ringing was coming from down the corridor, from his office.

He sprinted past his shocked assistant and to his office cellular phone. It was ringing insistently.

Randal Rumpp grabbed up a copy of *The Scam of the Deal* and slammed it onto the receiver, as if to block a rat trying to escape from a hole. He pushed down hard. The phone kept ringing.

"*Dorma!* Get a window open and throw something out!"

"But the windows don't open."

"Kick the glass out! *Anything!*"

The crash of glass came a moment later.

"Listen for it to hit the ground."

"I am."

"Anything?"

"No."

"Keep listening."

"It should have shattered by now."

Then the lights winked out.

"Great!" chortled Randal Rumpp. "It worked! It worked! My deal is still on! I'll be back on top yet!"

He dug out his attaché case and extracted his portable cellular phone. It took but a moment to reprogram it to ring when his private number was called. He felt empowered again. He was on a roll. Nothing was going to stop him now.

17

The first thing Cheeta Ching wanted to do upon disembarking from the churning BCN helicopter was to liberate the Rumpp Tower. She announced this in a triumphant screech that made everyone else reach for their eardrums.

"Nobody goes in until Cheeta Ching, superanchorwoman of our age, has done her duty!"

"So?" Remo asked. "What are you waiting for?"

Cheeta turned to her cameraman. "Is there enough tape left?"

The cameraman popped the cassette port, looked at the cartridge, and shook his head.

"Then load up a fresh one," Cheeta said impatiently. "I want every dramatic moment immortalized on half-inch tape."

"Oh, for crying out loud," Remo burst out, "just let's *all* go into the building, okay?"

"Not on your miserable life!" Cheeta flared. "Grandfather, please don't let him ruin my story."

"Remo, behave."

"Watch it, Little Father," Remo warned, "or I'll tell everybody how old you really are."

"I am not a day older than eighty!" Chiun screeched, in a voice whose tone clearly suggested that he had seen eighty a long time ago. In truth, the Master of Sinanju was more than a century old, a fact that he was sensitive about, inasmuch as he had never officially celebrated it. Somehow, by the logic of Chiun's ancestral tradition, this lapse denied him the right to claim that august achievement.

"Do not be ashamed of your advanced age," intoned Delpha Rohmer, "for in age there is wisdom. The druids knew this."

"Weren't they men?" Remo said.

"Warlocks. Male witches, which absolved them of the sins of ordinary men."

"Bulldookey."

Remo folded his arms while Cheeta and the cameraman fiddled with the videocam. Cheeta took possession of the old tape while the cameraman reloaded. That gave Remo an idea.

"Want me to hold that for you?" he asked helpfully. "So it won't get lost?"

"Sure, thanks," Cheeta said, handing it over her shoulder absently.

Remo reached out for the tape, a wicked smile on his cruel lips.

Suddenly, Cheeta let out a screech and her hand snapped back. Remo's reflexes ordinarily would have been equal to snatching it from her easily, but Cheeta's ungodly sudden screech had tripped his defensive reflexes and he had faded back from the horrific sound.

"Something wrong?" Remo asked innocently.

"Last time I let you near one of my cameras, a very important tape turned up missing. *Mysteriously* missing."

"Missing usually is mysterious," Remo agreed.

"I will be glad to safeguard the artifact," Delpha offered.

Cheeta hesitated. Then, saying, "I know I can trust a fellow woman," turned it over to Delpha, who promptly warmed the cartridge by slipping it down her swelling cleavage.

"It will be safe here," she intoned.

"Especially if it picks up traces of your animal repulsion," Remo said unhappily.

"You mean 'attraction,' " Delpha corrected.

"Let's split the difference and say 'aroma,' " Remo said.

The videocam reloaded, Cheeta Ching fluffed her raven-black hair. Strands of it clung to her fingers like a sticky spider web, and she pulled a small can of industrial-strength hair varnish and created a halo around her head. It not only tamed her hair but kept her thick pancake makeup from flaking off her flat cheeks.

She squared her padded shoulders and started for the entrance, saying, "BCN anchor chair, here I come."

Remo turned to Chiun. "So we just watch?"

"Emperor Smith instructed me to investigate and report on all I beheld."

Remo shrugged. "I guess that means watch. There are worse ways to spend Halloween Eve."

Cheeta got halfway to the door when one of her spiked heels struck a pebble. She stumbled, caught herself, and said, "Oh, damn. I gotta start over."

She went back to her mark, squared her shoulders again, and retraced the path. Her heels made sounds that made Remo expect to see sparks spit in her wake.

Then, walking backward, Cheeta's cameraman went before her, his lens capturing her every brisk, fearless step, the way her hair bounced determinedly. Cheeta narrowed her almond eyes at the camera until they glinted.

She came to an abrupt stop and said, "Okay, cut. Now move off to one side."

The cameraman obliged.

He repositioned himself so he could catch Cheeta's resolute profile as she reached for the door and flung it back.

That was not the image his lens captured. Cheeta

reached for the brass door handle. Momentum carried her into the glass. It didn't break. It didn't resist. Cheeta tumbled through it and fell on her flat face in the lobby marble.

Her face quickly sank without a trace, taking Cheeta's shoulders with it.

"The building! It went crazy again!" Remo said.

"Cheeta! My Cheeta!" Chiun screeched.

"Use your atavistic womanly powers!" Delpha called. "Levitate! Levitate!"

The Master of Sinanju reached the scene a second ahead of Remo. He grasped Cheeta by her wildly kicking ankles and pulled back.

Cheeta came loose from the marble floor like a big yellow tooth with legs.

"My God!" she said, wide-eyed. "It happened again!"

"We noticed that, too," Remo said, looking up at the building's face. The lights were going dim again. "We're back to square one."

Cheeta, fuming and flaring her magnificent nostrils, climbed to her feet and complained, "It's not fair! This was my moment of triumph. What the hell's going on here?"

"It is a puzzlement," Chiun said slowly, grasping his wrists firmly. His sleeves swallowed his hands.

Delpha Rohmer drew near, like a professional mourner approaching a vertical coffin.

"There is only one rational explanation," she said.

Everyone looked at her, their faces reflecting their combined thought that a rational explanation would be very welcome at this particular juncture.

"My magic worked, but it has now worn off."

"You call that rational?" Remo said.

"We must summon a greater magic to defeat these forces."

"Yeah?"

"We must join hands and form a circle around this building."

Remo looked at Chiun and back at Delpha. "There are only four of us, and the base of this thing must be the size of a baseball diamond," he pointed out.

"We will enlist others in our cause."

"Like who? Houdini's dead."

Delpha gestured to the line of barbed wire several blocks down Fifth Avenue. On the other side the huge crowd of gawkers, many dressed in Halloween regalia, stood watching. No one seemed to have any interest in approaching, not even the National Guard.

Remo growled, "I think you'll have a tough time drumming up volunteers. They look more scared than the people inside the building."

"I will appeal to their mystical natures," proclaimed Delpha Rohmer, throwing off her trailing garment.

Remo quickly moved upwind. Chiun looked away.

Delpha began chanting, "Sisters of the Moon, join us now! A mighty spell is needed to repair the rupture in our physical plane. Those who believe in the awesome power of womanhood unleashed, join hands with me now!"

To Remo's eternal surprise, those people who believed in the eternal power of womanhood unleashed numbered at least a third of the people behind the police lines, including several police officers.

They stampeded for the nude figure of Delpha Rohmer. Throwing her head back, she lifted her arms in thanks to the hunter's moon.

Almost at once the air changed flavor, and half the stampede came to a dead halt and grabbed mouths and noses. A number retreated. Others pushed ahead through those who were reversing direction.

They surrounded Delpha, whose voice rose from the pack.

"Sisters, join hands with me now!"

Hands grasped hands as a human daisy chain was

formed. It wound, sinuous and fluid, toward the Rumpp Tower.

As Remo and Chiun stepped out of their path and Cheeta Ching got her cameraman to record the display, the line of mystical convocation surrounded the Tower until its two ends, like a necklace joining at the clasp, completed the circle.

Delpha called, "Repeat after me: 'Diana, Goddess of the Moon, symbol of our sacred womb . . .' "

"Diana, Goddess of the Moon, symbol of our sacred womb . . ."

"Wait! Wait!" Cheeta cried. "Make room for me. I'm a woman too."

"That remains to be seen," Remo muttered.

The chant was resumed.

"Shine down your mighty light . . ."

"Shine down your mighty light . . ."

"So this shaft of misfortune is restored to sight!"

"So this shaft of misfortune is restored to sight!"

"Now," Delpha cried. "Move around it, closing the circle."

The circle moved. Not everybody moved in the same direction. Not everyone had a clear grasp of the concept of "left," but they soon got organized.

Delpha led the chant. "Repeat the following words of power over and over: 'Max Pax Fax.' "

"Did they have faxes in olden times?" Remo asked the Master of Sinanju.

"Hush! I must study this white magic. There may be something yet to be learned of value."

"I've already picked up a magic pointer. Use triple-strength Right Guard."

The circle went around once. Nothing much seemed to happen. It went around twice. The chanters grew hoarse.

On the third go-round half the chanters were croaking like toads and frogs, and Delpha was no longer where she had been.

"I do not see her," Chiun muttered, stroking his wispy beard.

"I do not want to," Remo said.

Altogether, the circle went around twenty times before the last voice gave out and people began collapsing on the cold pavement. Enthusiasm waning, the circle simply broke apart into clots of people standing around, breathing hard.

Cheeta came out of the group, checked her cameraman, and approached Remo and Chiun.

"It didn't work," she panted.

"Gee. Wonder why?" Remo said airily.

"Maybe Delpha knows," Cheeta said vaguely, looking around. "Where'd she go?"

Remo shrugged. "Search us. She disappeared on the second doe-see-doe."

Cheeta's dark eyes went to the spot where Delpha Romher should have been standing. But she was no longer there. She was no longer anywhere on the broad, empty stretch of Fifth Avenue, where old newspaper fragments skittered along the gutters, impelled by gusty winds.

Cheeta's quick brain registered the absence of Delpha Rohmer. Her exquisitely made-up face quirked in surprise. Her bloodred lips puckered in astonishment.

But from her mouth there came only these words: *"My tape! That bitch ran off with my tape!"*

Remo asked, "Don't you mean 'witch'?"

Cheeta turned like a angry lioness. "I mean *bitch* with a capital B! Do you realize how much that tape is worth?"

"What's the sweat? You still have the second tape."

"Of over a hundred New Yorkers making fools of themselves. Me included." She shouted over to her cameraman. "You! Erase that tape. Right now, buster!"

The cameraman obediently popped the tape. Instead of trusting his machine's eraser head to fulfill

Cheeta Ching's instructions, he smashed the tape under his pounding heel until loops of tape squirmed beneath his feet, like a nest of flattened brown worms.

For good measure, he kicked the tangled mess into an open sewer grate.

18

Remo Williams found a pay phone, put a quarter in the slot, and promptly lost his coin.

The next three NYNEX pay phones also ate his quarters. It finally cost him a dollar twenty-five to reach the long distance operator, who promptly asked him for an additional two dollars and sixty-five cents for the first five minutes of his long distance call to Folcroft Sanitarium in Rye, New York.

When Harold Smith's lemony voice came over the telephone, Remo said, "Bad news, Smitty. The Rumpp Tower is still an intangible asset of the Rumpp Organization."

"You can uncover nothing?"

"It's there, but it's not there. We went in, fell into the subbasement, and had to dig out again."

"Did anyone see you?"

"Only Cheeta Ching."

Smith's voice went stiff as a graham cracker. "Miss Ching is there?"

"Yeah, and she and Chiun have picked up where they left off."

Smith groaned. "Oh, no. Has security been compromised?"

"It's worse than that," Remo said cheerfully, enjoying getting a rise out of the colorless Harold Smith. "She has Chiun convinced that they are expecting their first child."

"My God! Chiun *is* the father. Do you know what this means?"

Remo rolled his dark eyes. "Do I ever. The rest of my life is going to be ruined by that lemon-faced shark."

"Remo," Smith said urgently, "I want you to get Chiun away from that woman. Away from the Rumpp Tower. Regroup. We will look into this from other angles."

"You calling us back to Folcroft?"

"No. Find a hotel. Contact me after you register."

"I'll give it a try, but Chiun's got Cheeta calling him 'grandfather.' This could be long-term problem."

"Is there anything else?"

"Did I tell you about the witch?"

"Witch?"

"Delpha Rohmer. Name excite a memory chip?"

Remo heard Harold Smith's fingers making hollow clicking sounds on his ever-present computer keyboard.

"I have her as the official witch of Salem, Massachusetts."

"You have her right."

"What is her role in this?" Smith asked sharply.

"As far as I can see, professional glory-hound. She ripped off one of Cheeta's precious videotapes."

"Is there anything on it that should concern the organization?"

"Not unless the thought of white night-gaunts running loose freaks you out."

"Excuse me?"

"Just witch talk," Remo said. "If I read Delpha right, it won't be long before she and that tape are on Horrendo Riviera or Nancy Jessica Repunsel."

Smith said, "Find a quiet out-of-the-way hotel and contact me directly, Remo."

"Gotcha," Remo said, hanging up. The phone immediately rang, and on impulse, he picked it up.

"This is the operator. Please deposit an additional seventy-five cents."

"Only if you refund the buck-twenty I lost to all your non-working pay phones."

"I cannot do that," the operator said primly.

"Then I cannot deposit additional funds."

"Then I must charge the receiving caller."

"His name is Smith, and he loves paying my bills," Remo said, hanging up.

The Master of Sinanju was not pleased at the instructions he was given.

"I will not abandon Cheeta in her hour of torment," he said tightly.

"Her hour of torment began the day she was born, and has poisoned everyone she ever came into contact with, not the least of whom is us," Remo said hotly. "Smith says we lie low. So do we lie low, or do we kiss off our current contract negotiation?"

"We lie low," Chiun said bitterly. "But if Cheeta refuses to speak with me after this incident, I will hold it against Harold the Smith forever."

"Gee, I was just talking to him, and he has his heart set on being the godfather."

Chiun's wispy facial hair trembled with surprise.

"Really, Remo?"

19

When Delpha Rohmer, Official Witch of Salem, Massachusetts, President of the Sisterhood for Witch Awareness, swept into the lobby of the Multinational Broadcast Company's New York headquarters, the Purolator guard looked up, frowned, and sighed.

"Aren't you a little old for trick-or-treat, lady?"

"I offer no tricks," she said haughtily.

The guard dug out a handful of butterscotch candies he kept behind the desk for his own use. "Okay," he said grudgingly, "put out your bag."

"You fail to understand, man-mortal. I have come bearing a prize that your news director will covet greatly."

"Covet?"

"Be good enough to inform him that Delpha Rohmer has footage of the haunting of the Rumpp Tower."

"Haunting?"

"Baphomet has declared it his domain on earth. And I have proof that Randal Rumpp is in league with the Great Horned One." From out of Delpha's cleavage came the black videocassette.

The guard looked at it. He recognized that it was no home VCR cassette, but a half-inch-tape cartridge. He picked up the lobby desk phone and said, "Mr. Graff. I have a . . . witch here to see you. Says it's about the Rumpp Tower thing. She says it's haunted and she has tape to prove it."

The guard listened a moment, then said, "Let me just say that she *sounds* serious."

Knute Graff thought Delpha Rohmer looked serious, too. He accepted her business card, winced, and swallowed his impulse to laugh. He said, "Come with me," and turned swiftly so he could relieve the stress of the moment with a half-repressed smile.

In the MBC viewing room, he ran the tape through.

"Who shot this?" he asked.

Delpha said, "Does it matter? I am offering it to you."

The news director watched as Cheeta Ching came on.

"Wait a minute!" he exploded. "I can't run this! That Korean Shark would eat me alive!"

"The most dramatic footage has nothing to do with her," Delpha pointed out, in a toneless voice that made the man think of sucked-dry flies in an old spider's web. Dead.

Graff watched the footage of Randal Rumpp claiming credit for the dematerialization of Rumpp Tower incident, and his eyes went wide. Then he came to footage that he could not explain.

"What is that thing?" he blurted.

"It is a negative night-gaunt," he was told.

"Looks more like a positive one."

"A positive night-gaunt would be black," Delpha explained. "This unholy creature is white."

"I can see that. But where the heck is its face?"

"It has none. This is how I know it to be a night-gaunt."

Eyes still wide, Knute Graff swiveled his chair around and looked at Delpha Rohmer.

"You know, if I use this tape, it might be called a gross breach of journalistic ethics."

"Yes?"

"On the other hand, that Korean Shark once shafted me good. How much do you want?"

"Ten thousand dollars. And as much exposure for myself and my religion as you can deliver."

"Religion?"

"Wicca was recognized as such long before the Burning Times," Delpha said in her sonorous voice.

"Exactly how long ago was that?"

"Before Christ was a corporal," she said flatly.

"You were an eyewitness to what's going on uptown?" Graff asked, switching the subject as fast as he could.

"I was."

"Deal." Knute Graff picked up the phone and made a quick series of calls.

"Payroll? Draw a check for ten grand. Payee: Delpha Rohmer.

"Editing? I have some tape you won't believe. I want it to lead our seven o'clock report.

"Security? Triple the guard. And if you see any sign of Cheeta Ching, fire a warning shot into the air. If she doesn't back off, shoot to wound. And *don't* miss."

Graff hung up and turned to Delpha Rohmer. "Lady, you're about to become the most famous witch since Elizabeth Montgomery."

Delpha Rohmer's smile was like moonlight falling across a row of tombstones.

"Fame is precisely what I want," she said hollowly.

20

The Rumpp Tower footage went out over the air at exactly seven o'clock Daylight Savings Time. It was repeated on the seven-thirty New York satellite feed to local affiliates in the western time zones.

CNN picked it up, and once they had it the entire world saw it. Literally.

ITAR—the Russian Information Telegraph Agency, once called TASS—ran it in the middle of the night, which, because they were on the other side of the international date line, was November 1 in the Russian city of Nizhni Novgorod.

Nizhni Novgorod was a grim industrial city, once known as the closed city of Gorky. A place where dissidents were exiled. It was very cold in Nizhni Novgorod. And it was especially cold in the apartment of Yuli Batenin, formerly chargé d'affaires with the former Washington embassy of the former Union of Soviet Socialist Republics.

These days, Yuli Batenin baked bread for thirty thousand rubles a day in an aging bread factory, which was enough to pay for a cold-water walk-up on Sovno Prospekt, but not to heat it. Even if there had been any fuel oil on the open market.

Yuli Batenin sat in his overstuffed sofa chair, trying to keep the loose spring from popping into his rectum, and shivered in a threadbare camel-hair blanket, which when he slept on a fold-down cot kept him no warmer than it did when he was awake.

The television reception made him shiver even more. There was so much snow he could only think of the coming Russian winter and shudder endlessly.

He was watching the news when the footage of the strange events in downtown Manhattan came on. The commentator was talking about an obscure American holiday known as Halloween.

The spring was worming itself into his left cheek, so Yuli shifted carefully. He was barely paying attention to what the commentator was saying. Under his breath he cursed the spring, the sofa, the apartment, the new Russia, and most of all the series of events that had turned him into a non-person.

It had been better in the old days. Before Gorbachev. Before Perestroika. Before Glastnost. When Yuli Batenin had enjoyed the privileges of being a major in the KGB at the same time as he enjoyed living among the comforts of the West. He didn't know which he missed most, the old Russia or the West.

Yuli Batenin happened to look up as the footage of the Western ghost came on.

Even through the snowy reception, and despite the fact that the tape had been duped several times and was as blurry as a Moscow drunk's speech, Yuli Batenin recognized the ghost.

He stood straight up and swore, *"Chort vozmi!"*

He put his face to the screen, as if to make out every detail, and fumbled with the broken contrast knob.

"Nyet, nyet, neyt," he moaned. "It cannot be!"

As the picture resolved itself, a low curse of a breath escaped Yuli Batenin's curling lips.

"Brashnikov!" he hissed. "You miserable thief! You are alive."

Yuli Batenin stood up, like a man who has seen his

own ghost. He stared at the screen until the picture was replaced with footage of the latest food riots in Omsk.

"Alive," he repeated.

Then a twisted smile crossing his lips, he added, "But not for long."

There was no phone in Yuli Batenin's apartment. Even if he had been a millionaire in American dollars, there still would have been no phone in Yuli Batenin's apartment. Yuli Batenin had acquired an incurable fear of telephones during his last posting. The very sight of one made him shudder uncontrollably.

At first Yuli Batenin's upstairs neighbor, Mrs. Biliandinova, did not want to let him use her telephone.

"This is joke, *da*?" she asked suspiciously.

"This is joke, *nyet*. I must use telephone."

"You are afraid of telephone!" spat old Mrs. Biliandinova. "So you tell me countless times. I am forced to muffle bell because it frightens you so."

Batenin made his voice firm. "*Babushka*, you will let me use telephone. I am former major."

"In defunct Red Army. There is no more Red Army. And I will not let you use telephone unless you first tell me who you will be calling."

"I will be calling Moscow."

"I cannot afford to call Moscow. You are mad."

"I will call collect."

"They have no more money for foolish telephone calls in Moscow than they do in Nizhni Novgorod."

"*Babushka*, I will break down door," Batenin warned.

Silence. A chain rattled. And a huddled, red-faced woman drew open the door and said, "Broken door will cost more than telephone call. Make call, Batenin. But if you cause me trouble, I will have landlord throw you out. That is one good thing about the new order. Tenants can be evicted."

Yuli Batenin had difficulty getting through to Moscow. That was not unusual. With the current state of the collapsing Russian infrastructure, he would have had trouble calling a downstairs apartment.

It also didn't help that he made his call with his eyes shut because even now, three years after the telephone phobia had seized him, he could not bear to look at one. He asked the local operator to put the call through. Dialing would have been too much for him. Just holding the instrument made his knees shake.

Finally, he got someone at the number he called.

"Is this KGB?" Batenin asked eagerly.

"No. This former KGB. Once great spy apparatus. Now clearinghouse for secrets to highest bidder. You wish to buy?"

"No. I wish to make you rich."

"I am already rich. Today I have sold Stalin's diaries to American film company. It is to be miniseries. We are hoping Bobby will take part of Stalin."

"Bobby?"

"DeNiro."

"Idiot!" Batenin snarled. "This is matter of national security. Soviet property of greater value than anything in your files is in United States and must be recovered."

"This is new?"

"Is greater than the method of preserving Lenin's corpse."

"Impossible! These is no such secret."

"Okay. We stole it from Japanese."

"That is better. Give me locator number. If we have not sold it, I will see."

"Locator Number 55-334. I will hold."

He held for over an hour, during which the *babushka* Biliandinova carried on something fierce, complaining bitterly of the cost. Yuli Batenin got so weary of it that he carefully laid down the telephone and brained her with her own wooden rolling pin, which she was waving threateningly. After she had hit the floor, he applied the hardest part of it to the back of her fat neck until he heard a satisfying crunching sound.

Thereafter it was very quiet in the apartment, and Yuli Batenin, formerly Major Batenin of the KGB, could at last hear himself think. He closed his eyes again, amazed that he had summoned up the courage to use the phone at all. Perhaps he was getting over it.

After a while, the voice came back. It sounded very impressed.

"You have told truth," it said.

"You have found file?"

"No. File was moved to new ministry. It must be very important, because everything else abandoned."

"What new ministry?"

"I have number."

Yuli Batenin called the number and got a crisp female voice that spoke only one word: *"Shchit."*

"Am I speaking to new ministry?" asked Batenin.

"Who is asking, please?"

"I am Yuli Batenin, formerly with KGB, calling on matter of gravest important to Soviet Union."

"Idiot! There is no Soviet Union. Where do you call from?"

"Nizhni Novgorod."

"Where?"

"Gorky."

"Oh. Hold the line."

"But—"

The unmistakable sound of being put on hold came over the long miles between Nizhni Novgorod and Moscow. Yuli Batenin had no choice but to hold the line. If he was disconnected, it might be weeks until the lucky connection was reestablished. If ever, given the pitiful state of his once-proud motherland.

He hummed "Moscow Nights" as he waited. Perhaps they would reinstate him. Perhaps he would no longer be required to live in disgrace in this dull city, which had once been the dumping ground for inconvenient traitors like Sakharov. Perhaps the clock would be rolled back and all of Russia would be reunited in socialism.

Yuli Batenin had less time to wait than he had dreamed possible. And when they got back to him, it wasn't through a crisp female voice over hundreds of miles of rusting cable but by crashing in the apartment door and seizing him roughly.

There were three of them. Plainclothes men. Very KGB.

"Yuli Batenin?" the tallest of them asked stonily.

"Yes. Who are you?"

"You will come with us," the man said gruffly, as the other two dragged him by his elbows down the dingy apartment stairs and out into the sterile autumn cold of Sovno Prospekt.

They flung him into a waiting car and, as the car sped off, Yuli Batenin found himself weeping with a mixture of pride and nostalgia. He himself had seized dissidents in just this fashion during the days of his youth.

"Is just like old days," he blubbered. "I am so happy."

They slapped him to quiet him, but he only smiled harder.

21

The Master of Sinanju was ignoring the prattling whites.

As he sat on a tatami mat before the hotel room television, with the incessant honk and blare of city traffic permeating the room, he bided his time, waiting for the glorious face of Cheeta Ching, *his* Cheeta Ching, rosy-cheeked with child, to appear.

The whites prattled on, disturbing his thoughts.

"I got it all figured out, Smitty," Remo was saying.

Over the miles of phone wiring, the brittle voice of Harold W. Smith buzzed. Its noise offended the ears of the Master of Sinanju above all.

"Yes, Remo?"

"It's a hologram."

"Pardon me?"

"The Rumpp Tower is a hologram," Remo repeated. "You know, one of those 3-D gimmicks."

Chiun snorted derisively. The whites prattled on, unheeding.

"What about the people trapped inside?" Smith asked.

"Holograms too," Remo said. "It's the only thing that makes sense."

"So far, you are not even making that," Smith buzzed.

"Follow my train of logic," Remo said, looking over to the bright television screen. His face was reflected in a wall mirror for the Master of Sinanju to see. His round white eyes grew interested in the image they beheld.

The Master of Sinanju casually reached up to change the channel.

Remo looked away with a frown and resumed speaking.

"Listen," he said. "Rumpp is about to be shut down. He's got an ego bigger than Lee Iacocca. He can't handle it, so he arranges for a hologram of his Tower to appear, to fool everyone who tries to evict him."

"Not likely," Smith said.

"And to make it really, really look good," Remo went on, "he has holograms of people planted so that when they seem to step outside, they fall into the ground."

"Explain how you and Chiun fell through the atrium lobby."

"Simple. Rumpp had the marble ripped up and laid down a hologram floor. We couldn't stand on it, because it was just light. The hologram people didn't fall through because they weren't solid either."

"Not plausible," Smith said sharply.

"Yeah? You got a better theory?"

"No," Smith admitted.

"Then let's go with mine until you do."

"There's only one thing wrong with your theory, Remo."

"What's that?"

"If the present Rumpp Tower is a three-dimensional illusion, where is the real thing?"

Remo's confident expression fell in like a black hole with a white face. He wrinkled his forehead unhappily. He pulled on an earlobe and scrunched up his right eye and that side of his face.

Remo snapped lean fingers. "Simple. He moved it."

The Master of Sinanju snorted and attempted to

return to his meditations. But he knew there would be no peace unless these whites were allowed to indulge their mania for trivia.

"Remo, it is not possible to simply move a sixty-eight-story office tower," Harold Smith pointed out in a firm voice.

"Maybe it was on jacks, and he just sent it dropping into the earth," Remo said with less confidence than before.

"Hardly."

"Okay, there are some weak links in my logic chain. But I still say the only rational scientific explanation is a hologram scam."

"Perhaps we should not be looking for a rational scientific explanation," Smith said slowly.

"What other kind is there?"

"What has Chiun to say about this matter?"

"Who knows? I'm still trying to get a handle on this baby situation."

"I spoke with Chiun earlier," Smith said.

Across the room, the Master of Sinanju cocked a delicate ear while feigning disinterest.

Remo brought the receiver closer to his mouth and lowered his voice. "Yeah? What'd he say then?"

"We did not get to the matter at hand. It seemed that the Master of Sinanju expects me to become the baby's godfather."

"Uh-oh."

"I told him it was quite impossible, for security reasons. He—er—hung up in a huff."

"Well," Remo said guiltily. "You know how Chiun gets these ideas into his head. It'll pass."

"It will not, liar!" Chiun hissed.

Remo, noticing something on the TV screen that interested him, grabbed the remote unit off the dresser and pointed it at the cable control box. He eased the volume up.

Chiun reached up and changed the channel manually.

Remo changed the channel back.

The Master of Sinanju, in response, lowered the sound.

"Chiun! Cut that out! That looked like a report on the Tower thing coming on."

"The only news that could be of interest will come from the divine lips of Cheeta Ching," he intoned.

Remo offered the receiver. "Here, Smith wants to know your theories about what happened tonight."

Chiun refused to move. "I will have nothing to do with a person who would turn away an innocent child."

"He, she, or it hasn't been born yet!" Remo called over. Cupping his hand over the mouthpiece, he added in a whisper, "Think how many points you can score with Smith if you can solve this mess for him. The President's on his back."

The Master of Sinanju hesitated between opportunity and stubbornness.

"And it'll sure make up for the way we screwed up our last assignment," Remo added hopefully.

"I screwed up nothing!" Chiun flared, leaping to his feet. "Your failure to dispatch the dictator allowed him to seize one of Smith's outermost provinces! No blame is mine."

Remo suppressed a grin. Last time out, Remo had been assigned to assassinate a deposed Central American dictator. Remo thought he had done the job, but weeks later, the man had resurfaced in an new identity as an office-seeker in the California governor's race. Chuin had been seduced into joining the campaign by a promised post as Lord Treasurer. When the truth came out the Master of Sinanju was embarrassed, and ever since he had been determined to restore himself to Smith's good graces.

"Tell that to Smith," Remo suggested.

Chiun grasped the telephone and brought the ugly device to his parchment face.

"Emperor Smith. The truth here is very simple, O all-seeing one."

"Yes?"

"The idiot Rumpp built his ugly tower on a cursed spot."

"Cursed?"

"All Koreans understand that one does not merely set a building down in any old place. There are lucky places and unlucky places in the earth. Restless spirits roam. Unmarked graves abound. This is why we employ *mudangs* to seek out efficacious places first."

"*Mudangs?*"

"He means witches!" Remo called over.

"Oh," said Smith, disappointment in his tone. "I do not think we are dealing with witchcraft here, Master Chiun."

"What other explanation is there? Even your white witches have emerged from their places of hiding to brave the hangman's noose to behold the awesome sight."

"I've been trying to explain about the Salem witch trials!" Remo called over. "Somebody forgot to tell him dunking stools went out with the Spanish Inquisition."

"Master Chiun," Smith went on. "Have you no ideas? This matter is beyond my ability to cope with it."

Chiun stroked his wispy beard, one eye narrowing thoughtfully. "White magic has obviously failed. It is time for yellow magic."

"Yellow?"

"Emperor, I have a certain trunk for situations such as this. Had I known more of this matter I would have brought it with me."

"You require it now?" Smith asked.

"You have it safe, do you not?"

"Yes, along with most of your other trunks."

"It is a sad thing not to be in possession of one's

most treasured belongings," Chiun said, voice quavering, "but when one is homeless in a foreign land, one must sacrifice for the good of one's employer."

"I have been in search of a suitable property for you and Remo," Smith said quickly.

"I vote for the Bahamas," Remo chimed in.

"I will sign no contract until this unresolved matter is settled," Chiun said sharply.

"I will have the trunk shipped immediately. Which one is it?"

"The green-and-gold one. And take care, Smith—its contents are very powerful. Allow no lacky to manhandle it."

"The trunk will arrive intact, I promise," said Smith, hanging up without another word.

The Master of Sinanju padded back to his tatami mat. Remo had claimed it. Chiun cleared his throat in warning.

Instead of vacating the mat with alacrity, as was proper, Remo asked a question.

"Why does the green-and-gold trunk sound familiar?"

"Because it *is* familiar," Chiun sniffed. "Sitter-on-mats-which-are-not-his."

"Huh? Oh, sorry." Remo got up and made way.

The Master of Sinanju settled onto his mat and fixed his hazel eyes on the television screen, his expression expectant.

"Waiting for Cheeta, huh?"

"It should not concern you, offerer-of-false-hopes."

"Are you saying that I fibbed when I told you Smith wanted to be godfather to the brat?"

"I am not saying that."

"Good," Remo said in relief.

"The tone of your lying voice is saying that."

"Bulldookey."

Chiun lifted a gnarled hand. "Silence! Cheeta appears."

In fact, it was the harried face of BCN anchorman Don Cooder that appeared on the TV screen.

"Good evening," he said. "Tonight, all New York is agog as one of its most famous—some say infamous—skyscrapers has reportedly been spectralized."

"Spectralized?" Remo muttered.

"For more on this breaking story, we turn now to our junior anchorwoman, our own fountain of fecundity, Cheeta Ching."

Cooder turned in his chair to face the floating graphic of the Rumpp Tower, which expanded and became the repressed-with-fury face of Cheeta Ching. She was surrounded by ordinary New Yorkers, some dressed for trick-or-treating.

"Dan, I'm standing behind police lines surrounding what may be the Halloween spooktacular of the century." Cheeta stepped aside, disclosing the brassy Rumpp Tower. A scarecrow slipped up behind Cheeta and made a two-fingered rabbit-ears behind her glossy head. Cheeta elbowed him hard, and after he'd doubled over in pain, pushed his head below the camera frame and held it down with one foot.

The other trick-or-treaters moved away with haste.

Cheeta went on with her report, every so often grimacing and jumping slightly as the scarecrow attempted to get out from under her heel.

"Over my shoulder can be seen the Rumpp Tower, where tonight perhaps thousands of residents and office workers are trapped by the latest gambit in the titanic financial struggle between Randal T. Rumpp and his legion of creditors."

Don Cooder jumped in. "Cheeta. What exactly has happened to the Tower? We can see it there, plain as day. Looks fine. What's the story?"

"The story, Don, is that Randal Rumpp is claiming to have turned his prime architectural trophy into an insubstantial asset. It is literally untouchable."

"I understand, Cheeta, that you've spoken with Rumpp this evening."

"That's right, Don, I—"

"Any footage?"

Cheeta Ching's face colored. Her bloodred lips thinned, and her black eyes snapped with fury. She muttered something under her breath that, out of the millions watching the broadcast, perhaps only Remo and Chiun, who both understood Korean, picked up on.

"Did she just call him a bastard?" Remo asked Chiun.

"Hush!"

Cheeta went on. "Don, whatever dark forces are at work here, obviously it affects videotape. My exclusive interview was ruined."

"Too bad."

Cheeta smiled through set teeth. A guttural fragment of sound emerged, too.

Remo asked, "Did she just call him a prick in Korean?"

"Be still!"

"But," Cheeta added, lifting a notebook into camera range, "I can quote precisely several of the things Rumpp had to say." She began reading off the pad. "According to the real-estate developer himself, the Rumpp Tower has been 'spectralized.' That is, made insubstantial to human touch. Rumpp declined to explain why he had resorted to this unique approach to protecting his assets from seizure, but it's widely believed in banking circles that this is the last, desperate act of a desperate man, a man who, only a decade ago—"

"That's fine, Cheeta," Don Cooder cut in, "but we have a follow-up report to get to."

"But—"

The angry face of Cheeta Ching winked out and Don Cooder turned to face his audience, saying,

"Spectralization. What is it? Can it happen to your home? Here with a full report is BCN science editor, Frank Feldmeyer."

The Master of Sinanju stabbed the OFF switch angrily.

"Hey, I wanted to see that report!" Remo protested.

"There is a saloon in the lower regions of this building," Chiun said. "I am certain if you cross his palm with silver, the saloonkeeper will oblige you."

"Crap," said Remo, turning on the TV again. Chiun retreated to the dresser and seized the remote. He stabbed the button.

A competing newscaster appeared. The anchor was explaining, as if it were a perfectly ordinary occurrence, how the Rumpp Tower had been "dematerialized."

Remo switched back to BCN.

Chiun ran the channel selector to another broadcast.

This particular anchor, in referring to the Rumpp Tower, called it "owl-blasted."

Remo and Chiun stopped their struggle for television supremacy and looked at one another.

"Owl-blasted?" they said. They began paying attention to the screen, as the camera pulled back and no other than Delpha Rohmer was revealed seated beside the boyish anchor.

"Here with exclusive footage of the apparent haunting is Delpha Rohmer, official witch of Salem, Massachusetts," said the anchor.

"Perfect," Remo groused.

"First, Miss Rohmer," said the anchor, "can you explain the so-called 'event' on Fifth Avenue?"

Delpha Rohmer parted her scarlet lips in a dry, empty smile. Her eye shadow had been replenished. It was an unappetizing color similar to canned mushroom soup.

"It is not an event," she said in a vaguely sinister monotone. "It is the sign of the second coming of

169

Baphomet, the Great Horned One. Soon all Fifth Avenue, then all of Manhattan, will become as the Rumpp Tower. More innocents will slip into the earth to roast in Baphomet's pitiless hellfires."

"You're not serious?"

Delpha's mushroom-hued lids settled, like an alligator's inner eye membrane. "It will be the fate of all who do not practice the craft of Wicca to fall into the Horned One's toils. Only by embracing the first religion can womankind be saved."

"What about men?" Remo asked the picture tube.

"What about men?" the anchor asked Delpha.

"Men," retorted Delpha Rohmer, "can be saved only by wise women. If the women out in the audience wish to be saved, or desire to succor their menfolk . . ."

"Here it comes," Remo said.

"I have a toll-free number they may call for information," Delpha finished.

"Actually, we don't have time for that," the anchor interjected hastily, "because we want to run that footage."

At which point Delpha Rohmer flicked her fingers in the anchor's face, causing him to fall into a sneezing fit. While the camera cut back to her, in order to spare the continental United States the sight of a star anchor's nasal distress, Delpha tore open her dress front, exposing two pale but generous breasts over which was stenciled a 900 number.

"A trick!" Chiun hissed, looking away. "I saw her fling some exotic herb!"

"If you call pepper 'exotic,' " Remo said dryly.

"To a Korean, Mediterranean spices are as alien as bubblegum." Chiun sniffed.

"Shall I change the channel, or do you want to copy down the number?" Remo asked.

"No! It is as the *Book of Sinanju* says: 'Never trust a *mudang*. Especially a white one.' "

"So much for magic," said Remo, grabbing the remote. But before he could bring it into play, the footage captured by Cheeta Ching's cameraman rolled. His finger on the channel-changer, Remo froze. "Chiun! Check this out!"

22

The long black Volga automobile carried former KBG major Yuli Batenin through the gates of a forbidding gray stone prison, causing his heart to leap with joy.

In the good times, the KGB sometimes had operated from behind the impenetrable confines of Soviet state prisons.

The Volga swept past the security gate and around to a rear entrance—another good sign.

Batenin was marched in. His feet were glad. The oppressive weight of Democracy seemed to be lifted from his square shoulders with every stumbling step.

He was taken into an office with only the modest legend SHCHIT on the pebbled-glass door.

"There is that word again, 'Shield'," Batenin muttered.

A hard truncheon jabbed him close enough to the kidney area to get his attention, but not near enough to cause blood in the urine.

His grimace did not look like a smile, but he recognized the blow with pleasure. A good old-fashioned KBG blow. Not like the sissies in the new Federal Security Agency, a toothless organization designed to sound like the American FBI in a stupid compromise between national pride and good PR. It disgusted Batenin, the way the new leadership aped everything American.

The door came open. Batenin was urged in.

Seated at a substantial desk was a dour, thick-set man in a jet-black uniform he had never before seen. The man looked like a Khazakh. It surprised Batenin. Since the breakup, most ethnics had returned to their homelands—there to await the coming civil war, in Yuli Batenin's pessimistic opinion.

"Sit," he was told.

Yuli Batenin sat.

"Batenin," said the officer—a colonel, according to his silver shoulderboards. The man looked like a Nazi, there was so much silver in his black uniform.

"Yes, *Tovarich* Colonel?"

"I am not your comrade," the colonel spat.

And former Major Yuli Batenin's face fell. Since the failed coup, the term "comrade" had fallen into disfavor. But to Batenin, it spoke of the days of pride in the motherland, now shattered and fighting amongst itself.

"You will address me as 'Colonel,' " the black colonel said. His desk was T-shaped, and bare but for a phalanx of off-yellow official telephones.

"Yes, Colonel."

The colonel in black shoved a manila folder across the green felt blotter.

Batenin recognized the KGB seal and the stark words, in Cyrillic letters, that were stenciled on the front.

UTMOST SECRET
TO BE STORED FOREVER

"It is the file of which I attempted to warn the Kremlin," Batenin said.

"You mean the White House," said the colonel.

"Yes. Excuse me. The White House. I had forgotten."

It was another public relations humiliation. In order to appeal to rich Americans, the Russian Parliament had renamed the parliament building "the White House." With all the bronze Lenins being torn down, Batenin half expected statues of Washington and Jefferson to one day sprout in their place.

The colonel in black went on speaking.

"This file contains report on Operation Nimble Spirit. What do you know of this?"

"I was case officer," admitted Yuli Batenin.

"It was your assignment to see that the agent in the field . . ." The colonel consulted the file. ". . . Brashnikov, fulfilled his duties to the motherland." The use of the honored phrase made Yuli Batenin blink. These men sounded genuine. But who were they? And what was meant by "Shield"?

"I performed my duty to the best of my ability," Batenin said stiffly.

"Which is why you were exiled to Gorky," the colonel said contemptuously.

"You mean, Nizhni Novgorod," Batenin corrected.

"If Shield fulfills its mission, it will be Gorky once more. And St. Petersburg will again be Leningrad, and the people will eat once again," the colonel said flatly.

Yuli Batenin's eyes became startled coins. "You are KGB?"

"No, Major Batenin."

Major! They were calling him "major"! Why?

"We are Cheka," the colonel said flatly.

"Cheka?"

"Then, VCheka. After that, OGPU, NKVD, NKGB, MGB, MVD and more recently, KGB. Now we are simply Shield. The name is no more than the fashion of the day. Our purpose remains the same: Protection of the Motherland, Holy Russia."

"You are good communist?"

The colonel only glared with his narrow black Khazakh eyes.

"I am Colonel Radomir Rushenko, and I offer you

an opportunity to be reinstated at your former rank with your former pay, in our organization."

Major Batenin almost leaped to his feet with joy. In fact his knees started to straighten, and the patched seat of his pants actually left the hard oak chair for a moment.

Then he remembered an important detail.

"A hummingbird could not live on my former salary, today."

"We pay in dollars, not rubles," said Colonel Rushenko.

"If you paid in nickels it would be better than rubles," Batenin admitted sadly. "But why me?"

"We have watched the same newscast as you did, Batenin," Colonel Ruskeno said firmly. He extracted a number of color photographs from the folder and slid them to Batenin's side of the desk.

Batenin took them up. They showed a manlike creature, all in white, with a smooth, bulbous head. A white cable looped up from sockets mounted on each shoulder, to disappear behind the creature's back.

The last photograph showed a black-haired Georgian, with shifty bright eyes and the sharp face of a ferret.

"This is Captain Rair Nicolaivitch Brashnikov, a special operative for KGB," the colonel said flatly.

"*Nyet*. This is Rair Brashnikov, who is thief. He ruined entire Operation Nimble Ghost. He cost me my career. And worse, he caused me to tremble at the very sound of—"

The telephone rang.

Major Yuli Batenin shot out of his hard chair and found refuge under the spread legs of a guard. Batenin had his hands over his eyes and was trembling from head to toe.

Colonel Rushenko let the telephone ring three times before picking it up. With cool dispassion, he noticed that each shrill ring had the same effect on the cowering major's body as would two live copper wires from a portable generator.

Ignoring Batenin, he listened to the voice at the other end of the telephone. Then he hung up.

"Your plane is ready, Major Batenin."

Batenin looked up. "Plane? What plane."

"The plane that will take you to America, where you will liquidate the renegade Brashnikov and recover the vibration suit that will restore the Union."

It was the most terrifying sentence Major Yuli Batenin had ever heard. Still, he found the strength to rise and salute.

"I am proud to accept this assignment," he said sincerely.

"You will be dead if you botch it," said the colonel, not bothering to return the salute.

And the cold, dismissive tones of Colonel Rushenko made Yuli Batenin's KGB-trained heart warm in response.

It was almost like being back in the USSR again.

23

Remo and Chiun stared at the image on the TV screen.

It was a floating white figure, with cables looping up from its shoulders like the transparent wings of a fly.

"It can't be," Remo said.

"The fiend," Chiun rasped.

"I don't believe it," Remo growled.

The sniffling anchor was saying, "This footage was shot from a helicopter, and purports to show a supernatural being inhabiting the Rumpp Tower."

As they watched the white figure, visible through a darkened pane in the southwest corner of the Rumpp Tower, it rolled in midair like a drowned corpse.

Probably no one watching the tape could make out the blocky object that hung in the white webbing knapsack on the back of the floating figure. It was too indistinct. The letters on the back of the boxy object were too faint to be read by normal eyes.

But the eyes of the only two living Masters of Sinanju were not ordinary.

And they knew exactly what to look for.

A logo that said: SEARS DIEHARD.

"I believe it," Remo said unhappily.

"The Krahseevah," hissed Chiun, making tiny yellow mallets with his bone-hard fists.

"Mystery solved," Remo said glumly, snatching up the telephone. He got Smith immediately.

"Smitty. Turn on Channel Four. Right now."

"One moment."

A moment later Harold W. Smith's surprised voice came back, saying, "What should I be looking for?"

"It shiny and white and trouble."

"All I am getting, Remo, are two rhinoceroses copulating."

"Your Channel Four must be different than ours. Try MBC News."

The sound of Smith's breathing went away. Then there came a hoarse, "Oh my God."

"Look like the Krahseevah to you?" Remo asked.

"I do not know. I have never seen this creature."

"Well, Chiun and I have. And it's the Krahseevah all right. I thought you call-wasted him."

"By all rights, Remo, the Krahseevah, as you call him, should have been atomically scattered through the nation's telephone system, after we tricked him into teleporting himself to a dead phone here at Folcroft."

"Well, he's loose in the Rumpp Tower. And five will get you ten, he's responsible for what's going on down there."

"I wonder," Smith said.

"Wonder what?" Remo asked.

"Remo, do you recall reading of system-wide telephone difficulties over the last few years?"

"Sure. Once La Guardia was shut down for over an hour, because flight-tracking information is carried between airports through Ma Bell's lines."

"These service interruptions date back approximately three years."

"Yeah. About that."

"The same length of time since we tricked the Krahseevah into, we thought, destroying himself."

"You don't think . . . ?"

"The Krahseevah, you will recall, possessed the ability to make himself insubstantial. This enabled him to steal into high-security installations throughout the nation and make off with valuable technology for his Russian superiors. It was one of the last-gasp efforts of the former Soviet Union to achieve technological parity with the U.S., before their system finally collapsed of its own backwardness."

"Don't remind me," Remo said sourly, glancing at the footage of their most aggravating opponent as it was replayed.

"A side effect of this property was that if he energized the suit that provided him with this ability while holding an open-line telephone, his unstable, dematerialized atoms and molecules would be sucked into the phone lines, much the way electrons travel as electricity, only to reintegrate, intact and alive, on the other end."

"Yeah," Remo said bitterly. "He was a human fax. Chiun and I couldn't touch him, catch him, or stop him."

"Until I devised a foolproof plan to destroy him," said Smith.

"So much for foolproof," Remo pointed out.

Smith's harsh voice softened, as if he were reliving the entire operation.

"We set it up perfectly. A lure on an Air Force base."

"I remember. We had a stealth plane that didn't exist. It was a hologram."

"Designed to make the Krahseevah, when he turned off his suit in order to steal the prototype model, doubt the status of his molecular state."

"It was good enough for me to get a good shot in."

Chiun squeaked contrarily, "A proper blow, and we would not be having this problem!"

"So? I only winged him. It happens."

"Your repeated failures will go against us at the next negotiation!" Chiun said loudly. "But at least no blame will attach itself to our emperor. His head will be spared by the President, whoever that person will be this time."

Remo said, "I think Chiun's trying to brown-nose you, Smitty."

Smith ignored the outburst and went on: "The Krahseevah reacted as I thought he would. He went to the nearest phone and dialed the Soviet Embassy in Washington, from which he apparently operated. But the phone was programmed to dial only one number. That of a Folcroft phone."

"Which you disconnected," Remo pointed out. "You said it would scatter the guy into a million dial tones."

"The only explanation is that the Krahseevah has been caught up in the telephone system, wreaking havoc, and somehow emerged through one of the Rumpp Tower lines," Smith said.

"Talk about a wrong number," Remo remarked glumly.

"And I am responsible for it," Smith said, his voice aghast.

"Okay, we know what's up. Now we just have to figure out how to stop this jerk."

"There is more to it than that, Remo," Smith said slowly.

"Yeah?"

"Recall that Randal Rumpp had claimed credit for the events of this night. We have every reason to believe that Rumpp and the Krahseevah have joined forces."

"So? Chiun and I are running a two-for-one Halloween special. We'll take them both out."

"Not until we better understand the situation. Sit tight. I will get back to you."

"Do not forget my trunk!" Chiun called, just as Smith hung up.

Remo snapped his fingers. "*Now* I remember. That trunk! It was full of your shaman junk. The stuff you used to exorcise that missile base, before we knew we were dealing with a Russian scam and not poltergeist."

Chiun gave his kimono skirts a resolute hitch. "We were dealing with dark forces. This time, we will deal with them intelligently and atone for our past failures."

"Chiun, this is science, not magic. We gotta fight it scientifically."

"White ignorance," Chiun scoffed.

The TV began scrolling vertically. Absently, Remo stuck out his two outer fingers and folded back the middle pair and his thumb. He pointed them at the rising black transmission line and said, "There's no such thing as magic."

The line followed Remo's fingers when he lifted them.

"Machine-worshipper," Chiun spat.

"Bulldookey," said Remo. The transmission line slipped back just before it got to the top edge of the tube and Remo caught it again. This time it followed his fingers until the picture was perfect once more.

"When Emperor Smith instructs us to seek out this enemy," Chiun said firmly, "I will have my herbs and bells and you may attack it with a turbocharged hot-cheese blaster, and we will see which is more effective."

"There is no such thing as a turbocharged hot-cheese blaster," Remo pointed out.

"By morning, some greedy white tinkerer will have invented one. You may be first in line to purchase the worthless thing. Heh heh heh."

Ignoring the dry cackling of the Master of Sinanju, Remo went to the hotel window.

The Rumpp Tower was visible only a few blocks away. It was as dark as Remo's mood.

"This is *not* going to be easy," he muttered unhappily.

24

The Aeroflot flight that carried Major Yuli Batenin of the supersecret Russian organization known only as "Shield" out of Russia had to refuel in Minsk because of insufficient fuel. And again in Warsaw, Oslo, Reykjavik, and Halifax, Nova Scotia, because Areoflot's credit standing was so poor no airport was willing to fill the Ilyushin jet's fuel tanks.

Inasmuch as few would accept Russian credit cards, they had to dig into their hard currency reserves at several stops.

This left them with seriously reduced operating expenses by the time the wheels touched down at Kennedy International Airport, chosen not only for its geographical proximity to the operations field but because it was more open to illegal entry than the Texas border.

"We must pool funds," Batenin told the captain in charge of the operation, whose name was Igor Gerkoff.

"It is for me to say these things; you are merely *osnaz*."

Which confirmed to Yuli Batenin the suspicion that had been growing since he had left the motherland. These men were not ex-KGB. Not all of them. They were Spetsnaz—*spetsialnoye nazhacheniye*. Special purpose soldiers of the GRU, military intelligence. They were the shock troops of the former Red Army General Staff.

By *osnaz*, they were mocking him as a mere secret policeman, which is what he had been in his KGB days, albeit a glorified one.

Whatever this "Shield" was, it was comprised of the most hard-core members of pre-Gorbachev forces. Every man was an athlete of Olympic caliber. This was good. It was also very intimidating to Yuli Batenin, whose background was in intelligence, not operations.

"I have forty American dollars and three kopecks," Yuli said, showing Captain Gerkoff the contents of his pockets.

"Give me dollars, and save kopeks for after next Revolution. When they will be valuable once again."

Reluctantly, Batenin did as he was told. He did not think kopecks would ever be worth anything. Even in good times, they were valueless. But he had no choice.

Others chipped in. Soon, nearly two hundred dollars had been amassed.

"Should be enough to obtain us each fine room in best American hotel," the captain said confidently.

As it turned out, when they presented themselves at the front desk of the Rumpp Regis Hotel, the two hundred dollars was barely enough to get them a single room in the back.

When Yuli Batenin broke the bad news to his Shield unit, few of whom spoke passable English, Captain Gerkoff said, "Is no problem. Take room, Batenin. We come back."

Less than an hour later, there was a knock at Batenin's hotel room door.

He called through the door cautiously. "Who is it?"

"Gerkoff. *Shchit*."

Batenin opened the door. There were all standing

there, in open-neck shirts whose pointed collars over-lapped their suit coats. Gold chains festooned hairy necks.

"We have registered, and are prepared to go among Americans undetected by them," Gerkoff said, stepping in.

"How did you register?" Batenin asked, marveling at their clothes.

"Credit cards. We strangle tourists and take theirs. Is no problem."

"Did you steal clothes, too?"

"No. Clothes foolishly donated by Americans to Russia through Project Provide Hope packages. They are latest fashion, no?"

"They are latest fashion, twenty years ago," Batenin said unhappily.

This assertion caused the Shield unit to huddle and converse worriedly. When they broke their huddle, Captain Gerkoff said, "We have decided clothes too fine to abandon. We will keep them."

And Yuli Batenin, looking at the only hope of reviving the Soviet Union assembled before him like extras from *Saturday Night Fever*, could only smile weakly and hope for the best.

After all, these were the finest killers produced by the Soviet Union. What matter their wardrobe, when it came time to make moist red spots on the carpets of America?

25

Randal Rumpp watched the sun come up through his magnificent office window.

The night had passed peacefully. Oh, there had been a few minor problems, such as the attempt by the mob below to storm his office.

Fortunately, Randal Rumpp had had anti-creditor doors installed on all access routes to the twenty-fourth floor. They were modeled on the waterproof sliding doors used to seal off flooded submarine bulkheads.

When his executive assistant burst in to warn him of the impending assault, he coolly reached into an open desk drawer and hit a switch.

A red light should have come on. None did. Then he remembered that the tower electricity was still off-line.

Rumpp came out from behind his desk, screaming, "Man the manual controls!"

They jumped on levers and turned big iron wheels concealed all over the floor, sealing off the two main points of invasion and later the remaining fire exits.

Randal Rumpp, not satisfied with having saved his own skin, hurled abuse through the thick doors.

"Go home, losers!"

That only made the pounding grow more heated.

The pounding continued for an hour or so. Then,

their rage expended, the mob had apparently withdrawn.

Now, with the sun up, and Randal Rumpp's enthusiasm, fortified by a wide assortment of candy bars ranging from a Skybar to a USA, restored, he was working his cellular phone. The USA company had gone out of business in the early seventies, and Rumpp, who had claimed in print that he hadn't really begun making money until he had tripled his sugar intake, had had a lifetime supply put into deep freeze for his personal use.

"Hello, Mr. Mayor," he said cheerfully, picking nougat out from between his front teeth with a monogrammed ivory toothpick, "have you given any further thought to Rumpp Tower II?"

"The plan is unworkable. Your FAR won't allow for two hundred stories."

"That's what the previous administration said about Rumpp Tower I," Rumpp countered. "The jerks said our permissible height was too much for our floor-area ratio. But I bargained for and got the max—21.6 FAR. And I didn't have an eyesore like this mess to cover up."

"According to some news reports, this mess, as you call it, is a haunting, not your responsibility," the mayor said.

"Hey! That's Cheeta Ching's version of events. She's got one in the oven. You know how that messes up those high-estrogen types. This has my fingerprints all over it."

"What on earth are you up to, Rumpp?"

Rumpp shrugged. "Hey, I do it to do it. I think that's what I'm gonna call my next autobiography. So what's the deal? Do I draw up a letter of intent, or what?"

"I have a nine o'clock with the planning commission."

"Listen, you tell those slobs if I don't get what I

want, all city property tax payments stop!" Randal Rumpp warned. "You're not dealing with just any chump here. You're dealing with a Rumpp."

"I know," said the mayor bitterly, hanging up.

"Hmmm. That didn't come out right. Dorma!"

Dorma Wormser raced in, her eyes expectant.

"Take a memo," said Randal Rumpp.

Her face fell. "Yes, Mr. Rumpp."

"I want a reminder in my personal reminder book never to use the phrase, 'You're dealing with a Rumpp.' It's bad for the image. Doesn't sound right, somehow."

"Yes, Mr. Rumpp," sighed Dorma, who had been hired because her boss was an "ass man."

The cellular phone rang.

Randal Rumpp reached for the handset. But his attention was distracted by his executive assistant's headlong leap under a glass coffee table. She huddled under it, in plain view.

"Get out of there! What's with you? You've been jumpy all night."

"I can't help it, Mr. Rumpp. Ever since that . . . *thing* jumped out of the phone, I've been a wreck."

"Be a wreck on your own time," said Randal Rumpp.

The phone continued to ring.

Dorma shrieked, "Please answer that thing!"

Randal Rumpp lifted the handset. Instantly, his assistant stopped trying to shrivel up into a cowering ball.

"Go ahead," Rumpp said into the mouthpiece. His scowl fled when he heard the tight voice on the other end. He brightened.

"Dad! Now, about those chips . . . Yeah, sure, I'll buy them back. I promise. A little misunderstanding. I fired the jerk who handled that deal. Listen, I need a hand up here. Can you front me some start-up money. Huh? Oh, not much. Maybe three-four million."

The earpiece buzzed angrily. Rumpp's mouth squeezed into a moist, meaty pout.

"Yeah, Dad. I know you're not made out of money. But this is an emergency. I got a problem with the Tower. You know, I think I've outgrown it or something. I need to trade up. How about a little interest-free loan?"

Rumpp listened, wincing on and off.

"Tell you what," he said quickly. "I'll name the new building after you. How's that? Yeah, I'll call it 'the Rumpp Tower.' "

Rumpp listened eagerly. His face resumed wincing.

"Then I'll issue a press release explicitly stating that it's named after you," he said soothingly. "No, I don't want to call it 'the Ronald Rumpp Tower.' Why not? You know these jerks on the planning commission. They won't let me put up a sign that big. If I could do it, I would. Honest. You know me."

The line went silent.

"Hello? Hello? Dad? Damn!"

Rumpp closed the antenna with an angry bat of his hand.

"That old fart! The nerve of him! I offered him the best deal of his life, and he walked way from it. His blood must be running thin, or something."

Randal Rumpp felt the stiffness of his joints as he got out of his executive chair. He decided to commune with his trophies. In his favorite room in the whole world, maybe he'd find inspiration. He took with him his attaché cellular.

"Hold my calls, Dorma," he said, as he marched out.

"Yes, Mr. Rumpp."

In the trophy room, Randal Rumpp pored over the takings of a lifetime of cutting corners, wheeling and dealing, and bait-and-switch at the executive level.

He paused to admire a rare Picasso hanging on a wall. He knew nothing about art, but someone had told him at a cocktail party that Picasso was the artist to invest in. He had bought it sight unseen. When it came in, he couldn't figure out which end was up and was afraid to hang it in a public place. Rumpp called the gallery to complain the paint had settled during shipping, and the work was ruined.

When the dealer refused to take it back, Rumpp had the signature painted over and "Property of R. Rumpp" inscribed in its place, figuring that would increase its resale value.

On his second circuit of the room, he noticed something missing. He ran to the door and stuck his head out into the corridor.

"Dorma!"

"Yes, Mr. Rumpp?"

"Did you take my monogrammed Colibri lighter?"

"Of course not."

"Well, somebody did. It's gone. And nobody's been in here except you and me and the—"

Rumpp's face acquired a sick look.

"Oh, God," he said thickly.

Randal Rumpp turned on his portable cellular phone. He lifted the receiver to his ear.

"Anybody in there?" he asked.

"Help me. I am lost in telephone," said a familiar voice.

"I know."

"You! You trick me!"

"There was a screw-up. But don't worry. I fired the jerk responsible. Listen, did you take my monogrammed cigarette lighter?"

"Are you calling me thief?" the voice demanded.

"It was either you or my secretary. And I saw you looking at it. You called it a funny name."

"I called it '*krahseevah*.' In my language, it means 'beautiful.' I like beautiful things."

"Case closed. Good-bye."

"I admit it! I admit it!" the voice said hastily. "I have lighter. I will be happy to return it to you."

Randal Rumpp hesitated. "Can you do that without coming out of the phone yourself?"

"I can try."

"How?"

"You lift up receiver. I hand out lighter. It is very simple. Like opening refrigerator door for ice cream cone."

Rumpp frowned. "I don't trust you."

"You trick me and talk about trust. You phony-baloney."

"Hell, *you're* the thief here!" Rumpp protested indignantly. "I'm a businessman. I don't steal. I just hoodwink people who don't do their homework. No law against that."

"You want pen, you must lift receiver. There is no other way."

"Forget it," said Randal Rumpp. "I'm not ready to cash in my chips just yet. I'll get back to you."

"Wait!"

Randal Rumpp hung up the telephone. Instantly, it began ringing.

From down the corridor Dorma Wormser shrieked as if in pain, and begged for mercy.

"Remind me to fire that weak-kneed bitch when this is over," Rumpp muttered, moving the bell lever to LOUDEST.

When his executive assistant's screams began to get on his nerves, Rumpp reluctantly suppressed the bell.

It was going to be a long, long day.

26

The Master of Sinanju's green-and-gold steamer trunk arrived by express at nine o'clock.

"Your trunk's here," Remo called.

"Do not let the messenger escape."

"Escape?"

Chiun bounded out of his bedroom, wearing a blue-and-white ceremonial robe. Ignoring Remo and the surprised deliveryman, the Master of Sinanju fell upon the ornate trunk. He examined every inch of its lacquered surface for nicks or blemishes.

Finding none, he threw open the lid and did a complete inventory with suspicious eyes.

Only then did he straighten his cat-lean back and address the waiting messenger.

"You may live, careful one."

"You mean 'leave,' " said the deliveryman.

"That too," sniffed Chiun.

After the man had closed the door behind him, Remo remarked, "He thinks you were kidding him."

The phone rang. Chiun ignored it. Remo scooped up the receiver and said, "Smitty?"

"Remo!" Harold Smith admonished. "You should never speak my name before I identify myself. Security."

"Like there aren't twenty million Smiths in the world," Remo muttered. "Okay, what's your problem?"

"The Rumpp Regis is about to be seized for back taxes."

Remo raised an interested eyebrow. "Oh yeah?"

"It just broke over the wire services," Smith added.

"So what do we do?"

"Sit tight. If Randal Rumpp has somehow turned the Krahseevah technology to his own use, it's possible he may move to despectralize it."

"That means we're at ground zero. With a capital Z."

"Await developments."

"What developments?" Remo asked.

"Any developments."

"Great," Remo said sourly, hanging up.

"What did Emperor Smith say?" Chiun asked absently. He was going through the contents of his trunk. Remo noticed he was holding some sort of feather-decorated wind instrument, whose flaring mouth promised an ear-splitting cacophony.

Remo decided the less the Master of Sinanju knew, the quieter the lull before the storm would be.

"He said we're to hang loose until something happens," Remo replied, trying to keep his voice toneless.

Chiun looked up from his trunk. "He said to do nothing?"

"That's about the size of it."

Chiun returned to his rummaging. "Then we do nothing."

"Not me. I'm going downstairs to get a newspaper."

"For an illiterate like you, that is nothing," Chiun sniffed.

Remo took the elevator to the lobby and bought a paper at the newsstand. He bought a *Post*, because the *Times* didn't have a comics section.

The lobby was busy with grim-faced official types

who were showing badges. IRS. They were giving the desk clerk a hard time.

"Are we being audited again?" the clerk asked.

"No, sir," said the IRS man said. "We're not auditors. We're revenue collectors."

"If you want to take money from the hotel safe, you'll have to speak with the manager," the clerk sniffed.

"No need. We're seizing the entire hotel."

The clerk paled and looked on the verge of fainting. "Does this mean I'm unemployed?"

"Only if you don't follow instructions. You work for Uncle Sam now."

Remo decided to read the paper in the lobby, seeing as the IRS agents promised to be almost as entertaining as Calvin and Hobbes.

An agent sauntered over and said, "No loitering in this lobby."

"I'm registered," Remo pointed out.

The agent flashed his badge and said, "Agency rules. Sorry."

"You guys are going to bankrupt this place with that attitude."

"I don't make the rules."

"I know. You just jam them down people's throats."

Remo got up and started for the elevator. He reached it a step behind a thick-necked man in a John Travolta ensemble.

The door opened and Remo got on. So did "Travolta."

"I thought Halloween was yesterday," Remo remarked dryly.

The man looked at the elevator indicator board and said nothing.

"Got a match?" Remo asked. The man looked down at his shoes. One hand—his right—rose slightly . . . and Remo became aware that the man was armed. He was no IRS agent. That was for sure.

In fact, he didn't even smell like an American. Remo's senses had been trained to the peak of perfection. But that was only the first step. Chiun had taught him to utilize his heightened senses in ways Remo himself still found amazing. One exercise involved guessing people's nationalities by their personal scents.

It was not as bizarre as it sounded. Personal scents were a mixture of hygiene, diet, and other organic constants. Diet was the predominate determinate, however.

The man in the elevator smelled of black bread and borscht.

A Russian.

In itself, it was not unusual to find a Russian staying at the Rumpp Regis. It was a four-star hotel. Its clientele probably included citizens from Canada to Tongo.

Still, an *armed* Russian was unusual.

When the elevator stopped at the fourteenth floor and the Russian got off, Remo kept the door from closing again with the toe of an Italian loafer and stepped out into the lobby.

He hung back, staying close to the walls, as he followed the Russian's distinctive scent to a room at the end of one corridor. The man knocked, spoke a thick word that sounded to Remo like "shit," and was let in.

Remo noted the room number and went to a corridor phone. He called his own room.

"Chiun. We got Russians."

"Turn on the lights and they will scurry away," said Chiun unconcernedly.

"I think this may be connected to the Krahseevah. Smith said we may have another Rumpp Tower here."

"He did?" Chiun squeaked. "You did not not tell me of this! I must make preparations!

"Wait a minute!" The phone clicked in Remo's ear.

"Damn," Remo said, racing to the elevators.

The doors opened on a cage going up. Remo ignored it.

The next elevator was going down. Remo knew that because, when the doors opened, there stood the Master of Sinanju, standing before his green-and-gold trunk, wearing a ceremonial white stovepipe hat.

"Little Father, wait!"

From up one sleeve, the Master of Sinanju withdrew the strange feathered wind instrument and brought it to his lips.

It made a sound that paralyzed Remo's supersensitive eardrums long enough for Chiun to stab the door's CLOSE button. It shut in Remo's unhappy face.

"Damn," Remo said again, racing for the stairs.

When he got to the lobby, the Master of Sinanju had placed the trunk in the center of the ornate lobby floor. He flung it open.

An IRS revenue collector came over to lodge a protest and found himself being escorted to the revolving doors by the pressure of two long-nailed fingers on his right elbow. The incredulous look on his heavy, muscular face—revenue collectors, unlike IRS agents, are chosen for their brawn, not their brains—was that of a man who has been seized by a giant tarantula. He was placed inside, and the door started revolving with him in it. Then it stopped abruptly, bumping his nose hard.

Nothing the man could do could unstick the revolving door. He was trapped. He looked almost relieved about it.

Remo warned, "Chiun! That's only going to create more trouble."

"Stand back," Chiun said, shrugging his kimono sleeves back, exposing spindly arms like bony, tanned leather. He dipped into his trunk and extracted with one hand a bamboo wand decorated with silver bells and with the other a drum.

Remo put his hands on his hips. "Let me guess. You're going to drive off the evil spirits with those."

"No," corrected Chiun. "*We* are going to drive away the evil spirits with these tokens. You may beat the *chang-gu* drum, since it requires no skill or cadence."

"I am not beating any freaking drum. I told you, we got Russians. I think something is about to break."

"Yes. Our contract, if we do not give Smith proper service. You will beat the drum."

"Will you listen to me if I go along?" Remo asked in a heated voice.

"Possibly."

Remo took the drum. He wrapped one arm around it and began slapping the tight skin with his palm.

"I feel like an idiot!" he protested loudly over the noise.

The Master of Sinanju pretended not to hear him. Remo paused and then began, "Listen—"

Chiun flared, "Keep drumming. It is important. Relatively."

Chiun lifted his wand and shook it. His head rocking from side to side and threatening to dislodge his stovepipe hat, which was tied about his wispy chin by a string, he began to move about the lobby, chanting and making other noises that brought to mind a tomcat caught in the rinse cycle.

Frowning, Remo woodenly beat the drum. With any luck, he thought, this is the five-minute exorcism.

In the middle of all this, Yuli Batenin returned from having breakfast in the hotel restaurant, Soup de Rumpp.

27

By eleven o'clock, Randal Rumpp had figured out that he was being stonewalled.

The mayor's office wasn't returning his calls. The Planning Commission wasn't returning his calls. No one was returning his calls.

Randal Rumpp's office suite included several televisions sets in elegant cabinets, and assorted sound systems. All useless in the blacked-out skyscraper.

"I can't stand this!" he complained. "I'm the lead story on every broadcast, and I'm missing everything. Dorma!"

"Yes, Mr. Rumpp?"

"Go down to the lobby and get me a newspaper."

"But Mr. Rumpp. The only papers would be yesterday's."

"Then get me yesterday's paper. The *Post*, not the *Times*. I gotta read something. This is driving me bugnuts."

"But the mob . . ."

Randal Rumpp's voice dropped to a throaty growl.

"Dorma, can the mob fire you?"

"No, Mr. Rumpp."

"Think the mob will hire you if I fire you?"

"No, Mr. Rumpp."

"Then go fetch, Chuck."

"Yes, Mr. Rumpp," said Dorma Wormser meekly.

She slunk away, slipping through one of the secret exits and closing it after her.

"Money always talks," said Randal Rumpp confidently. "She'll probably break the stair-climbing record, if there is one. Gotta remember to stiff her for the cost of the paper."

But when eleven o'clock became twelve-thirty and Dorma Wormser still hadn't returned, Randal Rumpp was forced to conclude that one of two things had happened: either she had deserted him, or she had been torn apart by the unruly mob below.

He privately hoped it was the latter. Dorma was single. He could probably get away with holding on to her last paycheck.

But that still left him out of touch. And Randal Rumpp hated to be out of touch. He roamed the twenty-fourth floor looking for a transistor radio. He doubted that he'd find one, inasmuch as personal property that cheap was banned from Rumpp Organization work space, but one never knew. Employees could be treacherous.

The ringing cellular sent him racing back to his office.

"Yes," he said, out of breath.

"Randy?"

"Don't call me that. The tabloids call me that. I hate it. Call me the . . . the Rumpporama!"

"This is Dunbar Grimspoon. The IRS has just seized the Rumpp Regis for back taxes."

"They can't do that."

"They did."

"Damn! Well, what are you sitting there for? Get on it! Get on their cases and make 'em cough back it up!"

"Uh, Rand?"

"Rumpporama."

"This is a bad time for you, I know. But about your last bill . . . It's overdue."

"Is that all you overpaid lawyers ever think about—money?"

"That's why we're overpaid. Look, if it were just me, okay. But the partners are bitching. This is a six-figure bill."

"Which will never, ever be paid if you don't jump up this seizure thing," Rumpp said heatedly. "Hear me, Chuck? You tell *that* to your partners, and get back to me within twenty minutes."

Fifty minutes later, Randal Rumpp was wondering if he had overplayed his hand. His called his law firm. When he identified himself to the switchboard operator, the girl's voice grew chilly and he was put on hold. For an hour.

Rumpp reluctantly cut the connection. "Okay, I overdid it. It happens. When you've been on a winning streak as long as Randal Rumpp, you're bound to screw up in insignificant ways. No big deal. The world's full of lawyers."

He ate three chocolate bars and immediately felt his confidence return. Idly, he picked up his dormant cellular and thumbed the bell button. It immediately began ringing.

Randal Rumpp, more for someone to talk to than for any practical reason, picked up his working cellular and said, "Hello, you still there?"

"Yes. And I still have cigarette lighter."

"Keep it. I got a better deal."

"What is that?"

"Come in with me."

"Come in where?"

"Become a vital player in the greatest deal-making organization on the face of the planet, the Rumpp Organization."

The voice grew interested. "You wish to hire me?"

"At a handsome salary. What say?"

"I say, how much salary?"

"Twice your previous one. I'll have to check references, though."

"I do not think KGB will give such things."

"I know they won't. There's no KGB anymore."

"Is true, then? Russia is no more?"

"Oh, Russia's still there," Rumpp said airily. "It's just a heck of a lot smaller."

"It shrink?"

"You might say that. Listen, this is chitchat. Are you willing to join the Rumpp team, or not?"

"Definitely."

"Okay. I'm going to pick up the other phone now."

"Before you do that, there are two things you must know."

"Yeah?"

"One, I will be unconscious when I leave phone. I will float."

"I saw that happen. You'll come out of it."

"Not if I do not turn off suit before battery runs out."

"Suit?"

"I am wearing suit. Vibration suit. It enables me to vibrate through solid objects. If I float into solid object, then battery runs low and rematerialize inside, explosion may be nuclear."

"What explosion?"

"The one that will result when atoms and molecules attempting to be occupying same space collide. Is bug in suit."

"That's a pretty big bug," Randal Rumpp said dubiously.

"That," the voice said, "is the second thing. I am ready to come out now."

Randal Rumpp thought a moment. He hadn't bargained on a nuclear downside. On the other hand, who would have thought a day ago he could have found a scam to make the Rumpp Tower safe from the banks? He decided to go for it.

"I'm picking up the other phone now," he said.

The static roar was brief, loud, and seemed to pierce Randal Rumpp's unwary brain like a noisy stiletto. The air about him turned white. Very white.

Randal Rumpp fell back in his chair and hit his head. The cellular phone fell from his fingers and struck the floor.

When Randal Rumpp regained conciousness, he was looking at the ceiling. The ceiling looked ordinary. It was tile. The initials RR had been laid in the tile so large that only Randal Rumpp could see them.

He saw them perfectly now. He just couldn't understand why he was looking up at the ceiling, when he had been sitting up straight at his desk just a moment ago.

He found out, when he tried to extricate himself from his fallen chair. His head hurt. The circulation in his legs had been cut off by the weight of his thighs on the chair edge.

"Damn."

Unable to climb to his feet, he looked around.

Then he saw it. The white creature. The Russian. He was floating limply, just inches before the big picture window that looked out over Central Park and the nearby Rumpp Regis Hotel.

"Oh, shit," said Randal Rumpp, realizing from the limp way the Russian's arms hung down that he was dead to the world. Dead to the world and about to float into the window. The solid window.

Randal Rumpp's legs refused to support him. So he crawled. He crawled hard. He got under the floating thing.

Its face was not expanding or contracting. It looked dead. And Rumpp, for the first time in his life, cared about a fellow human being.

"If that schmuck dies, I'm dead," he said bitterly. "Gotta do something fast."

He tried throwing objects at the floating apparition. All sailed harmlessly through him. He crawled to his computer and yanked out cables, trying to form a lasso. Desperation made him remember his Cub Scout knots. He flung the loop and actually scored a ringer on a left foot.

The loop dropped through the ankle like it was composed of fine mist.

"Gotta figure out a fresh scam," he muttered.

Then, the creature floated into the window.

Randal Rumpp covered his head with his hands and hoped for a painless death. He got, instead, utter silence.

He looked up. Eventually.

The thing was still in the office. It was moving toward the glass again. This time Rump couldn't tear his eyes away from it.

It touched and, like a balloon animal sculpture, bounced back.

Randal Rumpp was exuberant. "Back! It bounced back! This is fantastic! I'm not gonna go nuclear."

Then, like a patient who had been subjected to electric shock therapy, the floating creature started to wave its arms helplessly. The fat bladder of a face contracted. Expanded. It was breathing again. Somehow.

Reaching for its belt buckle, the white creature gave the white rheostat affixed there a twist. Immediately, it lost its fuzzy glow and fell to the rug.

"Ouch!" it said.

Randal Rumpp forced himself to his feet. His feet felt like they were walking across tacks and not carpet nap.

"You—ouch!—okay, pal?" he asked.

"I am fine. Happy not to be vaporized in nuclear fire."

"Same here," said Randal Rumpp, giving the thing

a hand. He pulled it to its feet. It grabbed its own shoulder as if in pain.

"You bounced off the wall. How come?"

The thing tested its footing. Rumpp noticed it stepped carefully, as if testing the solidity of the floor under its ridiculously thick boot soles.

"Building was insubstantial. I was insubstantial. We were on same vibratory plane, and so felt solid to one another." The manlike creature extended a rubbery white hand. "Here is lighter."

"Keep it," Rumpp said.

"Thank you. I can keep gold pen also?"

"You stole my graduation Waterman?"

"*Da.*"

"What are you, some kind of klepto?"

"*Da.* I am klepto. This is why I was sent to America by KGB. To steal. I steal much technology for KGB. And other things for myself, which I send to cousin in Soviet Georgia for black market. All lost now."

"Okay," Rumpp said impatiently. "Now that I know your work history, let's get down to cases. I wanna buy the suit."

"What about job?"

"I changed my mind. How much do you want for it?"

"I keep suit, all the same to you. Very valuable."

"Don't be coy. Everybody's got their price. Name it."

"I want job."

"And I want that suit. Five million."

"Dollars?"

"Yeah."

"Hokay."

"Take a check?" Rumpp asked.

"No."

"Look, I'm Randal Rumpp, the greatest financial genius since Rockefeller. You know I'm good for it."

"I know you are not," the other snapped. "I have

been trapped in your telephone system, and overhear every phone conversation. You are pauper."

"The hell I am."

At that moment, the lights came on.

Randall Rumpp looked up at the lights. "Oh, shit. Does that mean what I think it means?"

"If you mean, is building normal again, lights mean that, *da*."

"Damn. Okay. Forget my buying the suit, I want you to fax yourself over to my hotel."

"Why?"

"The IRS just seized it."

"Ah. The IRS. I have heard of them. They are more vicious that KGB."

"You're pretty smart for a guy without a face."

"Have face under helmet. Is for protection of eyes for when walking through walls."

"Right, right. Listen, if we can pull off spectralizing the Rumpp Regis, the IRS can't do anything."

"What about Rumpp Tower II?"

"On the back burner, until we get this straightened out. How about it?"

"I do not know if this will work. It is dangerous. Also, I do not trust you. You tricked me once already."

"Let me make you an offer you can't refuse."

"There is no such thing."

"When word gets out that the Rumpp Tower is back on line—so to speak—the mob is going to try to bust down my door and tear me limb from limb."

"Da?"

"If you're here when that happens, you get the same medicine," Rumpp pointed out.

The faceless Russian tilted his head, as if thinking. "You make excellent offer. I will telephone myself wherever you wish."

"Great. There's just one last thing."

"What is that?"

"Any way I can hitch a ride with you? I wasn't kidding about that mob."

"Nyet."

"That's Russian for no, isn't it?"

"Da."

"Damn."

"Sorry. Technology brand-new."

"Okay," Randal Rumpp said, offering the celluar unit, "I'll be in a better bargaining position when the Regis thing is taken care of. Let's give it our best shot."

Randal Rumpp repeated a number and the thing dialed it.

Then the Russian turned on the suit.

Randal Rumpp had seen it before, but it still amazed him. The thing went white, seemed to congeal and collapse, only to be drawn into the diaphragm like a movie image being run in reverse.

The hand was the last to go. After the fingers had released their grip on the handset, the hand practically evaporated.

Rumpp caught the cellular before it could hit the rug.

"When this is over with," he growled, "I'm gonna own that fucking suit. And I don't care who I have to screw over to get it."

28

Major Yuli Batenin took little note of the strangeness that was taking place in the Rumpp Regis lobby. There were two persons, one in some Asian native costume and the other a Western man, engaged in making a racket—to the consternation of the desk staff. No doubt, he concluded, it was related to the odd holiday known as "Halloween."

Batenin had just had his first American breakfast in three years, and cared little for watching street performers. He had ordered a Spanish omelet, blueberry pancakes, a side order of wheat toast, orange juice, and two cups of good Brazilian coffee.

It had cost him the equivalent of a year's salary at the bread factory—or it would have, if he'd had any intention of settling his room tab—and probably taken three months off his life span in cholesterol consumption. But Major Batenin didn't care. His first American meal in three years. His first decent meal in the same amount of time. It sat in his stomach like a warm mountain of pleasure.

It was good to be working—truly working—at his craft again.

He strode to the elevator and rode it, humming "Moscow Nights," to his fourteenth-floor suite.

The elevator was old, but soundproofed. So he didn't hear the insistently ringing telephone in one corner of the supposedly nonexistent thirteenth floor.

*   *   *

IRS agent Gerard Vonneau could hear the phone all too clearly. It had been ringing for fifteen minutes now. If he got his hands on the damned thing, he was not only going to give the caller hell, but personally audit him until the end of time.

Gerard Vonneau was an agent for the New York regional office of the IRS. It was his job, along with a team of other agents, to inventory the staid old Rumpp Regis and prepare its contents for auction.

His responsibility was the thirteenth floor, which hotel records indicated had been set aside for no less than Randal Rumpp himself. Somewhere, he knew, there must be an office where that damned phone was jangling. It was the only explanation.

He was going to enjoy answering that telephone. He was going to take extreme pleasure in giving the caller hell. If he ever found it.

There were rings under Cheeta Ching's eyes as she tore apart the morning paper. On the front pages were blurry photos of the white floating thing her cameraman had filmed the night before. Each was credited to MBC News.

"I could just spit!" she hissed, as she ripped the papers to shreds with her busy talons.

The phone rang and she snapped it up, saying, "What is it?"

"Miss Ching. This is Gunilla."

"Right. How are you?" said Cheeta, having no idea who Gunilla was.

"They say you're willing to pay five hundred dollars for information on that witch lady."

Cheeta brightened. "You know where she is?"

"Yes. I'm her maid."

"Maid?"

"At the Rumpp Regis. Her room number is 182.

But you'd better hurry. The IRS has taken over the place."

"The check's in the mail."

"But you don't know my—"

Cheeta Ching hung up and stormed from her Park Avenue penthouse.

Moments later, she burst out of a yellow cab in front of the Rumpp Regis Hotel, and stormed up the palatial steps toward the revolving doors.

She noticed a heavyset man in the revolving door. He was pounding on the brass-bound glass, as if he were somehow stuck.

Delpha Rohmer was doing phoners when a demanding knock came at her door. She tried to ignore it. She was speaking to a talk show in Fond du Lac, Wisconsin, and judging from the hysterical tones of the callers, witch awareness was reaching new heights.

The knocking continued.

When the talk-show host called for a commercial break, Delpha excused herself and hurried to the door. She threw it open.

The sight of a plump maid with a red worried face was not exactly what she'd expected.

"Can't this wait?" Delpha huffed.

"No, ma'am. Sorry, ma'am. My name is Gunilla, and I want to warn you that Ching woman is on her way right now. And she knows your room number."

If it had been possible for Delpha Rohmer to become more pale than her normal state, she would have done so. As it was, the only outward sign of her fright was a darkening of her mushroom eye shadow.

"Thanks," said Delpha, grabbing her coat. She thrust a five-dollar bill in the maid's plump hand and raced to the elevator, cursing the MBC news director, who had promised her absolute anonymity.

* * *

Remo Williams was trying to keep the beat on the stupid drum and at the same time avoid the bear hugs of various IRS revenue collectors.

Avoiding their clumsy grabs was easy. He barely had to pay attention. They tried to circle him, but he ducked and retreated effortlessly. They might as well have been wearing lead diving shoes while attempting to bear-hug a flock of doves.

Keeping time with the Master of Sinanju's jingling and caterwauling, however, was not easy. If there was a rhythm, Remo couldn't find it. If there was a beat, he couldn't keep it. So he just pounded on the stupid drum until the Master of Sinanju had finished his ceremonial spirit-chasing.

Then, suddenly, four strange and unexpected things happened at once.

First, Remo felt wrong. It was a kind of wrongness that was difficult to describe. His teeth hurt. His vision blurred for a microsecond, almost too quickly for an ordinary person to detect.

Chiun stopped in mid-warble.

"Remo!" he squeaked. "Something is wrong!"

"I know. I feel it, too."

They looked around. All seemed normal. Except for the persistent IRS operatives.

Then Remo noticed Delpha Rohmer hurrying from the elevator banks.

Simultaneously, the Master of Sinanju spied Cheeta Ching clopping in off the street.

Delpha and Cheeta were both headed toward the same thing: the revolving door.

They reached it simultaneously. Cheeta noticed Delpha, and Delpha spotted her mortal enemy. In between, the trapped revenue collector pounded futilely for release.

He, at least, got his wish granted.

Cheeta took a run at the door. Delpha, in the act of entering the revolving door, hesitated. Cheeta bulled through. Literally through. She passed through the door as if it were a brass and glass mirage.

The sight of that was enough to start the IRS man's adrenaline pumping. Like a slave lashed to a grinding wheel, he kept pushing the stubborn revolving door, forcing it to squeal and groan.

The door surrendered. The rubber weather stripping slapped and squeaked as Delpha, caught by surprise, was swallowed up and carried between two sheets of brass-bound glass.

The revolving door ejected the revenue collector onto the steps. He was so happy that he didn't realize he was sinking into cold concrete until he had reached the sidewalk and found he had no traction.

Delpha Rohmer saw the man standing—apparently—on his ankles, then looked down at her own feet and clutched for a brass awning pole, moaning, "O Ishtar, save your daughter!"

She was on the last step. It seemed solid.

The IRS man looked up to her with a beseeching expression on his wide face. "Help me!"

When Delpha recoiled, he grabbed for one of her pale wrists. Delpha tried to kick him. She lost her balance and fell into the sidewalk.

Delpha Rohmer had wanted to be a witch since she was a little girl. Witches were her role models. As she crouched on the intangible sidewalk, staring at her hands slipping into the gray concrete, her mind flashed back to childhood.

"Help me!" she screamed in a high, skittery voice. "I'm melting! Oh, I'm melting!"

In a matter of seconds, she was a pair of legs sticking up from the pavement and collecting a horrified crowd.

Oblivious to the fact that she had walked through solid glass, Cheeta Ching stumbled into the lobby yelling, "You'll rue the day you met me, Hortense!"

Seeing no sign of her prey, Cheeta stopped, her eyes raking the lobby.

She started sinking into the floor almost at once.

Chuin shrieked, "Cheeta! She is sinking!"

"We lost Broomhilda, too," Remo said. "What the heck's going on?"

The Master of Sinanju didn't reply. His face a knot of concern, he bounded for the helpless figure of Cheeta Ching.

"Do not fear, child. I am here."

Cheeta seemed not to hear. She was staring at her legs as they vanished into the lobby marble, taking the rest of her with them. Her arms were lifted high. They trembled.

The Master of Sinanju reached out to help her. His thin fingers grasped solid flesh, only to come away empty.

"Remo!" Chiun said in a horrified voice. "I am helpless!"

Remo jumped to his side, but found he could no more touch Cheeta Ching than the Master of Sinanju. He said, "Get down to the basement and catch her there."

Chiun flew off. Remo hit the revolving door. It was as solid as it looked. So were the steps. He took them in one leap.

At the last step, Remo reached out for the crying IRS man. He accepted Remo's outstretched hands gratefully. Remo pulled him to solid ground, then got down on his knees.

He was too late. Delpha Rohmer's kicking feet vanished like popped soap bubbles.

"Damn!" he muttered, rising again.

Along Fifth Avenue, passersby gawked and shouted. They made the same sound as silent movie actors. Which is to say, none.

"What in God's name is happening?" the IRS man moaned.

"Halloween decided to stick around an extra day," Remo said, pushing the man back up the steps.

Back in the lobby, Remo left the man to his fellow agents and went in search of the stairs to the basement.

On the way down, he felt weird again. His teeth chattered briefly, and his vision blurred. The sensation reminded him of the vibrating floor-plates in carnival fun houses he had visited as a boy.

"Now what?" he growled.

IRS agent Gerard Vonneau had gone through the thirteenth floor twice without finding the hidden office. On his third run-through, he decided to be scientific about it.

He located a suite where the phone sounded loudest. In the adjoining suite, it was equally loud. He stormed across the hall. Softer. Definitely softer.

So Vonneau went back to the first suite. Then it hit him. There was probably a connecting suite. Sure enough, what he had taken for a closet door opened on the most immodest office Vonneau had ever seen in a twenty-year career of auditing large corporations.

The telephone was a sophisticated model. He raced to it, snatched up the receiver, and shouted "Hello?" before the entire universe turned white and his right ear was filled with a roar that made him dream of diesel locomotives crackling with static electricity.

It was twenty minutes before the shock wore off.

By that time the floating, white, manlike thing had merged with the ceiling, like a melting ice cream bar. His dangling wrists and limp fingers were the last things to disappear from sight.

Yuli Batenin was seated on the wide, warm bed in his fourteenth-floor suite, watching the latest bulletin with his fellow Shield operatives.

The American anchorman Don Cooder was framed

in the screen, looking, to Batenin's eyes, like a well-barbered water buffalo.

"As yet there has been no explanation for the mysterious reversing of the Rumpp Tower situation. Less than twenty minutes ago, a sharp-eyed National Guard helicopter pilot noticed what no one else had—that his rotor blades were causing the trees decorating the lower building to sway. A team of rescue firefighters braved possible death to enter the building and liberate the people trapped on the ground floor. Efforts are now under way to evacuate the entire building before the uncanny events of Halloween Eve can recur. Of the man at the heart of the controversy, Randal Rumpp, ominously, there is no word."

Captain Igor Gerkoff turned to Batenin, his bulldog face dully curious.

"What does this mean, Batenin?"

"I do not know, but we must watch carefully. All channels."

"There is more than one channel on American TV?"

Batenin nodded. "There are hundreds."

And the men of Shield laughed at the hilarious joke. Until Batenin began running up and down the dial with sure clicks of his remote control.

A Russian muttered thickly, "It is no wonder we lost Cold War."

Gerkoff slapped him and Batenin settled on another channel, saying, "Go to other room and watch other televisions. They will bring Brashnikov out. That is when we will strike."

"By then it will be too late."

"No. We could not hope to succeed. There are too many people. Too many cameras."

"So? We kill them all. We have bullets."

"No. It cannot work. We will allow Brashnikov to show himself, and we will find him later. This is a so-called open society. It will be easy."

"I am in charge here, Batenin."

"And I am only one who is certain to recognize Rair Brashnikov when he shows his face."

Captain Gerkoff jumped to his feet angrily. Batenin stiffened where he sat.

The agents of Shield arrayed about the room perked up. Their two senior officers were about to settle a dispute over operational seniority. They licked dry lips, hoping to see blood spilled.

Instead, Major Yuli Batenin suddenly grew a third hand in the middle of his chest.

The hand was white, blurry, and seemed to sprout from the center of Yuli Batenin's breastbone.

Major Batenin, stiffening in anticipation of the fight of his life, seemed unaware of the phenomenon. The hand grew a wrist and, like some fast-growing, leprous vine, continued to emerge from the unaware ex-KBG major's person.

"Sukin syn!" Gerkoff swore, his eyes growing wide.

They had to point to the thing coming from Batenin's chest before the petrified major looked down and saw the phantom appendage.

The howl Batenin gave was like a hot needle piercing their eardrums. He scrambled off the bed as if it were afire, became tangled up in the loose bedding, and thrashed around on the rug.

"Brashnikov!" he screamed. "He is here!"

Of that, there was no doubt. A luminous white figure, its limbs spread like a crippled white starfish, continued to rise out of the mattress. It was still as death.

"What do we do, Batenin?" Gerkoff sputtered.

"We must capture him."

This proved difficult. They threw blankets on the slowly rising figure. They fell flat on the bed without impeding the thing in the least.

Each Shield man carried a white silk strangling scarf

under his shirt, which was imprinted with key commands in Russian and translations in the major NATO languages. They pulled these out and tried to ensnare the stiff limbs of the ghostly corpse of a thing.

They might as well have been attempting to capture moonbeams.

Gerkoff looked back, his face twisted in anger and superstitious fear. "Batenin, what do we do?"

"We pray."

"Why?"

"Because there is nothing we can do, and if Brashnikov's power is drained while he is in contact with physical object, it will be just like Chernobyl, but much worse."

This galvanized the men of Shield. They drew Tokarev handguns, P-6 silent pistols, and short-barreled AKR submachine guns from hidden holsters and opened fire on the untouchable apparition.

"Nyet nyet nyet!" Batenin screamed over the din. "You will awaken entire hotel and ruin mission!"

But the Shield men didn't hear. Or if they heard, they didn't care. They peppered the thing that threatened them with nuclear disaster, as if the sheer volume of their fire could affect this untouchable thing they could not understand.

29

The lowermost floor of the Rumpp Regis Hotel was the storage subbasement. It was crammed with the historical castoffs of the nearly century-old hotel. Everything from old brass mantel clocks to spittoons littered the dusty shelving.

It was dark. Remo closed his eyes and listened for the sound of a heartbeat he knew better than anyone's on earth. Chiun's.

He zeroed in on it and simply moved in the direction his ears indicated, oblivious to the solid-looking obstacles he breached with each step.

He passed through antique highboys and turn-of-the-century dining tables like a phantom wading through the history of furniture.

His bare arms felt the body warmth of two people.

Remo opened his eyes to see the frantic figure of the Master of Sinanju, bending over the prostrate figure of Cheeta Ching.

Apparently, Cheeta was drowning on the concrete floor. At least, that was the impression her body language gave Remo. She had landed on her back, and now strained to keep her mouth and wildly flaring nostrils above the level of the floor. Her hands threshed the air, and when her mouth came up above the floor level, it made shapes Remo mentally called "inarticulate."

Remo looked down at his feet. The floor supported his feet perfectly. It gave Remo a creepy feeling.

The Master of Sinanju was fussing helplessly.

"Remo! I cannot help Cheeta!"

"Tell her to stand up," Remo told Chiun casually.

"I did!" Chiun squeaked. "Cheeta cannot hear me!"

Remo folded his arms. "Oh, that's right. We can't hear them and they can't hear us. In this case, it's a blessing."

Chiun stood up. His wizened face was beseeching. "Oh, Remo, what do we do?"

"Look, she's not going to drown. She just thinks she is. Give her time. She'll figure it out."

Chiun stamped an angry foot. "Heartless one!"

At that moment, Remo felt the vibration again.

"Oh-oh. Don't look now, but the building's becoming glued again."

"Quickly! Cheeta will be trapped. Help me!"

"Help you how?"

"Take one precious hand."

"If you insist . . ."

Remo reached down. Chiun did the same. Their fingers attempted to capture the incapturable.

In a flash of a second, the insubstantial hands of Cheeta Ching grew palpable. Remo and Chiun each grabbed a flailing bunch of fingers.

"Now!" Chiun cried.

They heaved. Cheeta came up out of the floor. They set her on her feet.

In the darkness, Cheeta Ching swayed like tightrope walker.

"You okay now?" Remo asked.

"What? What? What?" Cheeta gulped. "Who's there?"

"It's me," Remo said.

"Frodo?"

"She's okay," Remo said.

"She is not!" Chiun flared. "She has been traumatized by machines. Cruel, white, oil-drinking machines."

"Fine," Remo said, starting off. "You comfort her. I'm going to look around."

"I am coming with you."

"You bring that barracuda, and there will be complications," Remo warned.

"Chico, don't leave me!" Cheeta pleaded.

At that, the Master of Sinanju rendered Cheeta Ching insensate with a simple application of pressure to a neck nerve. She collapsed with a rattly sigh.

Bearing the limp figure, Chiun followed Remo Williams back up to the lobby level.

"In her hour of need, she spoke *your* name!" he hissed.

"Technically, no," Remo pointed out.

"I am humiliated."

"Wait'll she names the baby."

"Argh!"

They found the Rumpp Regis lobby in an uproar.

The desk clerk was screaming at the IRS men, saying "They're shooting up the fourteenth floor! Do something!"

"Call the police," suggested one IRS man.

"But you're government agents!"

"Yeah, but we're tax collectors, not enforcers. We don't carry guns. Call the police."

Remo turned to Chiun. "The Russians are up on the fourteenth floor."

"Then that is where they will perish," said Chiun, placing Cheeta on a divan. She immediately rolled over and began snoring.

"There they are!" one of the IRS men shouted. It was the one Chiun had imprisoned in the revolving door. "You, stop!"

"Let's go, Little Father!" Remo urged. "The last thing we need now is tax trouble."

"Woe to him who touches the Master of Sinanju's trunk!" Chiun hurled back.

They flashed to the elevators, Remo racing and the Master of Sinanju floating along in an effortless series of leaps.

Three revenue collectors hit the closing elevator doors and bounced off like ping-pong balls.

Remo and Chiun piled out on the fourteenth floor and ran into a wall of frightened hotel guests, who pushed past them in a blind panic and commandeered the elevator.

"They will surely hinder pursuit," Chiun remarked, as the elevator started down.

"Follow me," Remo said grimly. "I know exactly what door to knock on."

Captain Rair Brashnikov floated in the middle of a bullet storm. He knew it was a storm, because all around him the fine gold-leaf molding and framed pictures were cracked and coming apart as assorted Soviet-made ammunition took their toll.

Assorted rounds pierced his brain, his lungs, and other major organs with no effect, other than to cause him to blink when the stray bullet crossed his retina.

Otherwise, it was quite peaceful up here under the ceiling. Much like the bathhouses of his homeland.

He faced an interesting dilemma. He knew that he could not float here forever. Yet to deactivate the vibration suit would be to become vulnerable to the angry bullets.

On the other hand, he seemed to be floating toward an outer wall. This was not good, Brashnikov knew. To float into a outer wall in this bodiless state would be to float out the other side. Depending on how high this particular floor was, he might find himself floating high enough off the ground that to turn off the suit would be to risk a broken neck or a completely pulverized skeletal system.

The third option, no less terrifying, would be to wait until the suit's battery power died. There was no telling how long that might be. He had been trapped in the American telephone system for a very long time—much longer than his reserve supply.

Somehow, the power had not been drained in all that time. This was good. What was not good was that he had no idea how long he had until the power went dead.

Then, in the tight-fitting confines of his white protective helmet, he heard an angry wasp's buzz. Looking down toward his midriff, he saw the red warning light illuminate the core of his belt control rheostat.

Rair Brashnikov knew two things then.

One, that he had only twenty minutes of power left.

The second thing he spoke aloud in a thick voice.

"I am dead man."

Even if Remo Williams had not followed one of the Russians to his hotel room, there would have been no question which door they were behind.

It was the one full of punch holes, from which the occasional bullet snarled out.

Remo dodged a stray round and dropped to one knee.

A step behind him, the Master of Sinanju hugged a wall, his eyes like steel.

"Game to crash the party?" Remo asked.

"Make haste. Cheeta awaits me."

"Never keep a hungry shark waiting."

Remo moved on the door. He drove a half fist ahead of him. It connected with the lock, which surrendered with a metallic clank. Remo brought his other palm around and spanked the door in its exact center, sending shock waves through the thick wood.

The heavy panel flew off its ornate hinges and became a wonderfully efficient room-clearer.

It flew true, unimpeded by the natural resistance of

the air, and pinned at least three unwary Russians against the far wall. Remo figured it was three because, in the instant he paused to assess the situation, that was the number of left hands he counted sticking out from the door edges.

Then Chiun bounded in.

The Master of Sinanju selected the nearest man, a Tokarev-weilding ox, and relieved him of his pistol with a high kick that shattered every bone of his gun hand, creating a kind of limp bag of bone-and-blood pudding at the end of the man's wrist.

His scream refocused the attention of every Russian in the room. Away from the floating target, and toward the two intruders.

It was exactly what Remo and Chiun wanted.

They harvested their foes with methodical precision.

A strangling scarf descended on Chiun's frail neck. One long-nailed finger snapped up, struck, and the heavy silk parted with a short snarl.

Two others tried to use Remo for target practice. He gave them a few seconds of his time, twisting and arching out of the way of their precise shots.

They were good. That is, they were skilled marksmen. But to Remo, they might as well have been cavemen attempting to brain a man on a motorcycle with stone hatchets.

Remo eluded each shot by sight alone. He could actually see the bullets emerge from each muzzle, compute the trajectory, and easily slide out of the bullet track.

Two shots from each man equaled two steps closer to each man. Remo didn't need three. He took one out with a two-fingered strike to his rotator cup that sent shoulder bone spears ripping through his major organs, and dislocated the neck of the second with a light tap to the point of his chin. His head snapped back so far on his suddenly elongated neck it was crushed under his broad back when he hit the rug.

The survivors took note of the carnage and, dropping their weapons, took man-to-man fighting stances.

"Guess these guys' taste in fighting styles matches their taste in clothes," Remo grunted.

"We will educate them," Chiun sniffed.

It took less than two minutes. But they cleared the room.

All except for a stark-white figure floating over their heads and another cowering behind the big television.

Chiun got under the Krahseevah and began leaping up at it, like a pit bull after a treed cat. His clawlike hands swiped futilely, and he hissed his anger.

"Nothing we can do about that one," Remo muttered, stepping over to collect the other. He dragged the shivering form of Major Yuli Batenin out by the collar of his shirt.

"At least this one is in fashion," said Remo, noticing his suit, "So who are you, pal?"

"I cannot say."

Face angry, Chiun stepped up and pinched a dangling earlobe.

"You can."

Suddenly, the man could say. In fact, he could sing. He began singing out a stream of information, evidently convinced, in his pain, that singing was faster than speaking.

"I am Major Yuli Batenin, formerly with KGB, come to America to capture Captain Rair Brashnikov, also formerly with KGB, and reclaim vibration suit for motherland before nuclear event occurs and we all die."

Remo turned to Chiun. "You make any sense of that?"

"He is off-key." Chiun squeezed harder.

Batenin screamed louder. He pointed toward the ceiling. "Brashnikov! Is Brashnikov! Vibration suit is running out of power. If he rematerializes inside wall, atoms will mingle and there will be nuclear event."

"He is making no more sense," Chiun warned.

Remo looked to the floating Krahseevah edging toward the wall and the burning red light at his belt buckle. "Wait! I think I get it. The suit is about to shut down. If the guy is touching anything, it'll be like the old atom bombs, only worse."

"More machine talk," sniffed Chiun.

"Maybe. But we gotta keep him from entering that wall."

"How?" asked Batenin.

"Like this," said Remo, going up to the wall. He made one hand into a spear point, and using it like a jackhammer, began chipping out a section of the wall. He cut a long horizontal line just under the floating figure, stepping onto an end table to continue cutting. Plaster dust and old lathe cracked and showered down in a dusty storm.

Remo swiftly completed a rectangle and pulled it inward. A square chunk of horsehair plaster came loose and hit the carpet, with a billow of dry white dust.

"Problem solved," Remo said, stepping down. "If he floats out, he won't hurt anything."

"But we still have not captured that fiend!" Chiun said harshly.

"The day's young yet," Remo said, returning to the shivering Major Batenin. "I recognize you," he said.

Batenin looked incredulous. "You do?"

"Yeah. Our boss once had us intercept you when you were trying to smuggle stealth technology out of the country in a diplomatic bag."

"I was never intercepted by you."

"Sure you were. Remember at Dulles International, we made you put your case through the X-ray machine?"

Major Batenin's suspicious eyes lost their narrowness. "That was you?"

"In disguise," said Remo.

"I was inside the machine," sniffed Chiun.

"We switched bags," Remo added. "You got one filled with junk."

"It was not Brashnikov's fault?" Batenin said bleakly.

"It was us. But enough ancient history. You said you were with the KGB. Everybody knows they went the way of the Berlin Wall. Who are you with now?"

"I will not say."

The fingernails bit into his earlobe again, and Major Yuli Batenin screamed, "I am *Shchit*! I am *Shchit*!"

"You got that right," said Remo, killing the Russian by the simplest means at hand. By killing his brain. Remo's steel-hard right index finger went in through the forehead bone and came out clean.

"Not bad, huh?"

Chiun made a disgusted face. "Check under your fingernail for brain."

Remo looked injured. "There's no brain under my nail."

"Did you check?"

"I don't have to check. That was a perfect stroke."

"Your elbow was not aligned perfectly."

"Are you saying it was bent? It was not bent!"

"I did not say bent," Chiun sniffed. "I said not perfectly aligned. It is not the same."

"It wasn't bent," Remo insisted.

"It was not perfect, either."

"Never mind. Let's finish up our business here."

The eyes of the two Masters of Sinanju looked up toward the helplessly floating figure of the thing Remo had years ago dubbed "the Krahseevah," and which they now knew was a Russian named Captain Rair Brashnikov.

Behind his expanding and contracting face membrane, Rair Brashnikov looked down at the pair of deadly eyes and came to a bitter conclusion.

"I am not dead. I am worse than dead."

He choice was as simple as it was stark. Turn off the vibration suit and be delivered into the hands of the same American agents that had tricked him into a purgatory of fiber-optic cables and American telephone cross-talk, or hope that the suit stayed powered long enough for him to float out into the clear air and drop to his certain death.

Rair Brashnikov was not a brave man. He was, in his heart of hearts, a common thief. It was his kleptomania that had gotten him cashiered from the old KGB in the first place, and the same uncontrollable urge that had compelled his old KGB superiors to reinstate him and unleash him, virtually untraceable in the vibration suit, upon the technological candy shop that was America.

He reached for the buzzing rheostat and gave it a twist. The buzz cut out.

His teeth suddenly hurt, and his vision went blurry.

Gravity took hold and Rair Brashnikov crashed to the carpet, taking a chunk of wall with him.

"I am surrendering peacably to you," he said, as swift hands more strong than Soviet leg irons took hold of his wrists. He was hauled to his feet unceremoniously.

"Gotcha!" said the Caucasian American agent.

"Your ugly head will be set before my emperor by sundown," threatened the Oriental American agent.

"I would like to be keeping head," Rair said thickly.

"That'll be up to our boss," the Caucasian said. "I'd better call him. Here, Chiun, hold both hands so he doesn't pull a fast one."

The Oriental took the wrist the Caucasian surrendered. Rair Brashnikov looked down at the old man through the transparent inner lining of the permeable face membrane, which enabled him to breath in dematerialized oxygen when he was in his bodiless state.

The old man looked impossibly ancient. His arms were like twigs coated by animal hide. He looked frail enough to snap under a kneecap's pressure.

But the strength in his long-nailed hands was anything but frail. And so Rair Brashnikov remained very, very calm. He had seen these two destroy whole buildings with their bare hands when attempting to seize him, and perform other dazzling feats. They were very dangerous.

And it was always better to lull a dangerous foe in the hours before one vanquished him.

The Caucasian was speaking into the telephone.

"That's right, Smitty. We just captured the Krahseevah."

Brashnikov cocked his featureless head in surprise. "Krahseevah?"

"You are misnamed, ugly one," spat the Oriental, tightening his grip. Brashnikov bit the inside of his cheeks to keep from crying out in pain. His shoulder was on fire, and he remembered the single blow that landed on him during their last encounter had struck there.

The Caucasian was asking, "What do you want us to do with him?"

Rair Brashnikov attempted to listen, but he could not hear the other side of the conversation. The conversation that was no doubt deciding his very fate.

"It's *what*?"

The Caucasian clapped a hand over the telephone mouthpiece and called over to his comrade.

"Smitty says there's new trouble over at the Rumpp Tower. It's sinking."

"Sinking?" asked Rair Brashnikov. "My tower?"

"Yours?"

"Randal Rumpp gave it to me."

"I think Randal Rumpp pulled the wool over your

eyes, buddy. You *do* have eyes under that blob of a face, don't you?"

"Yes. Would you like to see my eyes?" Rair Brashnikov asked hopefully.

30

Randal Rumpp learned that he was riding the largest elevator ever built straight to the center of the earth, as he was happily channel-hopping in the security of his Rumpp Tower office.

The electricity was back on. Lights shone, computers hummed, faxes spooled out unimportant transmissions, and the telephones rang and jangled insistently.

Everybody, it seemed, wanted to talk to Randal Rumpp. Just like in the long-ago eighties.

Best of all, the TV sets were working.

The early reports indicated that the Rumpp Regis had become "spectralized." Every channel was using the word, another source of pride.

"Gotta have it trademarked," Rumpp chuckled, "and charge those chumps for using it. This is great! I'm getting ink again. By Christmas, I should be a Barney's display."

It was so great, in fact, that he didn't pay any attention to the furious pounding on the creditor-control doors throughout the twenty-fourth floor.

What the hell are they using? Rumpp wondered. Their thick heads?

An American Networking Conglomerate news report answered the question, when Rumpp paused to check out the local ANC affiliate broadcast.

"At this hour," a reporter was saying, "the Rumpp Tower has been completely evacuated, except for the bankrupted developer himself, whom authorities believe is holed up on the twenty-fourth floor. Police spokesmen tell us that attempts are being made to batter down the doors. Meanwhile, a grand jury has handed down a seventeen-count indictment against Randal Tiberius Rumpp for criminal fraud."

Randal Rumpp jumped up from his chair, shouting.

"*Fraud?* Is that the best those jerks can come up with? Fraud! I can beat that crummy rap without my law firm. I didn't defraud anyone. I just exaggerated my involvement here and there. The worst they can nail me with is malicious mischief."

The reporter went on. "Adding to the sense of urgency is the bizarre fact that the Rumpp Tower appears to be settling."

"Settling!"

A live shot of the Rumpp Tower facade replaced the reporter's stern face. The brass lintel on which Randal Rumpp's name had been cast in gleaming letters was now at sidewalk level. The lower edges of the bold brass letters were bent and mangled from contact with the too-solid sidewalk.

Rumpp's astonished mouth imploded in an uncomprehending pucker.

"Settling?" he exploded. "I'm *sinking*! I'm headed straight for China!"

A voice-over added, "Scientists are unable to account for this latest phenomenon, but estimate that if it continues to settle at this present speed, the Rumpp Tower may be entirely underground by Thursday."

Randal Rumpp sat stupefied.

The pounding continued throughout the twenty-fourth floor.

The phone rang. Woodenly, Randal Rumpp picked it up.

"Yeah?" he said dully.

"Dahling . . ."

"Igoria?"

"Dahling, I am watching the news, and I see you are about to be arrested. How droll. Be sure to pack your toothbrush, and an extra set of those snug little monogrammed shorts."

"Igoria!" Rumpp bit out. "What do you want?"

"I was calling because I have a wonderful business opportunity for you, my pet."

Randal Rumpp blinked. Momentarily, he was caught off-guard. His better judgment invariably shut down when he smelled a deal in the air.

He made his voice sound disinterested. "Yeah. What?"

"Well, it seems there are these unhappy little S&Ls which you could pick up for a song."

"Yeah?"

"You could buy them all up and weld them into a superbank all your own."

Randal Rumpp perked up. "I could be my own bank. Make loans to myself. Interest-free loans. Duck payments when it suits me."

"Yes. And you could call them all BankRumpps. Because that's what you are, dahling." Tinkling laughter broke through the earpiece.

"Igoria," Randal Rumpp hissed, "you were only a trophy wife. You hear me? Just a trophy wife. I should have had you stuffed and mounted after the honeymoon!"

"Ta-ta, dahling. Give my best to Leona."

Rumpp hung up angrily. Down the hall, the pounding went on and on.

He stood up. Outside the window, a few blocks away, the ornate mass of masonry that was the Rumpp Regis looked the same as it always did. On the other hand the silvery skyscraper across the street, only a day before a single floor shorter than the Rumpp Tower, was now at least a head taller.

For the man who prided himself on being the biggest, boldest, and best at everything he did, it was a crushing blow to the outsized ego of Randal T. Rumpp.

"I'm ruined! I'm not only ruined, I'm sunk! Literally sunk!"

Rair Brashnikov listened to the American with the dead eyes. The American was not interested in seeing his Georgian face. This was unfortunate. It represented an opportunity for escape lost. For in order to remove the velcro-seals of his helmet, they would have to release his hands. Long enough to reengage the vibration suit.

"Listen, you know how to stop the Rumpp Tower from sinking?" the American asked.

"I am not sure," Brashnikov said carefully, thinking perhaps a new opportunity was presenting itself.

"Then we have no further use for you," snapped the Oriental.

Brashnikov brightened. "Sinking? Of course I can help. But I must speak with Randal Rumpp first."

"Got a number for him?"

Brashnikov indicated the phone with an eager nod of his head. "Yes. Give me phone. I will happily make call."

"No chance. Call it out."

Rair Brashnikov's cabled shoulders deflated. "It is 555-9460," he murmured.

The Caucasian dialed and listened a moment. He put the earpiece to the side of Rair's featureless head, not quite getting the spot where his ears were, but it was close enough for the ringing of the other line to come through.

Randal Rumpp's querulous, dispirited voice answered. "Who is it?"

"Ho ho ho," said Rair Brashnikov hollowly.

"You! What happened? The TV says the Rumpp Regis is back to normal, and my Tower is sinking into the ground. How do I stop it?"

"How am I to know? I am thief, not rocket scientist."

"Do better than that!" warned the Caucasion named Remo.

"Who is that?" Rumpp wanted to know.

"New friend," Brashnikov explained.

"So what do I do?" Rumpp pressed.

"Try calling Moscow. I give you number."

Rumpp grabbed a pad and paper. "Shoot."

The long-distance operator was very helpful. She got through to Moscow in under an hour. Normally it took two, she explained. On a good day.

The voice that picked up on the other end at first denied any knowledge of the vibration suit.

Then Randal Rumpp said, "I'm Randal T. Rumpp, and I see a lot of investment opportunities in your country."

"Ah. Vibration suit. Why did you not say so? I will put you through to Vibration Suit ministry. We are only KGB liquidation unit."

"You're killers?"

"It is not that kind of liquidation we are doing."

"Oh."

The line clicked and hissed and hummed, and Randal Rumpp watched the ever-changing TV screen to keep from being bored.

Finally a low female voice said, *"Shchit."*

Rumpp said, "I guess some words are universal."

"Who is speaking, please?"

"Randal Rumpp, famous billionaire."

"The one whose building, it is sinking?"

"The very same. And it's all the fault of your crummy vibration suit. It got into my Tower electrical system and screwed it up somehow."

"Vibration suit?"

"Don't be coy. Your guy was just captured."

"Which guy?"

233

"I don't know. I didn't catch his name. But I do know who I'm gonna sue if I don't get some satisfaction."

"USSR did not invent suit," the woman said crisply. "You should take this up with manufacturer."

"Who's that?"

"Nishitsu Corporation. Osaka."

"The Japs? How did you guys get hold of the technology?"

"KGB steal it."

"Oh," said Randal Rumpp, hanging up.

The long-distance operator put him through to the Osaka research and development plant of the Nishitsu Corporation in Japan.

Rumpp identified himself, and asked to speak with the department that designed the suit.

At first, the thick voice at Nishitsu denied any knowledge of the invention.

Then Randal Rumpp said, "The Russians say they stole it from you."

The man at the other end said, "Ah," and asked a simple question. "You possess device now?"

"Could be," Rumpp said cagily. "And I might be willing to do a trade."

"Prease continue."

"First, I want my skyscraper to stop sinking."

"How does *bakemono* suit have anything to do with that?"

"Bakemono?"

"Means gobrin."

"Spell it for me."

"G-o-b-l-i-n."

"Good name for it," said Randal Rumpp, going on to explain how it had all started with a funny Russian voice in his telephone system, and what had squirted out when his secretary picked up a certain receiver.

The voice at the other end said "Ah" again, and in

the background a number of people could be heard conversing in rapid, unintelligible Japanese.

Finally a different voice came on. It said, "It appear person wearing gobrin suit was captured by your buirding terephone system, much rike virus in broodstream of a riving person."

"Makes sense," said Randal Rumpp, wondering how a people who couldn't pronounce their L's could be so successful in international business.

"The properties of suit were transferred to buirding."

"That much I figured out by myself," Rumpp said dryly.

"Now person has reft, but your Tower is sinking?"

"You got the picture."

"Perhaps probrem remain in terephone wires," the Nishitsu representative suggested.

"Could be. So what do I do?"

"Ask terephone company to shut off power."

"And if it doesn't work?"

"Carr back."

"Count on it, Chuck."

The AT&T service representative listened to Randal Rumpp's odd request.

"We will be only too happy to comply," the rep said smoothly.

"Great. Do it now."

"However, there is the matter of an unpaid bill due four months ago." Rumpp heard a clicking of a keyboard. "The current outstanding balance is $63,876.14."

"What is this crap! You've been threatening to shut off my lines for weeks over that bill!"

"I imagine so."

"Well, I'm still in arrears. So shut me off, Chuck!"

"Not without payment."

"You can't do this! It's un-American!"

"Continued service is entirely an AT&T decision,"

the infuriatingly unruffled voice said. "In this case, we elect to continue to serve your telephonic needs."

"I demand to be disconnected! Right now!"

The line went *click*, and Randal Rumpp found himself listening to a dial tone.

He hung up the telephone, with no life left in his eyes.

"I'm dead," he said dully. "I'm sinking into the earth and I'm dead."

A thought occurred to him.

"Where the heck am I *going*, anyway?"

Rumpp went to a hand-carved globe and spun it. He picked out the longitude and latitude of Manhattan, spun the globe, and found their counterparts on the other side. It was in a mountainous border region of what was once the Soviet Union.

"Great," he muttered. "I'm heading for 'Kazakhstan.' I never even heard of Kazakhstan. They probably don't even speak English there. Maybe I'd better just surrender."

But the pounding at the credit-control doors made him think again. It was getting louder. Louder than the insistently ringing office telephones. They really wanted him. Wanted him bad.

"What the heck!" he told himself. "Can't hurt to call those riceballs at Nishitsu again. I haven't threatened to sue them yet. Maybe I can hose them into building Rumpp Tower II."

Grinning, Randal Rumpp reached for his portable cellular phone.

31

Rair Brashnikov was attempting to induce the two American agents to let him remove his helmet.

"No," said the Caucasian.

"I am having trouble breathing."

"Then die quietly."

The Oriental was arguing with the Caucasian. They were arguing over his head. The Oriental wanted it removed from his shoulders, and the Caucasian was in favor of letting Brashnikov keep it.

In the meantime, they were waiting for the telephone to ring. And then it did.

The Caucasian picked it up.

"Yeah, Smitty. What's the deal?" The Caucasian listened.

He looked up and said to the Oriental, "Smitty says the Rumpp Tower is still sinking, and they can't get Rumpp out."

"Offer to Smith our services to extricate the schemer, Rumpp."

"Smitty. Chiun says we can get Rumpp out." He listened again. "Okay. What do with do about Ivan here? Gotcha."

The Caucasian hung up.

"Smith says we grab Rumpp."

"And this monstrosity?"

"Put him on ice until we get back."

The old Oriental was still holding on to Rair Brashnikov's aching wrists, pinning them together as irremovably as shackles. Now he manipulated his long bony fingers, transferring both wrists to the unshakable grasp of one amber hand.

All around him, the bodies of the many Russian agents sent to recapture Brashnikov lay still and waxy as a Disco museum after an earthquake.

"What means 'on ice'?" Brashnikov asked.

Silence.

"Does 'on ice' mean dead? I must know. Am I allowed a final prayer? I know some very short ones."

The cold-eyed Oriental reached for his throat.

Down the corridor the elevator doors rolled open.

Remo called, "Shake a leg, Chiun!"

Then came Cheeta Ching's voice. "Grandfather Chiun! Where are you?"

Chiun started. "Cheeta?"

But the corridor was suddenly filled with the tramping of heavy footsteps.

"We can't leave him now," Remo hissed. "That's either the IRS or the cops."

The Master of Sinanju stepped toward the open doorway. The helpless Russian came with him, unable to free his pinioned arms.

Then the tiny Korean lifted one foot. A simple gesture barely noticed. Remo moved to the edge of the door, hands high, ready to strike if need be.

A clot of Manhattan's finest clopped up the corridor, guns drawn.

"Grandfather Chiun!" Cheeta shouted. "It's all right! I brought the police!"

"Some one shut her up," a voice growled.

And the Master of Sinanju pivoted on his one planted foot.

The thick-soled white boots on Rair Brashnikov's feet buzzed the rug, as sudden centrifugal force brought him around in a standing arc.

Incredibly powerful fingers released his wrists.

By that point, momentum had set his legs at right angles to the walls. His feet flew through the bullet-gnashed doorway, taking the rest of him with it.

The Russian bowled over four policemen before they could react or retreat.

Remo and Chiun jumped out into the corridor, their feet busy. Their heels stamped pistol muzzles flat and broke cylinders from their frames.

"Remo!" Chiun squeaked. "See to the Krahsee-vah!"

"Right."

Remo reached into the tangle of blue and white and came within a hair of grabbing the Krahseevah by its rubbery neck.

That hair made all the difference. For Rair Brashnikov had fumbled for his belt rheostat. Remo's reaching hand dipped into a sudden blur of white shine.

"Damn!"

Chiun turned. "What?"

"Lost him."

"Idiot!"

Rair Brasnikov remembered his KGB training. In his disembodied state, he had to be careful. Only micron-thick wafers in the bottom of his boot soles enabled him to stand on solid ground when the vibration suit was operation. He could not use his hands to lever himself up.

He could only unbend himself until the boot soles found traction.

Unfortunately, that was not as easy at it sounded.

He realized that his rear end was sinking through the hall carpet, when all around him dazed American policemen recoiled and shouted hoarse curses.

Rair Brashnikov decided to go with the flow.

The flow was taking him through the floor, much to the frustration of the Caucasian American agent, who frantically tried to grab him by any handy extremity.

The level of the floor soon crept up to Brashnikov's chin, his nose. Then he shut his eyes—and did not open them until the subatomic darkness had gone away and he could see pink light through his closed lids.

Remo was taking his frustration out on the hapless police.

"You guys couldn't have waited another lousy minute," he said, grabbing ankles and pulling the police into his inexorable grip. Remo put them all to sleep with simple nerve pressure, while the Master of Sinanju confronted a shocked and wide-eyed Cheeta Ching.

"It is all right, my child. This was not for your eyes."

"My God!" Cheeta gasped. "That witch-bitch was right. It *is* a night-gaunt!"

"No, it—"

Remo straightened. "Exactly. A night-gaunt. And we want you to spread the word. Tell the world that the night-gaunts have broken loose into the waking world. You're the only one who can convince people."

"Yes, yes, I must!"

"But leave us out of it."

"But . . . but you're part of the story."

"Chiun," Remo said.

The Master of Sinanju took Cheeta Ching's cold hands in his.

"Child, you must do as Chico says."

"Frodo," Remo corrected, straight-faced.

"No word of us must be spoken aloud. Have I your word on this?"

Cheeta Ching had never been known to squelch a story in her career. She was being asked to do so now.

It was a complete violation of everything she thought she stood for.

Silently, she nodded, her lids lowered demurely. She bowed. Twice.

The Master of Sinanju bowed in return. Once.

"We must go now, to seek out other night-gaunts," said Chiun solemnly.

Cheeta Ching brushed away a tear. "Go in peace, Grandfather!" Her wet hand got stuck in her sticky hair, and refused to come loose.

Remo and Chiun slipped to a fire exit.

"Good move," said Remo. "Now we just gotta capture that Krahseevah without raising a ruckus."

"This is all your fault," Chiun spat.

"Why? You let him go."

"But you failed to seize him. A mere Russian, faster than a Master of Sinanju? My ancestors would disown me for having lowered myself to instruct you in proper breathing."

"I had my hands full. The police were loaded for bear."

They reached the thirteenth floor. Chiun led the way to a point along the corridor.

"It is here he should have fallen," Chiun said, looking up at the paneled ceiling. There was no sign of the Krahseevah under the ceiling, or along the carpet.

"Split up?" Remo said.

They split up, breaking down doors, moving from room to room like unstoppable juggernauts.

When they had worked their way down the corridor, a white shining bubble emerged from the wall near where they had paused. The bubble continued to grow until it became a smooth rubbery head, whose blank face expanded and contracted like some gruesome external lung.

Then the Krahseevah tiptoed across the hall with soundless ease. It melted into a door as if it were a gossamer curtain painted to look like wood.

Rair Brashnikov was in luck. There was a telephone in the room he had chosen. He strode up to it and put his hand to the belt rheostat. It was buzzing angrily and emitting a warning red shine. He would have to move fast, he knew. There was no telling how much power he had left in his reserve supply.

Grasping the knob, he turned the rheostat.

Down the hall, Remo and Chiun both heard the sudden sound of a heartbeat that had not been audible on the thirteenth floor before. They flashed out into the corridor, nearly colliding, and plunged up the hall.

They hit the door at the same time. Simultaneously they burst into the room. Their eyes read the figure of the Krahseevah—which was not shining—a telephone receiver clamped to its bald head.

"Hold the phone!" Remo shouted.

And as their reaching hands traveled the space between the door and their quarry, the creature acquired a nimbus like a frosted light bulb.

The Krahseevah turned.

"Too late Americans! Speed-dialing!"

Then it began.

"Damn!" said Remo, slapping at the vaporous mist that was oozing into the mouthpiece. It was drawn from sight like inhaled smoke.

"Again you have shamed me!" Chiun squeaked, stamping a tiny foot on the receiver as it hit the rug.

"Me? You had the same shot as me."

"You were in my way."

"My left foot."

"Which is that, clod-footed one? For I count one at the ends of each of your clumsy legs."

"Har de har har," Remo growled.

Remo noticed a blinking light on the telephone console. There was a menu of speed-dialing buttons, and the blinking light was the button marked: RANDAL RUMPP.

"Looks like we may have another crack at the guy," Remo pointed out.

"I insist upon no interference this time," Chiun said sternly.

Remo rolled his eyes skyward. "Done. Now let's get cracking."

32

Randal Rumpp had one finger in his ear and the free
ear to his cellular handset.

He was trying to reason with the Nishitsu technician
over the pounding on his creditor-control doors and
the telephone-orchestra accompaniment. It killed him
to ignore all those ringing phones. Probably all report-
ers hot to quote him. But if he was going to walk out
of this clean, he had to get a handle on this sinking
setback. If he knew why the Rumpp Tower was acting
like a mole, maybe he could stop it. That would be
his bargaining chip with the courts. Lighten up, and
the Rumpp Tower won't end up in Kazakhstan.

The Nishitsu technician was trying to explain his
theory in layman's terms.

"Buirding has great weight," he was saying. "Many
tons. But when buirding rose mass, there is no weight.
Ground rerax."

"Ground what?"

"Rerax. Take it easy."

"Got it," said Randal Rumpp.

"When buirding regain weight, it exert downward
force. Rike pire driver."

"Like what?"

"Pire driver."

"What the heck is a pire driver?"

"You are construction man. You do not know?"

"Oh. Pile dliver," said Randal Rumpp, after writing

the words down on a pad and substituting L's for R's. "Why didn't you say so?"

"Did."

"Right. So you're saying that the skyscraper is literally pounding its way into the ground?"

"Yes. You must not ret it demateliarize."

"Spectralize. Get it right."

"Spectrarize. Yes. You must not—"

"Hold it," Rumpp interrupted, hearing a beep in his ear. "My other line just beeped."

Randal Rumpp tapped the handset switch hook and got a familiar staticky roar in his ear. He jumped out of his chair and under his desk just in time.

The light was a cold flare that soon abated. Rumpp crawled out. The Russian in the vibration suit was hanging suspended in the air, his belt buckle as red as if it were on fire. A cold chill went through Randal Rumpp's trim body.

"Oh, shit. Forget ending up in Kazakhstan. We're about to go nuclear."

Over the next ten minutes, Randal Rumpp did everything he could to capture the floating white apparition before it merged with anything solid.

A luminous foot slid into an oaken coat rack. Rumpp knocked the rack over. The top of its head merged with a ceiling fixture, and Rumpp got up on a chair and shattered the frosted glass globe with a paperweight carved in the shape of his own initials.

He got under it and tried to blow it away from the wall with his breath. He was close to fainting before he gave it up.

He tried sucking the thing down with a Dustbuster he found in a maintenance closet, but the thing was impervious to suction, too.

Finally, as Randal Rumpp lay under the thing, out of breath, it came to life. Its arms and legs started waving crazily. One hand reached for its belt buckle.

Realizing what was coming, Randal Rumpp tried to roll out of the way. He was too late.

"Oof!"

When he regained his senses, the white thing, no longer luminous, was standing over him, its expression even more blank than usual.

"You almost killed me!" Rumpp roared.

"Sorry." The white creature cocked a head in the direction of the door. "I hear pounding."

"The police are trying to break in. We're trapped."

"It is worse than that. American agents are coming to liquidate you."

"Liquidate me how?"

"How do you think?"

"Well, I'd like to think they're coming to liquidate my assets."

"It is not your assets they are coming to liquidate, but your ass."

Randal Rumpp groaned. "How do you say 'damn' in Russian?"

"Proklyatye."

"Proklyatye," Rumpp repeated. "What do we do?"

"Surrender to police at door."

Rumpp sat up, aghast. "And be lynched?"

"Better than being killed dead," said the Russian.

"You got a point there," the Rumppmeister said, getting to his feet. He looked around his office frantically.

"There's gotta be another option. All my life, I've found other options." His eyes fell on the faceless Russian agent.

"That suit got any more power in it?"

"Probably."

"Buy it from you?"

"No sale. You are broke."

Randal Rumpp shrugged. "Okay. Just thought I'd ask. It can't hurt to ask, can it?"

"No. It cannot hurt to ask. Suit not for sale."

Randal Rumpp picked up the heavy paperweight in the shape of his initials. His eyes were on that blank white head, which suddenly looked as fragile as an eggshell.

"On the other hand, I can just bash your stupid head in, Chuck, and take it."

"You would not do such a thing. Would you?"

"Bet your ass."

Just then, the pounding at the door grew in intensity and fury.

"They must have brought up a battering ram," Rumpp mumbled.

The pounding turned into the screech of metal.

"Sounds like tank coming," said the Russian.

"I don't think a tank would fit on the freight elevator."

"Then it is not tank. It is American agents come to liquidate our asses."

Something that sounded like a hull plate of a battleship clanged to the floor. The entire floor shook.

Randal Rumpp stiffened. The paperweight dropped to the carpet. He didn't know what to expect, never having been liquidated—in any sense of the word—before.

Then two strange figures appeared at the door, moving fast. One was a tiny wisp of an Oriental and the other a lean American not exactly in business dress.

They split off. One came toward Randal Rumpp and the other toward the Russian, who had snatched up his cellular. The other hand was going to his belt buckle.

"You are mine!" the Oriental screeched.

Randal Rumpp didn't see what happened next. He was staring at the approaching eyes of the tall skinny guy. His eyes were as dead as a loan officer's. A hand came up and took him by the throat and kept going.

Randal Rumpp was slammed into the big picture window behind him.

"You," said the cold voice of the dead-eyed man, "have caused enough trouble."

"Urkkk."

"What?"

"I made it all up!" Rumpp said breathlessly. "I didn't make any of this happen! I lied! You can't liquidate my ass over a lie!"

"That's the biz, sweetheart," said the man, as he gave Randal Rumpp a harder push. The back of his sandy head banged the wobbly glass.

"But I didn't—" Randal Rumpp attempted to say. The hand constricted, choking off the words. Randal Rumpp wanted to tell the man that it had all been a scam. That he had not caused any of this to happen. He had just taken advantage of events to engage in a little creative restructuring of his debt load.

But the man wasn't listening. He was using his free hand to manipulate Randal's Rummp's helpless limbs. He forced Rumpp's left arm against his side, his palm flat with his thigh so they formed a straight standing line. Then he crooked Rumpp's right arm at the elbow and set his fist on his hip. Lastly, he made his right leg stick out straight at an angle from his pelvic bone.

Randal Rumpp's couldn't see what he was doing, but when the man was done Rumpp was standing on one leg, frozen in the awkward pose.

"Guys like you," the dead-eyed man was saying, "used to have the courtesy to jump out of their offices when things went bad."

The man's hand rose. Randal Rumpp's polished shoes left the floor.

Then he was being forced out through the bronze solar window glass. It made a sudden crack, but strangely didn't shatter as it should have.

Randal Rumpp flew twenty feet straight out, and saw why.

His nerve-stiffened body had punched out a perfect silhouette. It was in the shape of a six-foot letter R.

Rumpp smiled. It was perfect. A classy touch. The guy was a real pro. He wanted to salute the guy on his taste, but his arms were still stiff and gravity was starting to exert its inexorable influence.

As the ground zoomed up to meet him, Randal Rumpp's life flashed before his eyes. It was such a kick to relive it all that he completely forgot about his predicament—until he went *splat* on the sidewalk in front of the mangled letters RUMPP TOWER.

Remo Williams waited until the pulpy sound had reached his ears before turning to check on Chiun's progress.

The Master of Sinanju was using a delicate sandal toe to kick apart the cherry wood desk that dominated the cathedral-like office.

"Missed, huh?" Remo asked.

"The fiend resorted to his machine trickery again."

"Well, I got mine."

Chiun sniffed. "The unimportant one."

"The big cheese. Rumpp was the big cheese," Remo said, picking up the fallen receiver.

He put it to his ear. The line was still open. He heard voices shouting and screeching in confusion at the other end.

"Here, check this out."

The Master of Sinanju snatched the handset from Remo's grasp and listened, fuming.

He made a face.

"Pah! It is nothing," he snapped.

"What makes you say that?"

"It is only Japanese complaining."

"Just the same," Remo said. "Let's take this phone to Smitty."

"Yes," Chiun said bitterly. "Let us take the evi-

249

dence of our ineptitude to Mad Harold. No doubt he will wish us beheaded for our miserable failure."

A relentless pounding continued to come from down the hall. Remo indicated it with his head.

"Think you can keep it down, until we can slip out of the building the same back way we got in?"

"Who could detect us over that racket?"

Harold Smith was very interested in the telephone.

He looked up from his shabby oak desk at Folcroft Sanitarium later that day, his gray, pinched face thoughtful.

The cellular unit had been partially disassembled and was now connected to his computer system.

"According to the memory chip," he said, "the last number dialed was that of the Nishitsu Corporation in Osaka."

"Nishitsu?" Remo said. "Weren't they the ones behind that crazy invasion of Yuma, Arizona, a few years ago?"

Smith nodded. "A rogue operation. Or so it was claimed. But recall, Remo, that before that we had intelligence on an event at Nishitsu Osaka which was laid at the KGB's doorstep."

"Right. You thought that the suit was a Japanese invention, and that was how the Soviets got hold of it."

Smith nodded. "No doubt Rumpp was attempting to gain more information on the suit from Nishitsu. When you and Chiun burst in, the Krahseevah simply hit the redial button."

"And faxed himself to Nishitsu. Damn!"

"Not necessarily, Remo."

Remo and Chiun looked interested.

"Then where did he go?" Remo asked.

"Recall that prior to this, the Krahseevah traveled through fiber-optic cables and short-distance cellular transmissions. In order to reach Osaka, he would have to be uplinked to an orbiting communications satellite and relayed back to a ground station. It is not clear that his atomic structure would retain its integrity during such an extreme transfer."

"You mean he might have had his molecules scrambled?"

"It's possible."

Remo folded his arms. "Last time, you were sure he was never going to come back to haunt us again."

"And I am not certain of his fate this time. But it is a possibility."

"Yes," said Chiun. "That must be what happened."

"Since when did you become the technology expert?" Remo asked dryly.

Chiun surreptitiously kicked Remo in the ankle. Remo went silent. Chiun went on.

"Obviously the Russian fiend is no more," he said firmly. "And since we dispatched the schemer Rumpp, this assignment has been successfully accomplished and all glory and credit is ours."

"I imagine that it has," Smith allowed.

"And contract negotiations may continue," Chiun added.

"Er, yes," Smith said carefully.

Chiun beamed. "Then I suggest we begin now."

"If you do not mind, I have a few loose ends to tie up."

"What could be more important than contract negotiations?"

"Briefing the President."

"Yes. Do that. And be certain to speak our names prominently and often."

"Of course, Master Chiun."

"You know, there's one thing I still don't get," Remo said slowly.

The others looked at him.

"Who *were* those Russians?"

"That is a good point," said Smith. "You had no chance to interrogate them?"

"Yeah. The head guy said he was shit."

"He did?"

"So I obliged him."

"No," Chiun interjected, "he said he was 'shield.' "

Remo frowned. "I thought I heard the other word."

"Your mind is a sewer," Chiuh sniffed.

"One moment." Smith turned to his ever-present computer terminal and called up his Russian lexicon file base.

"The only Russian word that transliterates into that term is *Shchit*."

"That's the word I heard. What's it mean?" asked Remo.

Smith looked up, his face puzzled.

"Shield."

"Means nothing to me."

Smith switched to another file. Keys rattled. "There is no such Russian organization on file, past or present."

"Maybe they're new, Smitty."

Smith's lemony face grew more bitter. "I believe I will create an active file under that name. Strange things are happening over there now. If there is a new Russian group or organization known as 'Shield,' it may be a problem for the future."

"Emperor, what will be the fate of the mighty building of the schemer Rumpp?"

"It has been condemned. Demolition experts are going to wire it with shaped charges and implode it into rubble."

Chiun nodded. "It will be an improvement."

Remo said, "One last thing, Smitty."

"What is that?"

"Those people who fell into the ground when the Rumpp Tower first spectralized. What happened to them?"

"Officially, they will be counted among the missing."

"And unofficially?"

"Unofficially, we have no idea. They may have simply slipped into the earth some distance. Or they may continue falling until they emerge from the earth's crust at some point on the other side of the globe." Smith consulted his computer briefly. "Which would appear to be Kazakhstan."

"*Then* what will happen to them?"

"I have no idea. And it is not something I care to dwell on," said Harold W. Smith, closing the file and pressing the concealed stud under his desk edge that sent his CURE terminal slipping into the concealment of his desktop receptacle.

Epilogue

With the coming of winter, the Kazakh hill men of Kazakhstan came down from the gray folds of the Tian Shan Mountains to dwell with their herds in the valley.

Bulbul, leader of his people, led them off the mountains, as he had every winter for twenty-two years. Come the spring, he would lead them back up. It was the way of the Kazakh hill men of Kazakhstan.

After they had pitched their felt tents and set the bullocks to grazing, they cut the head off a sheep and played the last game of *buzkashi* until the spring.

It was a rough, sweaty game. The men on their horses would swoop down on the carcass, and fight with one another for the privilege of carrying it from a circle drawn at one end of the great winter valley to a pole at the other, and back.

It was a tradition as old as the mountains.

Bulbul, as always, was the first to reach the dead animal. Leaning over his pounding pony, his weathered hands snatched up the thing by its wooly white coat just ahead of the others.

Laughing and calling, they thundered after him. They seldom caught him. But this year, Pishaq bumped his horse against Bulbul's own and grabbed a sheep leg.

Tugging and struggling, they rode hard, the sheep carcass straining between them. The man who had it firmly in hand when he reached the end of the valley would be declared the winner.

In past years, for twenty-two winters, the winner had been Bulbul. This year, he felt, for the first time, the strength of a new champion in opposition to his own. It made his blood run hotter, but somehow his spirit grew sad. He did not yet wish to become old.

They never reached the end of the sheltering valley, still green with grazing grass.

Directly before their pounding hoofs, something came up from the earth.

It looked like a man. A strange, dead man.

Bulbul gave a warning shout, and immediately all horses were reined in.

Through the dust they watched as the dead man floated up from the grass, as if he were a ghost arising from some long-forgotten grave.

Their narrow eyes tensed, in the wonder of it.

"A ghost!" Bulbul hissed.

"Look at its eyes! They are dead!"

It was true.

The eyes of the ghost were open and staring, but its pupils were like pinpoints. Dead.

As they watched, it floated up toward the sky.

A rider shouted.

"Another ghost!"

It was so. This ghost wore a blue uniform, like a soldier. His eyes, like the other's, were round in a way they had never seen.

A third ghost, too, soon emerged from their ancestral grasslands.

They watched in stolid silence, these men of the mountains, rough of face and hard of eye.

They had seen strange things in their lives. But none stranger than this. Yet such were they, that they did not retreat or betray cowardice. Only the horses were skittish.

The three bodies floated up to the sky and out of sight.

Later, an ugly dog resembling the forgotten *buzkashi* sheep was seen floating in the sky. Then there came a long, white wheeled object one man said resembled the machines men drove through distant Kashgar, followed by another dead man-corpse.

The last ghost to emerge from the cursed earth was that of a woman, wide of eye and black of garment.

Bulbul grunted at the sight of her.

"Truly," he said, "she is of the grave. Look, cave spiders have spun their webs in her dusty garments."

This was indisputable.

The dead woman quickly disappeared from sight.

They held vigil all night long, but no more spirits rose into the heavens toward the cold stars.

At dawn, they held council. It was decided that the valley was a cursed place, and no more could they play *buzkashi* there.

It was a sad thing to accept, for this was the land of their forefathers. But they were clear-eyed and unsentimental.

There was no dissent.

As they rode back to their tents and their bullocks and their worried women, the Kazakh hill men of Kazakhstan made a compact never to speak of this to any whose eyes had not beheld the unforgettable sight.

It was a pact made by men of honor, and it was kept.

And so the world never learned of the floating ghosts of Kazakhstan.